ALMOST AS MUCH

Book 3 in the Cherished Memories Series

By
Linda Ellen

Continuing the story of Vic and his Louise, *Almost as Much* touches on the funny times, the sad experiences, the frightening events, and the magic that life can be when two people love one another and love their family and friends. It's a fond voyage through the wonderful days of the 1950's.

Reviews

"A truly heartwarming read! Oh, the memories! This book was a refreshing walk down memory lane for me. Even if you weren't around in the 1950's you'll still enjoy everything about this book and the series. What intrigues me most while reading it is that it's based on true events. You can even go to Linda Ellen's Pinterest page and see pictures relating to the book with the real people. That, to me, is fascinating. The book is so well written that you feel you are there with them. You cry when they cry, and laugh when they laugh—or at the "I Love Lucy" style antics that sometimes appear in the book. I laughed at some of the scenes, especially one about taking a trip in a stick-shift vehicle that the driver had never driven. I could picture it all. Hats off to Linda Ellen for sharing her family stories with us. What a delightful romp, and I'm sorry to see the series end. After reading book 3, I want to go back and read the other two again! One thing for sure, I fell madly in love with Vic. He wasn't a perfect person, but he sure tried hard to be. Wouldn't we all love to be loved like Louise was by Vic? This was a truly unforgettable book. Thank you, Linda Ellen."

~Romance Author Barbara Goss

"I couldn't wait to dive into this 3rd of Linda Ellen's trilogy. As each chapter delved into more of their relationships and struggles, Linda's writing made me feel as if I was being pulled back in time and sharing the experiences with them. My heart beat faster at each danger and I couldn't contain the laughter during the carefree moments. I struggled with Louise and her burning desire to have what she feared she wouldn't have, through to her steadfast belief that her dream would become a reality. I felt for the family members when her obsessions affected them. Mostly I enjoyed how this family got through many struggles, some life threatening, but their love never wavered."

~Beta Reader Judy Glenn

"Every time I enter the world Linda Ellen has created I feel like I'm going home. Home to characters that feel like a family I've been away from and get to visit with again. Getting to follow Vic and Louise as they traverse the hardships and the blessings of life invariably seems to mirror something very close to my own. There is always hope in these stories, and always truth. And underneath it all, there's the excitement and humor of an era gone by; an era of music, classic cars, and family holidays that were done up like they never will be again. With these stories and this book, especially, those times live once more."

~Author Venessa Vargas

Almost as Much
Book 3 of The Cherished Memories Series
Written by Linda Ellen

Copyright © 2016 by Linda Ellen
Trade Paperback Release: August 2016
Electronic Release: August 2016
www.facebook.com/LindaEllen.Author
ISBN: 978-0-9909044-4-1
Print Edition

Although this book is a work of fiction, the story was partially based upon events in the lives of the author's family. Names were changed or details altered; characters, places, and incidents are products of the author's imagination, or are used fictitiously. Brands are used respectfully. Details regarding Louisville as it was in those days were taken from the memories of those who lived then, as well as photographs and other documents.

The following story contains themes of real life, but is suitable for all ages, as it contains no explicit sex or profanity.

Cover design by Kari March Designs
Cover photography by Linda Bullock
Formatting by BB eBooks
Editing by Venessa Vargas
Proofreading by Kathryn Lockwood

Table of Contents

ဢၣ

CHAPTER 1

A Little Trouble in Paradise

August 1955

L OUISE MATTHEWS CAREFULLY removed the hot cake pan from the oven. Straightening and reaching over the open door, she placed it next to its twin on the stovetop.

Glancing at the clock on the wall by the doorway, she nodded in response to her thoughts. *Everything's under control; I'll have this cake frosted and ready for the party when Vic gets home...* "I hope he's on time tonight," she muttered under her breath.

It had been a year since Vic opened the station, thus fulfilling his life-long wish of experiencing his own *Bold Venture.* After so many years of being jobless, or working for low pay, and for bosses that didn't appreciate him, Vic was finally master of his own livelihood. None of his jobs had ever seemed completely secure – there was always that fear that some*one* or some*thing* could come along and hi-jack it. Now, the amount of money he brought home depended mainly upon how long and hard he worked – and how many customers he had – not the whims of those in authority over him.

But what an arduous year it had been; way over and above what Louise had been prepared to endure. She couldn't withhold her sigh of frustration as she thought about the grueling hours her husband put in, working so hard to make Louisville's newest Phillips 66 service station a success. He wanted so much to make everyone proud, and to please the company's board of directors. Deep down, she knew he longed for the coveted *Manager of the Month* award – and why not, even the esteemed *Manager of the Year* title. He deserved them.

"They dang well ought to give it to him, he's worked hard enough for it. His customers see him more than his *family* does," Louise grumbled as she moved around the kitchen preparing food for the party and striving to push away the loneliness her husband's absences caused. She missed the early days of their marriage…the romantic gestures…the sweet-nothings whispered in her ear as she cooked a meal or did the dishes…and the longing looks across the supper table when they couldn't wait for little Tommy to go to sleep so they could be alone to snuggle, among other things.

It was a hot afternoon, not a breeze stirring, and Louise paused for a moment to walk over and stand in front of the window fan, with its warm air ruffling the strands of damp hair lying against her forehead. *Not exactly a good day to be baking, I guess,* she mused with a smirk. But she was determined to bring some joy into the house. The stresses of daily life had become extraordinarily heavy as of late.

Suddenly, a sound like a herd of elephants approached at a fast clip across the back porch, just before six-year-old Jimmy and nine-year-old Buddy came busting through the back screen door. The boys nearly bowled Louise over as they ran past, the older directly on the heels of the younger.

"Boys!" she fussed as she held a large jar of mayonnaise up out of the way.

"Gimme those, you little fart!" Buddy hollered as Jimmy's teasing peal of laughter rang out. Jimmy was clutching the set of toy bongo drums his brother had received for his birthday in May.

Lilly chose that moment to step into the dining room doorway, dust mop in hand. The youngsters nearly collided with her. "For Heaven's sake, boys! Watch where you're playing, somebody could get hurt."

"Sorry Gramma!" Jimmy squealed as he darted around her, nearly making it past before his brother reached out and grasped the back of his shirt, jerking him to an abrupt halt.

"Get 'yer own if you want to play drums," Buddy growled as he yanked his prize possession back. "Take 'em again without my saying you can and I'll pound you," he added for good measure, leaning over his smaller brother, his face scrunched into a menacing scowl.

Jimmy, only slightly intimidated, shrugged as he took a half step back. "I just wanted to see if I could do it…as good as you," he added, his hazel eyes giving off a soft sparkle as he saw a fleeting glimpse of pride ignite in his brother's eyes.

However, refusing to give in to his little brother's charms, Buddy growled, "Well, you *can't*. So, keep your mitts off."

"Boys, get along!" Louise hollered from the kitchen as Lilly placed her hands on her grandsons' shoulders and directed them through the house to the front door. "You two go on outside and play – nice. It's too hot to run roughshod through the house."

"But Gramma!" "I'm hungry!" the boys fussed simultaneously.

"I want a cookie," Jimmy added, gazing up at his grandmother with his most precocious smile.

As usual, Lilly softened at the charm of her youngest grandson. "Alright, you two go on out to the front yard and I'll bring you each a cookie."

"Yippee!" they yelled in unison as the screened door banged shut behind them.

The grandmother turned and met her daughter's eyes, both of them shaking their heads in heat and adolescent-induced irritation.

Louise turned to head back into the kitchen, one hand smoothing back the damp, short-cut strands of her hair. Her mother followed her into the room and retrieved two cookies from the cookie jar on the counter. After delivering the items, she returned and opened the utility closet to put away the dust mop.

"Vic knows about the party tonight, right?" Lilly queried, forgetting that she had already asked the same question three times that day.

Her back to Lilly as she continued peeling potatoes, Louise nodded. "He promised he and Tommy would knock off around five-thirty and leave the new guy to close up."

The older woman snorted softly as she removed the string mop and bucket from the closet. "That's what he said last night."

Louise turned her head and shot an aggravated look at her mother. "He couldn't help that. You heard him – he wanted to get that big job finished. The customer owns a delivery business with six trucks and promised Vic could have all of his mechanic trade if he got that first job done in one day," she stated, staunchly defending her husband even though deep down she was fighting her own battle against resentment. It seemed that all her husband did anymore was work – and seven days a week at that.

Living out Vic's *Bold Venture* wasn't turning out the way she had imagined. She knew she was being unreasonable – her husband was working so hard to provide a home and a good living for her, the boys, and her mother to boot. She knew he loved them all, fiercely…she just couldn't seem to fight off the encroaching feelings of neglect and disappointment.

As if reading her mind, Lilly mused as she filled the mop bucket at the sink. "Well, if you ask me, it seems as if Vic thinks he's married to that *station* now, instead of a flesh and blood wife and family."

"Mama! That's not fair. And I don't want to talk about it right now, it's too hot to argue."

Louise reached for the cake pans, holding them carefully with a towel to cushion against the heat as she began the process of turning the layers out onto the cooling racks. Today was a milestone in their lives and she was determined there would be a celebration. Their friends Fleet and Alec Alder, Earl and Ruth Grant, Doc Latham and his wife Florence, Irene Waller, and even Vic's brother Jack and his wife Liz had promised to come…whether or not the guest of honor would be there on time. *No, he will. He promised.*

An hour later, the cake frosted and decorated, and the food finished, Louise glanced at the clock again, noting the time as Lilly came through the back door with a basket of laundry fresh off the backyard lines.

"It's five o'clock, I'm going to go take a bath and get dressed," Louise informed her mother as she slipped past, untying her apron and placing it on the counter.

Performing a quick tour of the house to make sure it was ready for company, Louise eyed the living room with Tommy and Buddy's bunk beds and double chest of drawers nestled against one wall. She was satisfied that everything looked as neat as could be. Surely their friends understood the logistical problems of six people living in a one-bedroom house.

When they had first moved into the little house at Thirty-Eighth and Herman, Lilly and Tommy had shared the bedroom, and Buddy had been less than a year old. He had slept in a crib in the corner of Vic and Louise's sleeping area, which they had carved from the back half of the large dining room. Now Grandma and the youngest shared the one small bedroom.

Hard to believe that much time had passed.

Retreating behind the curtain separating their sleeping area from the rest of the dining room, Louise quickly gathered her necessities and scurried into the bathroom for a cool, quick bath. As she soaked for a few blissful minutes, she could hear Lilly giving the boys orders, probably to change into clean clothes. Speedily washing her hair, Louise gave it a quick rinsing and then stepped out of the tub to dry off.

Back in her room a few minutes later, Louise stood in her underclothes and combed her hair at the mirror, relishing the breeze from yet another window fan. Running her fingers through the shortened locks, she grimaced at the unaccustomed brevity of the strands.

In a way, it felt kind of good to be in fashion for a change; after all, it was 1955 and the restrictions of the Depression and the War years had lifted. However, she still had mixed feelings about her decision to have it chopped off, at Fleet's insistence – and Vic's expression when he had first seen it hadn't helped. She could tell he was a bit shocked and disappointed. He'd always told her he loved to run his fingers through her smooth sable hair. The only consolation was that this shorter style was much cooler against her neck in the late summer heat.

Picturing her grinning friend with her new short hairdo as she had practically dragged Louise into a nearby salon to get hers cut the same way; Louise shook her head with a rueful half smile. *That Fleet, she's always been able to talk me into just about anything.*

Fleetwood McDougal, now Fleetwood Alder – had been Louise's best friend since they were girls in school, in spite of the fact that Fleet, as she was affectionately known, was a full three years older. Oh, the wonderful times – and mischief – they had gotten into together. Most of it still unknown to Lilly…*and* Fleet's own mother and grandmother, Blanche and Myrtle McDougal. Louise frowned when she thought of those women – Fleet's *family* – and she shook her head sadly.

Fleet had been raised on Seventh Street – in a notorious section where many of the houses sported a red light on the porch. Her mother and grandmother had both made their living doing what was unseemly to the decent people of the city – at least the females of the city, and many of the men. Those who chose to frequent such houses and women, well…

Louise shook her head regretfully as she thought of her friend now without a mother, grandmother *or* father for that matter, since Fleet had never even met the man. Blanche had caught pneumonia the previous winter and passed away down at the old

City Hospital, and Myrtle had come down with a fast-acting case of tuberculosis. Although the authorities had taken her out to Hazelwood Sanatorium for treatment, they hadn't caught it in time and she had quickly followed her daughter in death.

Shaking her head free of those sad thoughts, Louise aimed her mind at Fleet's husband – Vic's best friend, Alec. Although the jokester of the gang, he nonetheless loved his wife, son, and new baby daughter, and had never left his wife's side during the losses of her immediate family. In a way, it had been surprising that Fleet had mourned as she had, since she had never been particularly close to her parent and grandparent. But, Louise figured, perhaps Fleet had nurtured dreams and hopes that things would change – and now it was too late.

Her hair nearly dry, Louise stepped over to the bed and lifted her new dress, a soft wide-strapped white sundress with tiny purple grapes in the design, and purple corded trim around the perimeter of the wide skirt, the rounded neckline, and arm holes. A narrow matching belt synched in Louise's small waist.

Styling her hair into attractive waves that curved at the nape of her neck and around her ears, Louise retrieved her amethyst necklace from the dresser top and fastened the clasp around her neck before searching her jewelry box for a pair of earrings to match it. Unaccustomed to wearing earrings unless she dressed up, a frown creased her brow as she tried to remember where she might have a pair. *Maybe my memory chest...*

Opening the bottom drawer of her dresser, she retrieved the little cedar hope chest that held her most treasured memories and schooled herself to look through it and not sink into reminiscences of the past. Gently placing it on the bed, she caressed the intricately engraved top, faltering at the small cigarette burn on one edge, courtesy of her younger brother, Billy. Oh, how she had fussed at him for that!

She lifted the clasp opening the top, the mirror inside the lid immediately reflecting back the attractive picture she made in her new dress. Her image smiled in satisfaction as she began to rummage through the contents for the sought-after earrings.

Over the years, more items had been added to the small treasure-trove inside the box. Valentine cards Vic had given her, each one with a cute private note; tiny envelopes with a snippet of baby hair from each of her babies; post cards from her brother, Sonny, when he had been in the Merchant Marines during WWII; a leftover ration booklet from the War years; photographs of her daddy, Willis, and of her sister Edna, her husband, and her children, who still resided in Brooklyn, New York; two small photo booklets from their one big vacation trip to Miami Beach two summers before. Louise paused in her search to take these out and flip through the black and white pictures of herself and Vic, along with their good friends, Detective John Womack and his wife Josephine.

Louise's eyes lingered on a photo of a sun-bronzed, virile Vic, wearing dark plaid swimming trunks and reclining on a tiny towel, squinting up at her in the hot Florida sun. There had never been another man who could stir her feelings with just a look and a wink from those twinkling brown eyes – and he could still do it when he chose. And that strong, barrel chest, oh my...

Memories flashed in her mind as she gazed at his like-ness...Vic had laughed and reached out to take the camera from her, tossing it on the towel. He'd grabbed her hand, and ran with her toward the water. She had squealed with delight as he had scooped her up and slung her into the ocean waves before diving in after her. They had spent quite a while frolicking in the warm seawater, and indulging in stolen kisses and fond caresses until their friend John had teasingly hollered that he would arrest them for indecent shenanigans in public.

Louise brought the photo to her chest for a quick hug before closing the paper case and continuing her search. *Where are those blasted earrings?*

At last, in the bottom right corner, she found what she was

looking for – a pair of clip-on's with purple stones – costume jewelry, but quite pretty. *Maybe some day Vic will get me a real set to go with my necklace…*

Just then, a knock sounded at the front door. Louise's eyes flew to the clock on the nightstand. It was 5:45! *I bet that's Earl and Ruth and the kids. He always likes to get everywhere early.*

Quickly replacing items back into the little chest, Louise closed and stashed it away again in the bottom drawer, dabbed a spot of Emeraude behind each ear, checked her hair one more time, slipped into a pair of white sandals, and hurried to the living room.

As she swung the front door open and stepped back with a big smile to allow their friends to enter, she fumed silently, *I hope Vic and Tommy are on their way!*

೫೦෬

CHAPTER 2

The Celebration

THE BODY OF the old '48 Chevy half-ton pickup shimmied as Vic pressed the brake and clutch, shifting into neutral as the cars ahead stopped for another stoplight.

Glancing over at the teen in the passenger seat – his beloved stepson and co-worker, Tommy Blankenbaker – Vic blew out a frustrated huff as he reached into his shirt pocket and pulled a cigarette out of the pack. "Blasted rush-hour traffic gets worse everyday," he grumbled out of the side of his mouth as he held the flame of his polished Dunhill lighter to the end of the cigarette. The sweet, pungent smell of lighter fluid wafted quickly away. "That's one thing that's good about headin' home at nine o'clock – it's a smooth sail straight down Shelbyville Road, all the way to the house."

"Yeah, and cooler when the sun goes down. Just wish home wasn't a half hour away," Tommy replied as he raked a hand back through his damp hair, the moisture making it look darker than its actual light brown. Vic gazed at him, thinking his hair was a bit too long, but knowing that with helping out at the station full-time every day since school had let out, the boy hadn't the time to go for a haircut. He'd have to soon. Vic knew Tommy's thick wavy mass of hair always made him feel hotter in the humid dog days of summer.

"Yep," Vic agreed, flipping his lighter closed with a clink and running his thumb over the engraved letters of his father's name. It was an unconscious habit he had maintained for decades. The lighter he had inherited from his father was still one of his most prized possessions.

Waiting for the light to change, Vic wondered, as he had many times in the past, what his father, if he had lived, would think of the man his youngest son had become…

Tommy's bright blue gaze flickered toward his stepfather's profile for a moment, watching as he drew on the cig and turned his head to blow the smoke out the open driver-side window. He debated for a moment whether or not to speak what was on his mind.

"Hey Chief…" he finally murmured, using the nickname he had called his stepfather since the day Vic and Louise had married. "You think Oscar'll remember everything you told him to do when he closes up for the night? I mean…what if he don't shut the pumps off, or…" he paused, his eyes squinting a bit when he saw the muscle at Vic's jaw twitch as he ground his teeth together.

"Let's just hope he does."

Picturing his latest employee's clumsiness and happy-go-lucky naiveté, Vic shut his eyes with a grimace. He hadn't wanted to entrust the station to the new guy so soon, but he had promised Louise he'd knock off early. Maybe he should have just closed up ahead of schedule and not worried about the lost profit…

As the light changed, cars began to move, and he laid his hand on the small gearshift knob, maneuvering it into first as he added, "Guess it wouldn't hurt to write out a checklist of how to close up…post it on the wall by the door."

"Good idea," Tommy mumbled in agreement, turning his head to gaze out the window at the passing streets as they rolled along toward home.

Vic glanced over again at the young man, a half smile curving one side of his mouth as he thought of what a blessing he had turned out to be. The fact of who the boy's sire had been never crossed his mind anymore. Tommy was a hard worker, a quick-learner, and sharp as a tack. Vic didn't have to worry if he might forget a step. Oh, he wasn't perfect – who was? But Tommy was darn good.

Vic knew he was fortunate not only to call him his son, but also to have him on his team. He didn't want to even think about the fact that school would be starting up in a few weeks and he would lose his right-hand man. Eyes forward again, Vic mused for a moment at how fast the years were whooshing by, kind of like one of those MiG-15 jets Korea had used in the last war. How could sweet little Tommy, his little Kemo Sabe, already be sixteen, as tall as Vic himself, and *driving*?

With that thought, Vic glanced over at him and murmured, "Hey pal, I forgot I was gonna let you drive home…"

Tommy flashed him a grin, raising one hand in a wave-off gesture. "Don't worry 'bout it. For once, I'm too beat to cruise."

Vic let out a soft chuckle as he focused again on the road.

Going through the motions of driving, his mind dwelt on the myriad of ever-present responsibilities. He never felt truly "off duty", as even when he was at home and in bed, his mind was still at work, worrying about the hundreds of details of running the service station. Would there be enough gas to last until the tanker came again; would he get enough business to pay the bills for the month; would he be able to handle all of the mechanic work, especially since he was practically teaching himself as he went along; would he get many more impossible customers like one he'd had last week – elderly Mrs. Dorchester – who put on airs like she was one of the Vanderbilt's, and treated him like a servant. Then to top it off, she had complained loud and long about the bill, when he had to replace a dozen parts on her car! It had taken every bit of control he could muster not to lose his temper while dealing with her. But he'd held it. Used up half a pack of cigarettes doing it, but he'd done it.

Raking his hand back through his hair with a soft snort, he thought about the string of part-time help he had hired. One after another had proven less than desirable. The first guy, as soon as Vic would leave the lot, would pull his own car in a bay and work on it, or fill it up with gas, oil, and who-knows-what-else, without asking or paying. The next had stolen tools when Vic had left him to close up, and the guy hadn't bothered to show up for work the next morning, having skipped town. That had taken a chunk out of the week's receipts, replacing what was pinched. Another fellow had the absolute worst customer service personality and had practically run off many of Vic's regulars – and man oh man – he'd had to really bow and scrape to make that right again. He lost count of the free lube jobs and free car washes he had doled out to get back into their good graces.

After that, he had hired John Womack's son JD – who turned out to be one of the laziest young men Vic had ever encountered. He'd even caught the guy taking naps in the middle of the day! Vic suspected the boy was hooked on marijuana or something, as several times he had thought he'd smelled it on him. Thank Heavens, JD had found something else to do and Vic hadn't had to risk his friendship with John to get him out of there.

Now, however, he had Oscar. The poor, clumsy fellow seemed to have two left feet, two left hands, and tended to see everything upside down or backward.

With a tired sigh, Vic shook his head, negotiating the transition to Story Avenue. Flexing his shoulder muscles, he reached up with his left hand to try and rub away a crick that was radiating across both shoulders – a result of reaching overhead for an extended period as he struggled to break loose a rusted bolt on the underside of a car on the lift.

The thought of what awaited him at home made him almost wish he had called Louise and told her to cancel, as he was so tired all he wanted to do was rest. But...he couldn't do that to her. He knew she had put a lot of time and effort into planning this party for the one-year anniversary of the opening of the station, and he didn't want to disappoint her. As it was, he had headed home later than he'd promised, so she was probably fit to be tied right about now...

Louise...picturing his wife made the corners of his mouth tip up in a smile. Even when she was irritated and griping about something, she was still the best thing in his life. Still a looker even after three kids and fourteen years of marriage, her beautiful smile lit up a room. He had to admit, she had made a great wife. She was a good mother and a great cook. She kept the house clean...well, Lilly helped too, but Louise did most of the work. Louise always had something interesting to say, and she usually knew what he was thinking and feeling, as was true of the reverse.

A tiny frown furrowed his brow when that thought passed through his mind. Lately, something had been kind of...off...with his lovely wife. He wasn't sure what it was. She seemed...frustrated? Dissatisfied? On edge? He'd been so preoccupied with his unending responsibilities at the station and hardly ever having had time off that he found himself in the position of not being privy to his wife's thoughts and feelings.

Pursing his lips, he thought back on the changes in these past few weeks...

She'd been snappy and cross with him on quite a few occasions. With no advance warning or a word that she was even thinking about it, she had suddenly cut her hair short. He knew his reaction when he had walked in the door that night and looked at her wasn't what she had been hoping for, but it had been such a surprise. She had bought quite a few new dresses and outfits lately – which they could barely afford – and she seemed to be experimenting with new recipes and foods. It used to be that he knew what they would have for supper that night by what day of the week it happened to be, however, now it could be almost anything...some good, some downright terrible. Of course, not wanting to hurt her feelings he never let on if he didn't like something she'd made. And since he normally didn't make it home until 9:30 or later, he often had to eat his food warmed over, which hadn't helped.

Frustration threatened to overwhelm him. He hadn't exactly planned on keeping the station open seven days a week – hadn't given that aspect much thought when he'd been hot on the heels of pursuing his *bold venture*. But he had quickly realized that the weekends were his biggest moneymaking days – and who closed a service station during the week? Of course, the plan was for him to find help that he could trust so he could take a day off now and then, but so far, that hadn't worked out. Had that been *his* fault? *Why can't she see how hard this is for me? Sometimes I feel like I'm in way over my head and I'm worn out treadin' water...*

His eyes narrowed as he stewed.

❦

THE SMALL HOUSE seemed to be overflowing with people, making the temperature inside the structure just that much hotter. It wasn't long before they all spilled out into the back yard, where the air was a few degrees cooler now that the sun was a bit lower in the sky – and where one could feel at least a tiny breeze now and then. That was probably due to the fact that they weren't all that many blocks from the river.

Oh bless him, that Ol' Man River, who was at times both Louisville's friend *and* enemy.

Louise backed her way out onto the back porch holding a tray piled high with picnic items – potato salad, baked beans, sliced fruit, and hamburger buns ready to be filled with juicy burgers hot off the grill.

She smiled her thanks at John Womack as he held the outer door for her, and even reached to relieve her of the tray.

"I got this, where do you want it?"

"Over here," Louise indicated a well-used, borrowed picnic

table Lilly had covered with a checkered cloth to hide the stains and gouges. Scattered around the table sat folding chairs and stools.

Earl, Alec and Doc stood together at the grill, laughing at something Alec had no doubt said as he flipped burgers – in Vic's stead. He had been right, though, when he'd said Vic would have probably been too tired to perform the duty, even if he was there. So, being the friend that he was, he offered to oblige.

Louise glanced down at her watch. 6:15. She could feel her aggravation trying to rise to the surface and boil over. *Couldn't he drag himself away from that blasted station early – just once?*

Forcing a smile at her friend Ruth as she appeared by her side, the two began unloading the tray and arranging items on the table as Ruth murmured, "Relax. He'll get here when he gets here. Everything'll be okay."

Buddy and Jimmy ran by, along with Ruth and Earl's two youngest, Gina and Terry. Fleet was still in the house, feeding a bottle to her youngest – a little girl they had named Alexa.

Everyone was laughing and having a good time…except that the guest of honor hadn't arrived yet.

₲)ℓ℞

FIFTEEN MINUTES LATER, Vic turned the pickup into the alley and let it roll to a stop in the parking area behind the back fence.

"Mama! Daddy and Tommy are home!" Buddy hollered as he jumped up from his seat at the table and trotted back to open the gate.

"Everybody's here Daddy…and Mama's mad cause you're late," the boy informed his dad as Vic passed through the opening.

Vic smiled down at his namesake, Victor Herbert Matthews, Jr., nicknamed "Buddy" by a neighbor friend when the boy had been only weeks old, and reached out a work-roughened hand to feel the top of his head, specifically the close-cropped hair.

"Your mama got you scalped again, huh son?"

Buddy giggled as he stepped near to give his dad a quick hug around his waist. "Yep. School's gonna start in a few weeks," he replied, tilting his head back to gaze up at his beloved daddy. His eyes twinkled happily that Vic was finally home for the night – and earlier than usual. He was glad that it wouldn't be one of those evenings when he would have to feign wanting a glass of water, to steal a few moments of greeting with his father.

"She said she wanted to beat the rush down at the barber's."

"Mmm," Vic answered with a nod as his friends began to holler and wave for him to join them. Vic nodded and waved back, sharing a quick, tired glance with Tommy as they made their way forward.

Jimmy came running for a hug and reached to relieve his daddy of his lunch box. Vic let him take it and then bent to scoop his youngest up into his arms as he moved forward. The boy began to chatter about his day and the excitement of the party.

Louise met Vic halfway up the long, narrow back yard. "You're late. We had to start eating before the food got cold," she stated without preamble as Vic leaned to give her a kiss hello.

"Sorry, had some last minute stuff happen…" he mumbled, but he could see in her eyes it wasn't the time for explanations. She took his arm, urging him forward. "You want to go in and clean up a bit?" she hinted.

"If I go in the house, I might not make it back out," he tried to joke, only her eyes sparked hazel fire and he knew what she was thinking. His uniform was stained and dirty from working on cars, changing oil, and pumping gas all day – while everyone else at the party was scrubbed and clean. But right then, he just didn't care. All he wanted was some of that good smelling food and a place to put his feet up to rest.

The scent of grilled hamburgers wafted his way, making his mouth water and reminding him that lunch had been too many hours ago. His belly growled in response.

Alec came toward them then, hand outstretched and saving the day. "Hail the conquering hero! We'd about gave up on you, Chief. But we saved the best seat in the house…uh, I mean *yard*, just for you."

Louise resumed her seat and the others welcomed Vic to his celebration as he lowered himself into the chair at the head of the table.

The rest of the evening went well. Laughter, good friends, and good food rejuvenated his tired spirit. It was great to laugh with the others as they each told a funny "Vic" story or shared something from the past and their friendship with the couple. Even Jack and Liz seemed to enjoy themselves and participated in the fun.

The only drawback was the slightly frosty vibes emanating from Louise whenever she met Vic's gaze, or when she came to stand by him while the others raised their soda glasses in congratulations.

He knew that after everyone went home, he was more than likely in for an earful…

༄༅ ༈

CHAPTER 3

The Decision

Louise hugged Fleet and kissed little Alexa on the cheek before helping her friend into the passenger side of their car.

Carefully shutting the door, Louise fought back feelings of envy as she watched her friend cuddle the baby. Oh, how she missed the all-consuming preciousness of having an infant…that sweet clean ambrosia of baby powder and milk, and that indescribable innocent essence unique to newborns.

"Thanks again for coming," she directed at both Fleet and Alec as he reached to turn the key and start the motor. Louise leaned down to make eye contact with Alec. "And thanks for grilling the hamburgers, they were great."

"No problem-o," he grinned back at her as he put the car in gear, then added with a wink, "Don't be too hard on old Vic for being a little late, he's plum tuckered out."

Fleet laughed and gave him a soft smack on the arm. "*Old* Vic? Look at the pot callin' the kettle black."

"Yeah, but compared to him I've got a gravy job," he answered, suddenly serious – which was a rarity for him. "Nine to five and home on weekends. I can leave the job at the job. Vic's got a monkey on his back that never sleeps."

The women each pressed their lips shut and exchanged glances. For Louise, his words caused a moment of concern, but she soon brushed it off as her friends' car pulled away. She stood at the curb waving, one arm around little Jimmy's shoulder, until the Alder's car turned the corner.

"Can I have 'nother piece of cake, Mama?" the little boy asked, smiling sweetly up at her as he gave her hips a loving squeeze. "I'm still hungry."

She lowered her gaze to meet his, hazel eyes just like hers, and lovingly smoothed his coal black hair, which had been cut short for the start of the school year. *His first year of school…my baby will be a schoolboy in a matter of days. What'll I do during the day with no kids underfoot?* Trying to push away the melancholy thought, she answered, "No, it's too late for more cake, honey. It's time for bed."

"Aww Mama," he whined as they started up the sidewalk toward the front door. "Please?"

Louise stuck to her guns, shaking her head. "Not tonight. You can have a piece in the morning."

They moved on into the living room and Jimmy took off like a shot through the house as Louise shut the door and locked the deadbolt. Glancing over, the dim light from the hallway allowed her to see that her oldest was already stretched out on the top bunk.

"Thomas Joseph, did you bathe?" she queried, crossing her arms over her chest as she thought about how much dirt and grease he and Vic dragged home each night.

A bit muffled, his tired voice answered, "I washed up. I'll take a shower in the morning. Right now I'm beat."

Her arms relaxed down to their sides as she considered his words. *Well…it must have been some day if even Tommy is this tired…* "Alright honey. Goodnight."

" 'Night," came a slurred reply as he turned over toward the wall and made himself comfortable.

Louise walked on through the room, headed for the bathroom. The shower was running and as usual, Buddy and Jimmy were play fighting – this time jockeying for a place at the sink to brush their teeth.

"I was here first!"

"No you wasn't, I was!"

"Boys, *share*," Louise admonished. "Hurry up now and get to bed, we're all tired."

Stepping into the kitchen, she smiled in relief to see that Lilly had everything under control. The leftover food had been put away, and she was finishing up the dishes. During times like this, she was truly grateful that her mother did, indeed, live with them. Sharing the household duties was such a blessing.

"Thanks, Mama," Louise murmured, walking a few steps to give her mother a hug. "It was a good party...in spite of a rough start..." she ventured. The older woman merely met her gaze, choosing to keep her opinions to herself. However, even with no words spoken aloud, Louise could still see the I-told-you-so look in her mother's eyes, regarding Vic getting home later than he promised.

As the boys finished up, giggling and shoving one another, Louise stepped back around the corner. "All right, that's enough. Buddy, now you be quiet as you get into bed, your brother is already trying to sleep."

"Okay, Mama."

"Jimmy, you get on into your room and get ready for bed. Grandma will be in soon to tuck you in," she ordered the youngest. He scurried around the corner.

The shower was still running, steam building up in the bathroom in spite of the door being open. Louise stepped in leaving the door ajar a few inches for ventilation. She couldn't see any movement behind the curtain and the thought crossed her mind that her husband was hiding, purposely trying to avoid having a confrontation. She knew he realized she was aggravated at him. Slowly moving up, she put out a hand and moved the curtain just enough to peer through the steam, her face set with a frown...

What she saw gave her heart a twinge. Her husband...her

hard-working man…was standing with his back to the streaming hot water, allowing it to beat down on his neck and left shoulder. So much so that the skin was bright red from the heat. Thinking of her teenaged son already in bed and exhausted from his day at the station, for a crazy moment, she wondered if Vic had managed to fall sleep on his feet. His hair was plastered to his head, and his face wore a grimace. Then, slowly rotating his arm, she watched as he shifted to allow the water to beat down on the other shoulder.

After a few moments, as if he felt her gaze, his eyes opened and met hers as he blinked water from his lashes. Then his lips turned up in a tiny smile. "Sorry I was late gettin' home…"

Louise smiled softly and shook her head. The remnants of her anger from earlier had fled the moment she had seen the extent of his exhaustion.

"That's okay." After a few beats, she added, "Want me to wash your back?"

He let out a groan. "That'd be heaven."

She closed that end of the curtain and reached up for the washcloth he had stashed over the curtain rod, taking a moment to make it good and soapy. Then opening the curtain again, she pushed it back a bit. "Come here…turn around," she murmured over the sound of the water hitting the floor of the tub. He obligingly came forward, turning and bracing his hands on the shower wall, and letting out a soft moan as she began soaping and massaging his back and shoulders. When she was finished, she scrubbed his elbows and the backs of his arms free from ground-in grime.

Memories seeped in of the many times she had scrubbed his back during their early days. They were so much in love back then… With a soft sigh, she handed him the washcloth. Leaving the bathroom, she shut the door and slipped behind the curtain into their sleeping area.

Slowly removing her party dress and jewelry, she allowed her mind to wander over first one subject and then another. She wondered why she felt so restless of late. Was it because the boys, her babies, were getting so big? Both of them would be away from her in school soon and not with her and not under her protection every day. Thoughts of her friends having babies crossed her mind and for a moment, she wondered why she hadn't gotten with child again after Jimmy – it wasn't as if they had begun taking precautions again, because they hadn't. She paused in contemplation, wondering if having another child would make her feel fulfilled. Then, for the first time in a long time, thoughts of the baby she had lost on the banks of the Ohio so many years ago crossed her mind. The memories of pain, loss, and the accompanying conflicting emotions, had been buried so deep, they seldom surfaced...

Placing her hands up to her cheeks, she stared at her reflection in the bureau mirror. *Oh, what is my problem?* Was it that she and Vic didn't seem as close as they used to be? They had been so happy for so many years. It wasn't that she didn't love him or that she felt he didn't love her...*I know he does.* It was just that they never had time to spend together anymore...like they were two boats floating down opposite sides of the Ohio, but in the same direction.

Louise heard the shower stop and several minutes later heard him brushing his teeth as she stood running her brush through her hair, allowing her mind continuing to flit from one subject to another.

Not long after, Vic slipped through the curtain. Putting down her brush, she gathered her things to ready herself for bed, before she turned, emotions warring within. Wearing nothing but a pair of boxers, he stood gazing across the bed at her, his expression carefully neutral, as if bracing himself for a tirade.

All day, she had been planning on having it out with him over a great many things, but now...all the wind seemed to have left her sails. She could see the fatigue lines around his eyes and the guarded air of his posture.

With a sigh, she averted her eyes and slipped out past the other side of the curtain, pausing for a moment to gaze back over her shoulder before making her way to the bathroom. He hadn't moved, except to follow her movements with his eyes. After a moment, he shifted his focus onto the light blue sheets invitingly turned down.

When she joined him in their bed twenty minutes later, he was sound asleep.

For her, however, sleep was a long time coming.

ℒℂ

AT THE STATION the next day, Vic stood at the large windows of the office. Feet braced apart and hands shoved deep in his trouser pockets, he gazed out across the drive at the pouring rain of a late summer storm. He had flipped the outer lights on, as the rain had made everything dark and gloomy. With a sigh, he silently admitted that for once he was glad for the rain, as it had slowed what would normally be a steady stream of customers.

Today, he was in no frame of mind to put on his "customer service" smile and go out in the sopping wet to attend to his patrons' needs and wishes; although, his bright yellow slicker and rain hat hung ready on a peg next to the closed door. Inside his office, it was bright, warm, and dry. This day however…his mood more closely matched the outdoors.

It was Sunday, and Vic actually had been able to sleep in for two hours. When he awoke, the house was quiet and he knew the family had all gone to church. With a certain amount of shame, it pained him to realize that since he had started his own business, his family had almost stopped attending worship. Louise always said it was something they should do as a family and he knew she had tried to use that as leverage for him to go in late to the station, or not at all. Thus far, it hadn't worked. However, he did miss going, as he always seemed to feel better after one of Doc's rousing sermons, and glad he'd made the effort to attend.

Louise must have really worked hard to keep everyone quiet so I could keep on sleeping as she got 'em all ready to go... He knew she was a stickler for making sure each boy — even sixteen-year-old Tommy — was scrubbed clean and looking his best to go to God's house on the Sabbath. That normally involved quite a bit of arguing between the youngest and fussing from Grandma.

The evening before, at the party, Doc had made casual mention of their continued absence, although he had phrased it teasingly that they were tired of his preaching. This had prompted his good friend John to offer his services as chauffeur. It was a blessing that they all were members of the same congregation. Momentarily, Vic wondered why it had taken them so long to offer. He assumed everyone had been waiting for him to find a reliable employee so that he would be free on Sundays to take his family to church. Alas, that had not happened, so his friends were stepping in to bridge the gap. The thought pricked his conscience.

His eyes on the traffic out in front on Shelbyville Road, which was a scant few cars at that point, he hazily registered that it was only 11:30 and the churches hadn't let out yet. Since it was raining, he wagered most people wouldn't go for their customary Sunday drives — and therefore wouldn't stop in to fill up on their way out. *I might not have many customers at all today if this rain keeps up...maybe after lunch, I'll close on up and go home...*

The only reason he had driven the thirty minutes in the rain to open the station at all — and he would remain a one-man operation all day — was that bills were due and he needed the extra cash Sunday would normally bring. However, if virtually no customers came in...what a wasted effort it would be. It had taken quite a bit of resolve to roll out of bed and put his uniform on that morning.

Ahh well, he sighed, drawing in a deep breath and letting it out slowly. The now familiar smells of engine oil, rubber tires, and hoses, filled his nostrils. The station had become his home away from home…but was that good or bad? For his family, it wasn't turning out all good. His long-held dream of having his own business had proven to possess a dark side. It was good in many ways, no doubt. It just wasn't everything he had always dreamed it would be. *Almost as much…but not quite.*

Things that his friends had said the evening before now came back to him. Alec and Earl had even joked about a few things the boys had done over the past year, and it had hurt that Vic hadn't been there to witness them. His sons were growing up too quickly! Little Jimmy, the baby of the family, would be starting school in a matter of days. When had he changed from crying baby, to crawling tot, to curious toddler, on to bright and inquisitive child – now a school-aged boy? It seemed to have happened overnight. Vic keenly felt the regret that he was missing out on way too much.

He was so very proud of his sons – all three of them to be sure – but especially the two he had conceived with Louise. His namesake, whom they all called Buddy, was a handsome, bright boy who was already showing signs of being musically inclined, like his mother. Quiet and serious, he was studious and made good grades in school. Vic was sure he would prove to have a great many talents. He didn't enjoy getting his hands dirty, however, and in that way the older was very different from the younger.

Little Jimmy already seemed quite enamored with everything about the station, although he hadn't had many opportunities to visit. Usually Saturdays would be a day when Louise and Fleet would venture out to the shopping center down the road, and Jimmy would beg to be allowed to stay with Daddy at the station while they shopped. The boy seemed a natural, and even at his young age, he could fetch tools and roll tires across the bays in surprisingly competent help. Company policy wouldn't allow one so young to pump gas out at the islands, or Vic was sure the determined and precocious child would attempt that, as well. He did, however, go out and watch his older brother perform that task. They had even fashioned a long pole onto a squeegee with which he could wash a customer's windows while his brother checked their oil and fluids. Many a customer had tossed the boy a nickel or dime tip, which thrilled him no end.

Vic's thoughts meandered to his wife and his brow furrowed a bit. Louise's indifference regarding the business had him worried. Since the station's opening day, when his wife had stayed nearly the entire shift and helped to greet customers – and they had teased and flirted with one another – she had not been back out to stay any length of time. She had promised that on Saturdays, she would come to clean the restrooms and tidy up the office area, but those occasions had been few. It concerned him as he had assumed the station would be a family enterprise and that all of them would spend much time working side by side, being a family. It hadn't turned out that way. Sure, he and Tommy spent long days there together – or at least this summer they had as soon as the teen was out of school. But Vic realized he almost felt separated from the rest of the family, being so far away at work.

Another sigh escaped Vic's mouth and he unconsciously rubbed his thumb on the engraving of his father's name etched into the cool surface of the lighter in his pocket, an action that somehow always gave him comfort. It was something he found himself doing, almost as if he could conjure up his father like a genie to give him some much-needed advice.

I gotta make some changes. I don't want my life to just fly by, doing nothing but working. Pondering the dilemma, he knew that the long trip to and from home was part of the problem. He had toyed with the idea of moving closer, but had been afraid of rejection at the bank. Did he make enough money to qualify for a loan? *Well...they loaned me the grand to get the station outfitted...*

Nodding as the thought cemented in his mind, he made the

decision to call the bank first thing in the morning and see about the possibility of actually buying their first house.

He couldn't wait to close up and go home so he could tell Louise the news.

If that'll put the spark back in those beautiful hazel eyes of hers...the sooner the better!

ℰᴑᴑᴒ

CHAPTER 4

An Empty Nest and an Answered Prayer

L OUISE HELD THE screen door open for Lilly to step inside, both of the women carrying brown paper sacks full of groceries.

"I'll go back out and get the rest," Louise murmured as they headed on into the kitchen. She wiped a bit of perspiration off her forehead with the back of one hand. "I sure miss the boys helping," she added, fighting off the melancholy that threatened to consume. Little Jimmy starting school the week before had been difficult for her – indeed, vastly more distressing than either of the other boy's first day. She had stood gazing through the little window of the door to his class with tears running down her cheeks as he settled in, so excited to actually be in school like his brothers. When she had finally made herself leave, she had gone home and thrown herself on the bed for a good cry. Everywhere she looked in the house, something reminded her of one of the kids. *My babies are growing up too fast!*

With a huff of determination, she shook off her gloomy thoughts and headed back out to the car. *It isn't like me to be so weepy. I can't understand...why can't I get a hold of myself?* One would think by the way she was acting that she was pregnant, but she knew with certainty that she was not.

Lilly glanced over at her daughter as she came through the back door a few minutes later with the last of their purchases. Angling her head in a knowing nod as she perused Louise's face, she murmured, "It's just a touch of empty nest syndrome. You'll get over it." With that, she gathered things to put away in the bathroom and hall closet, and left the room.

Louise watched her mother's retreating form with a wry shake of her head. *All business, just like always. If a person didn't know better, you'd think that woman didn't have an ounce of sympathy in her veins.* But even as those words entered her mind, she felt guilty. Louise knew her mother's life hadn't been a happy one – married at sixteen to a man she didn't love who ended up being abusive, running from him with her two children and having to make a life for herself, then marrying Louise's father, Willis, who was twelve years her senior – not to mention the trauma surrounding her sister Edna's birth. Over the years Lilly had softened some, especially after their heart-to-heart talk when Tommy had been only two. Even so, there were times when Louise had to sternly remind herself to consider the source in regard to anything her mother might say or do.

Setting out the ingredients for that night's supper – fried chicken – Louise forced herself to think on good things. The dinner would be a celebration, both of little Jimmy's first week in school, and Vic's wonderful news that the bank had okayed a loan amount for them to begin looking to buy their first house. They were already scouring the newspaper daily for houses for sale, although the kind of house Louise wanted – and the location – versus what they could afford, was presenting a problem.

Pausing and raising her eyes to gaze out the window over the sink, Louise let her mind drift back to the evening after the anniversary party when Vic had come home early to tell her his news.

They were snuggled together on the cushioned glider on the back porch. The rest of the family was inside the house watching their second-hand RCA television, which Vic had acquired from a customer in exchange for some car repairs not long after he had opened the station. Black and white, with only a twelve-inch screen, it was nonetheless an exciting step-up for the formally radio-only family. The kids adored watching their favorite shows and seeing the characters in action rather than just listening and using their imagination. Little Jimmy immediately became the official 'rabbit ears' adjuster, a responsibility he performed with earnest care.

Drifting on the evening air, the couple could hear the boys' laughter as they watched the antics of the Jack Benny program. It warmed the parents' hearts to hear their children enjoying themselves.

The late summer storm from earlier in the day had slowed to just a drizzle, the water dripping mesmerizingly off the eaves of the house and the roof of the porch. It was soothing and comfortable. With a relaxed sigh, Louise nuzzled against her husband; arms around his ribs, her head nestled in the curve of his shoulder and neck.

"It's so nice out here," she murmured softly, eyes contently shut. All during the day, she had been giving herself a stern talking to, and was immensely relieved that the stresses of late had receded some. Then to have Vic walk in the door hours earlier than she had expected him seemed like an answer to prayer. "I know we need the business, but...I'm glad you closed up early and came home. It's been so long since we could just relax together like this...I've missed it."

"Me, too," he murmured, tightening his arms around her and pressing a kiss to her forehead.

They were silent for a few minutes, just enjoying the night. The clean fresh scent of the air after the day of rain, the good meal Louise and Lilly had prepared, and now the sound of the giggling joy of their boys, all worked together to provide a little bit of heaven on earth.

"Babe...I'm sorry things haven't been workin' out like I thought they would. You know I don't wanna be spendin' every day away from you and the kids, don't ya?"

She nodded, turning her head a bit to press a tiny kiss to the warm skin above the neck of the tee shirt he had donned after his evening shower. He'd even put on aftershave, and the heavenly scent of Old Spice wafted around Louise and made her snuggle in more. She almost felt like purring.

"I did a lot of thinkin' today and I made some decisions," he continued. "I'm gonna call the bank in the morning and talk to 'em about getting a loan so we can buy us our first house – closer to the station. That'll ease the stress of travelin' so much every day...and I can come home for lunch once in a while...maybe even have some dessert with my baby," he added in a husky, sensuously teasing tone, squeezing her a bit tighter.

She leaned her head back and met his eyes, smoky and dark in the dusky light of evening. "Oh Vic, that sounds wonderful."

A soft smile made his eyes twinkle in the dim light as he brought up his left hand and gently touched her face with his fingertips. "You're my world, babe. I love you...and I hate it that it seems like the station has been driving a wedge between us lately." He had stopped short of admitting he almost wished he were still employed by Hap at the downtown parking lot. That would sound like he was giving up on his dream and he didn't want her to lose faith in him or in his abilities.

"I love you too, Vic," Louise whispered, her eyes stinging a bit as the beauty of the moment resounded deep within her heart. She hadn't realized just how much she had missed her husband's normally romantic words and gestures. This was more like the Vic she had always known. The thought crossed her mind that she had begun to feel as if he wasn't the same person, but had turned into a tension-filled workaholic.

He smiled lovingly, leaning to press his lips softly against hers. After the sweet, love-affirming kiss, he pulled back a bit and resettled her into his arms. She grasped his left hand and brought it up to her lips as she laid her head against his chest, absently pressing a kiss to each finger – including the one that was missing its tip from the frightening accident he'd had at the CCC camp so many years ago.

Vic drew in a deep breath, letting it out slowly as more of the tension evaporated from his body. He rubbed one hand gently up and down her arm as he stared out into the wet backyard, past the slow drips from the porch's eaves. "Oscar did okay closing last night," he murmured softly, almost as if he were thinking out loud.

Glad that for once in a long while, talking about the station wasn't causing more stress, Louise opened her eyes and just listened, focusing on his words as he continued. "I couldn't see anything he forgot when I opened up this morning. But…I need somebody sharp that I can rely on when I drive off the lot."

"I know…" she sighed softly.

"Trouble is, those kinda' men cost more than I can pay right now…" he began.

"Doc mentioned to us as we were leaving church this morning that he's going to pray hard that you find the right man for the job," she admitted, adding with a soft smile, "I think he was worried about us last night during the party."

"Yeah…I feel so torn sometimes about not goin' to church. I ought to be *taking* my family to church. Once we find a place and move, maybe I can open at 1:00 on Sundays or something…"

"Yes, that would…" she paused as Jimmy came running out of the kitchen door and flung himself onto the glider with them.

"You gotta come! The Ed Sull'van Show is comin' on next! They're gonna have Dee Martn' an' Jerry Lews on!" he gushed. "Jerry Lews is so funny. C'mon! You're gonna miss it!" he insisted, grasping a hand from each of his parents and trying to tug them up from their comfortable spot.

Vic laughed and reached over to ruffle the closely trimmed

hair of his youngest, giving him a wink. "That's *Dean Martin* and Jerry *Lewis*, son. You go on, we'll be there in a few minutes."

"Okay Daddy!" Jimmy giggled, scrambling off the settee and retracing his steps. His boundless energy never seemed to abate.

The parents looked at one another and Vic shrugged good-naturedly. "So much for relaxin' on the porch, huh?"

Louise opened her mouth to suggest that they linger in their comfortable spot with the hopes that their presence would be overlooked, but they both heard their youngest bellow from inside, "Scoot over, Buddy – *Daddy's* gonna watch Ed Sull'van with us!"

Vic shook his head with a fond chuckle and stood to his feet. Reaching down to grasp both of Louise's hands, he tugged her up, immediately enveloping her in a tight, full embrace. Pulling back, his mouth covered hers for a toe-curling kiss that absolutely took her breath away. Before releasing her, he growled playfully in her ear, "For once, tonight I don't give a flyin' flip about who's on Sullivan."

Louise laughed softly as her arms wound around her husband and squeezed tightly…

"I'm glad to see you smiling again," Lilly's voice murmured nearby, bringing Louise out of her daydream to realize she was still standing at the sink, her arms wrapped around her middle.

Focusing on her mother, Louise sent her a soft smile.

છ૭ન્દ્ર

Vic grunted as he strained to break a bolt loose, under yet another car balanced on the lift. As he heard the driveway bell sound off with its double ding, the wrench slipped, causing him to bang his knuckles against the frame. He clamped his teeth together and ground out a choice word, but was glad that Oscar was on duty to pump gas for the apparent customer. Flinging his hand back and forth to lessen the pain, he forced himself to focus on the music coming from the radio on the workbench in the corner. His favorite singer/musician, Louie "Satchmo" Armstrong was, at that moment, belting out the lyrics to *Dream a Little Dream of Me*. Vic drew in a deep breath and clamped his hands on his hips.

Lately, his thoughts had been constantly straying to his fetching wife, whom he had left that morning a bit saddened by the rut she had found herself in since their youngest son was now in school. She had clung to Vic as he prepared to head out to work, and it had taken quite a bit of restraint not to stay home and be a comfort to her. Humming along with the gravel-voiced jazzman as he sang to his ladylove of fading stars and craving her kisses, sunbeams and leaving all her worries behind her, Vic glanced over at the round clock on the wall and wished it was time to close up shop and go home.

"Still goofin' off instead 'a workin', huh Chief?" a familiar voice drawled from the direction of the open bay door.

Vic turned as he reached for the ever-present rag in his back pocket, his face transforming into a wide flashing grin. A familiar lanky form relaxed against the edge of the doorway, hands shoved deep in his trouser pockets and one foot nonchalantly crossed over the other.

"As the kids say nowadays, *What's buzzin', cuzzin'?*"

"Floyd Grimes, you seven times a son of a gun! Where'd you come from?" Vic greeted his long time friend, moving forward and reaching out to shake the man's hand. "I ain't heard from you since I saw you last year, down at the parking lot. You still in the service?"

Vic grinned at his old pal from his days in the CCC's – the Civilian Conservation Corps – taking silent assessment of how good or bad the years had been. Floyd's white teeth gleamed from that familiar face, still a pleasant hue of café au lait. His round eyes, the shade of rich dark coffee beans, were fringed with black lashes and twinkling merrily, although Vic could see lines of age and strain around them that the years had inflicted. But then, Vic knew he bore the same signs of maturity on his own face. Floyd had filled out some since his days as a carefree skinny youth of twenty-one, and his close-cropped hair showed a hint of gray in the soft charcoal.

"Mustered out this mornin'," Floyd answered, turning to see what vehicle had tripped the driveway bell again. The late-model Ford honked and Vic raised a hand in greeting, even as he watched Oscar amble over to see to the customer's needs.

Indicating the large Coca Cola chest-type cooler situated on a concrete slab outside the wall between bays one and two, Vic offered, "Somethin' to drink?"

"Sho' thing," Floyd answered, watching as Vic opened the cold bottle of coke and passed it to him before securing one for himself and shutting the lid.

"So…" Vic began, pausing to take a long draw of his drink. "You got a place to stay yet?"

Floyd gulped down a mouthful of Coke and wiped the back of his hand over his mouth. "Not yet. Figured I'd grab me a room down at 'de Y fer now. Gots my saving's in my wallet, and all my worldly goods packed in my ride," he added, jutting his chin over his shoulder toward a 1950 mint green Packard, parked off to the side of the lot.

"That's yours? Nice car, man," Vic complimented, casting an eye toward the vehicle. "Goin' in the army was a good choice for you. You did good for yourself."

Floyd gave a carefree shrug. "Might say."

"Where'd you get your Packard?"

Floyd flashed one of his mischievous grins. "Won her off a sergeant playin' poker, on the base back in Jacksonville."

Vic whistled, muttering a few colorful words. "You jokin'? Aw man, you ain't still pullin' that *I don't know nothing, I ain't no good at this game* swindle, are ya?"

Floyd tipped back his head and laughed. "Naw man. Was just

a case of I was lucky and he was cocky. Won that babe with a
straight flush. He was holdin' three aces and thought he had me
by the short hairs. Dude shouldn't a' tossed his pink slip in on
that last call, but hey – I ain't one to look a gift horse in the
mouth, know what I'm sayin'?" he chuckled as Vic let out a laugh
and raised his bottle in salute.

"But hey…what'd *you* put up?"

Before Floyd could answer, a car pulled into the station's lot,
dinging the bell, and causing Vic to remember his duties. "Aw
man, I gotta get those shocks on. I promised it by six, and I don't
have any mechanic help, so it's all on me." As he headed under
the rack again, he glanced at his friend, "You got plans?"

Floyd reached up to give his head a scratch, an unconscious
habit Vic recognized from their younger days. "Well, Chief…I
been thinkin' a lot about it…you know I gots me some 'sperience
workin' on 'dem army trucks…" he paused, gesturing toward the
two vehicles parked in the station's bays.

Vic realized what he meant and it saddened him that he
would have to turn his friend down. His eyes met the other man's.
"Floyd…look…I'd like to take you on. More than anything, I
would. It'd be great to work together again. I know you'd be good
at it, but…I just ain't makin' enough profit yet. I can barely afford
to meet all the bills, keep a roof over my head, and pay Oscar
there," he added with a nod toward the man pumping gas. "Why,
thing's been so bad, it was just last week that I got a business
telephone in here. From the day I opened last year, I was stuck
with a pay phone. You talk about a pain in the you-know-where."
He chuckled and shook his head, muttering a colorful word. "Just
to save a dime, if I wanted to call home, I'd let it ring twice and
hang up and Louise'd call me back for free!"

Floyd opened his mouth to answer, but Oscar chose that
moment to holler, "Hey Boss! This man here wants to talk to
you."

Vic, who had picked up a wrench to begin working under the

elevated vehicle, let it drop with a clang and did an about face, making his way out to meet and shake hands with the visitor. Mr. Jason Lockridge, was a stocky, balding, well-dressed, cigar-smoking man who appeared to be in his middle fifties. He turned out to be a representative of the U-Haul Trailer Rental System, a ten-year-old company that provided one-way rental trailers to customers nationwide.

It couldn't have worked out better – one would even think the timing was God-engineered. On the very day that Floyd showed up hoping to hook up with his old CCC pal, Vic was offered a way for the station to make extra money. One catch was that the U-Haul venture operated strictly on a cash basis, no checks or credit cards, and precise paperwork needed to be kept. However, the profit potential sounded like a dream come true. Vic didn't have to think twice about the endeavor, since the fact was at least once a day, sometimes twice, somebody came into the station asking if he had any kind of trailer they could use to move their furniture. No one wanted to pay the moving companies' big fees.

So, it was decided. As Vic shook Mr. Lockridge's hand and signed the papers, he suddenly found himself with a man whom he could trust to oversee the station when he had to be away – *and* a way to guarantee his salary.

They closed up the station together that night and Floyd promised to be on duty first thing in the morning.

As Vic climbed into his old pickup for the ride home, he couldn't wait to tell Louise the good news.

CHAPTER 5

The House in Buechel

"TWO FORTY NINE, there it is…" Louise murmured as Vic allowed the car to slowly roll past a mid-sized house with a for-sale sign in the front yard. "What do you think? I like the flower boxes…"

Louise had been scouring the real estate section of the paper every day since Vic told her of his decision to buy a house, and this was the first property that had become available in their price range. Or rather…this was the first one worth looking at – the rest had been dumps. Quickly calling the telephone number, a Buechel Terrace exchange, she made an arrangement to view the house without Vic's knowledge. With his busy schedule, however, Vic was relieved and grateful that his wife had taken the initiative to get the ball rolling.

Now, on the following Sunday after church, with Floyd taking care of the station and Lilly minding the boys, Vic turned the car into the driveway and shut off the engine. His eyes scanned the front of the house, recalling the newspaper ad that had said it was a three-bedroom ranch. It had tan siding, two crank-out windows with white shutters and cute little flower boxes to the left of the front door, and a large three-pane window on the right that presumably was the living room. Alongside this was a one-car, three-sided carport.

Immediately the front door opened. A short, stocky man,

who looked to be in his early thirties, sporting a military haircut and khaki work clothes, stepped out and walked toward the car.

"You the Matthews?" he asked.

"That's right," Vic nodded and began to climb out on the driver's side. The man flashed a friendly smile and extended a hand to shake.

Vic took his hand in a firm greeting and then turned back to reach in and help Louise scoot over the seat as he said over his shoulder, "This is my wife, Louise."

The man greeted Louise with another smile and a handshake, introducing himself as Bill Hazelwood. Turning toward the house, he began, "Well, let me show you the outside first, and then we'll go on inside so you can take a look."

They spent the next few minutes taking a tour of the yard, with the man pointing out the features of the house and explaining details as well as the improvements he had made to the property in the three years that he had owned it. Knowing the man had purchased and had it built with a G.I. loan, Vic asked, "So, why are you sellin' so soon after buyin' it?" His tone suggested he wondered if there was something unseen, even unwanted, about the house.

"I hate to, because I really like it here and it's a great house, but my job transferred me to Evansville. I'm set to start work up there by the first of next month."

Vic and Louise exchanged smiles at that – Evansville; both thinking it was a small world. Just the name of the city in Indiana brought back memories for Vic – of Al and Goldie, his brother and sister-in-law, and of friends and places he'd visited while he lived there. Vic wondered for a moment where the man was going to work and if it was anywhere near Diamond Dry Cleaners, his gravy job he once had thought would be the career from which he would retire.

The man glanced from one to the other, briefly wondering at the secret joke, but only shrugged. "Well, let's go inside and see what you think," he continued. "Now, I built this porch last summer…"

Mr. Hazelwood described, in detail, everything that had occurred with the house, and even his dreams of someday being able to expand, perhaps adding another bedroom out the back thereby utilizing some of the ample space in the back yard.

After the tour, Louise wandered the rooms as the men talked. She inspected the closets; the bathroom with its modern shower; the size of the rooms as she pictured their furniture filling the space; the kitchen cabinets and counters, imagining herself and Lilly working to prepare meals. As she envisioned their future there, she pushed back the thoughts of what the house *didn't* have and she had wanted – namely a basement, more living space, and *two* bathrooms. However, she had quickly found out that what she wanted did not correlate too well with their budget. *But*, she reminded herself, *the house would actually belong to us, and no one would ever be able to tell us to find another place to live. We could do what we want with it.* That thought gave her a pleasant feeling of satisfaction as she pictured painting and wallpapering several of the rooms to suit her own tastes. No more all white walls or old, peeling wallpaper.

Her thoughts were interrupted as Vic called from the back door, where he and the owner had been lounging in a set of chairs on the back porch while they chatted over possible deals. "Hey babe? Where are ya?"

"I'm back here, in the master bedroom," she responded, struggling with a measuring tape as she sized the window.

Vic appeared in the doorway, a slow grin taking over his face as he watched her – his industrious little wife. He had left Mr. Hazelwood on the porch so they could have a private chat.

"Well? Whatdya think? Do you like it?"

She turned from the window and met his eyes. "Yes, I do like it…do you?"

He glanced around at what would be their room and down

the hallway with a slight shrug of one shoulder. "Yeah, it'll do. And I think it's a good deal for the price. He mentioned that we could assume his loan. That'll keep the payments low. But the main question is…will it…make you happy?"

Louise drew in a quick breath at the look in Vic's warm brown eyes. At that moment, more than at any other time in their marriage, she realized how much her husband adored her – and would do anything he had to do in order to keep her satisfied. A memory surfaced of Vic, on one knee, pledging that he would work his fingers to the bone to take care of her and the children. The realization gave her conscience a pang.

In a split second, she knew she had a choice – stubbornly hold out for a bigger place, essentially believing they would receive some kind of miracle – or go with what they could afford and make it work. Instinctively, she knew if she did the former, it would result in Vic working more hours and their money being stretched impossibly far.

Walking over to her husband, Louise slipped into the circle of his arms and leaned her head back enough to meet his eyes. "Yes, I think so. I like that it's right down the street from Earl and Ruth. Getting this place would mean we would live closer to the station, we would finally be out of the west end, and best of all…we would finally have a bedroom with a door – and a lock!" she teased, grinning when he threw back his head and laughed before tightening his arms around her.

"Well, all right then. What say we go talk turkey with Mr. Hazelwood?"

With a teasing little smile, Louise murmured, "Sounds like a great idea."

He leaned down to give her a quick kiss and with an arm around one another's waists, the two strolled down the hall from the bedroom.

ഖᏇ

THAT EVENING, THE couple stepped out onto the porch of what would be the first home they would own, and watched as their youngest two boys frolicked in a giggling game of chasing lightning bugs and each other.

Two young voices instantly yelled out, competing to be heard. "Mama! Wait till you see how many fireflies we've got!" "Almost a whole jar full!"

"There's lots more here than our yard back home has," Buddy added as he ran excitedly up to his mother and thrust the glass jar into her hands, its interior alive with the delicate flashing insects.

She held the perforated top tightly and smiled down into his eyes as he looked up at her adoringly. Then she murmured, "That's good, honey."

"You go on back and play with your brother, now," Vic gently instructed, tussling his son's hair. "We'll be gettin' on the road for home in a few minutes."

"Okay, Daddy," Buddy answered, reaching out and grasping the jar again as Jimmy hollered, "Got another one! Bring the jar!"

Vic watched them, a soft smile adorning his lips as he remembered catching lightning bugs with his own brothers in days gone by – carefree days of his early life before first his mother and then his father had passed away and he had spent a long succession of years shuffled from one relative to another.

Shaking off that thought, he reached out and pulled his wife close to his side as he concentrated on the here and now – his first home purchase.

Although the couple had gone ahead and signed the papers to assume Mr. Hazelwood's loan, deep down, Vic was a bit concerned about meeting the payments. Specifically, an extra twenty dollars a month they had agreed upon as a second mortgage, because the owner had insisted he wanted another $1,000 above the original loan for the improvements he had made to the property. Due to the fact that Vic and Louise didn't have that much money saved, the man had agreed to accept monthly payments to be sent straight to him to make up the difference.

At an original price of $12,000, a loan percentage of 3.5% on a fifteen-year loan meant the payments were nearly eighty-six dollars a month. That was almost double what they were paying John Womack to rent the house on Thirty-Eighth Street. Then with the extra twenty, it would be over $100 per month. The amount made Vic's head feel light and his stomach feel queasy. He had never imagined, in his wildest dreams, that he would ever sign his name to a promissory note for such a monthly amount. The thought of having slow months or a reduction in customers at the station – and as a result a decrease in their profits – made Vic's stomach do somersaults.

Doc would say to pray about it…but maybe we shoulda prayed about it before we signed the papers…? Well, what's done is done. And if it'll make Louise happy, that's all that counts. With an unconscious shrug, Vic pushed the concerns to the back of his mind.

As Vic watched the boys' carefree play, a doting twinkle in his eyes, Tommy walked up from the side of the house and slouched at the edge of the porch. Casting a sideways look up at his parents, he asked off-handedly, "So, when do we move in?"

Without taking his eyes off the cavorting youngsters, Vic answered, "Hazelwood and I decided on thirty days. That gives us both time to get everything packed and ready. He's got to make a trip to Evansville to secure a place to live, and your mom wants to have time to scrub the place from top to bottom and do some sprucing up before we move in."

Tommy nodded in reply to the answer, his features thoughtful as he watched his younger brothers. He grinned and shook his head at their antics as they both scrambled after the same lightning bug, resulting in one crashing into the other as they landed in a chuckling, tangled heap in the grass.

Lilly walked out of the back door at that moment, sighing in the early September heat as she lowered into one of the chairs on the porch and began to fan herself with a discarded newspaper. She had put on weight in recent years, something easy to do considering her short, stocky frame. Her penchant for wearing dark colored dresses and knee-high stockings only exacerbated the situation. "It's not as big as I hoped it would be," she commented to no one in particular.

Vic and Louise exchanged a look, and Louise answered over her shoulder, "No, but we'll make it work."

"No basement. And it doesn't look like I'll be having my own room…" Lilly grumbled under her breath, omitting the rest of her sentence, which would have been along the lines of, "Like you promised."

Vic knew she was miffed that they hadn't included her in their decision and he half turned toward his mother-in-law, feeling the urge to explain, "We looked and looked, Lilly, but just couldn't find a four-bedroom place we could afford…and even this one's payment'll be a stretch to meet…" he stopped, not wishing to air his fears.

Tommy turned his head and looked at his parents' expressions, as his concern turned from the fact that he would have to change schools and leave his friends, his girlfriend, and everything familiar, to a niggling worry and hope that the family hadn't bitten off more than they could chew.

Emotions beginning to heat up, Louise opened her mouth to send her mother a sharp retort when they all heard a voice shout, "Hey! What's this I hear? They're letting just about *anybody* buy a house in this neighborhood!"

The boys stopped playing, and the adults all turned toward the carport side of the house before reacting in smiles and laughs as a familiar face peeked around the edge.

"That's right, Grant. Somebody's gotta keep the peace around here, seein' that the neighbors have to put up with *your* nonsense," Vic shot back, causing his long-time friend, Earl, to burst out laughing and head on into the back yard. Ruth followed behind, swatting at her husband's arm in a joking attempt to get him to behave. Gina and Terry, the Grants' son and daughter, ran over to see what the boys were doing.

Moving over to the porch to give Louise a hug as Vic headed toward Earl to shake his hand in greeting, Ruth gushed, "I'm so happy for you, Louise! I know how exciting it is to finally be able to buy your first place. And it's so keen, right down the street from *us*." Glancing around, she remarked without thinking, "Of course, it's not as big or as nice as ours, but it's got potential…"

Louise forced a smile and glanced at her mother, who had emitted a decidedly un-ladylike snort at Ruth's clumsiness. Realizing the unintended slight, Ruth quickly backpedaled, her words tumbling over one another, "I…I mean, this is a nice place. The back yard has lots of room, and so many trees – and backs right up to that giant cornfield. Since ours is across the street, our yard backs up to the yard of the house behind us, and it's not nearly as deep, and only a few trees. You guys could put in a garage, or even add on to the house if you wanted…I've always wished for more backyard space, with ours being on the corner like it is…" she practically sputtered, obviously feeling bad that her previous statement had caused a bit of a dimming in Louise's countenance. "You'll like it here, it's a great neighborhood. The people are nice, there's lots of kids for Buddy and Jimmy to play with…" she continued on and on, extolling the virtues of Buechel Terrace.

Her momentary disgruntlement abating, Louise turned with her friend and they entered the back door, Louise nodding in agreement and making an occasional small comment as Ruth plowed on with observations and ideas. In no time, Louise's level of excitement about actually buying and moving into their first home began to rise again and she looked forward to starting their new adventure.

Outside in the backyard, Vic, Earl, and Tommy stood with their arms across their chests, watching the youngsters laugh and play a game of tag. It was obvious little Jimmy was feeling frustrated that he couldn't seem to catch any of the others. Finally he came trotting over to his father, a pout on his sweet face as he fought to hold back tears lest the other kids begin teasing and calling him a crybaby.

"Daddy, they won't let me catch 'em. Makes me so mad," he grumbled as he flung himself against his father's leg. Vic chuckled and laid a hand on his youngest son's head, ruffling his crew cut hair as he crooned, "Aw, don't you worry, Jimmy. Some day you'll be as big as them and you'll be the cock of the walk. You just gotta give it time, and let yourself grow a bit, son."

Jimmy tipped his head back and gazed up at his father, thinking he was the biggest, strongest, most wonderful man in the world, and he wanted to grow up to be just like him. With wide-eyed innocence, he asked, "What's a cocka the walk?"

Tommy snorted a chuckle as Earl threw his head back and laughed.

Before Vic could find the words to explain, Tommy stepped over and reached down to his youngest sibling, scooping him up and situating him on his shoulders as he answered, "It means the biggest and the best, little brother. Here, let's go see if we can chase us down some meanies."

The teen took off at a trot with Jimmy bobbing up and down on his high perch, clasping onto his big brother's chin with both hands. The little boy released delighted giggles as Tommy made snorting noises like an angry bull. Buddy and the two Grant kids squealed and scattered in three different directions.

Vic watched with a twinkle in his eyes, breathing deeply of the late afternoon air. It seemed to him that it smelled a bit sweeter and cleaner, there in the back yard that he actually owned and wasn't just renting – and out in the suburbs, away from the 'old' smell of downtown. Looking out past the edges of the yard with its large trees, he could see acres and acres of mature feeder corn, ready to be harvested. It was like having the pleasures of the country with the conveniences of the city all rolled into one. Taking a moment, he counted the number of trees scattered in his yard – sixteen! *Sixteen trees…wow. That will be a heck of a pile of leaves to rake in a month or two…*

His keen ears then picked up on the two women in the house, in a back bedroom where a window was open, allowing their voices to float out to him on the evening breeze. He smiled as he heard Louise's sweet voice discussing with Ruth what curtains she planned for the room and what color she wanted on the walls.

With a slight nod, he drew in another deep breath, feeling the familiar stress that always seemed to dog his every waking moment begin to melt away.

Good. Maybe now she'll get back to being the sweet wife she's always been.

As he only half listened to the story Earl began telling him about something that had happened at his work, Vic pictured what the future would be like once they moved into their new house.

With the U-Haul contract and his trusted best buddy, Floyd, now working with him, he looked forward to the next chapter in their lives.

ℬↄↃ CↃↄↄ

CHAPTER 6

Unexpected Visitors

LOUISE STOOD UP straight from stooping down to put her pots and pans away in the bottom drawers of her new kitchen's GE range. It sported four burners on the left side, surface space to prepare on the right, two ovens, and a window in the door. It was the newest cooking stove she had ever owned – and the first electric powered. Having always used gas ranges in the past, she couldn't wait to prepare a meal on it. Briefly, she wondered how different cooking with electric would be, but dismissed the thought, assuring herself that she would get the hang of it in no time.

Her new kitchen was so modern and clean, with pale mint green walls, sparkling white cabinets (which she and Lilly had scrubbed to a polished shine), bright green counters, a white porcelain double sink – the first she'd ever had – and shiny white appliances. Matching corner shelves, on which she had placed some of her prettier knickknacks, bracketed a large window behind the sink overlooking the back yard. She was grateful that Mr. Hazelwood had taken such good care of the house while he had occupied it.

It's sure a far cry from some of the places I've lived…and some of the kitchens I've had to cook in… With a shiver, she remembered one of the places she had lived with her first husband, T.J. – a dark, drafty, depressing place, and they couldn't seem to get rid of the roaches. While living there, she had come down with tonsillitis, twice! Thankfully, they hadn't lived there long. Even with Vic, she'd had her share of not-so-pleasant experiences in the places they lived – like their visit from Mr. Rat at their second apartment. *Ewww! One time seeing him was enough!*

Wiping her hands on her apron and smoothing her hair back with one hand, she gazed around at the room, pleased with how everything was shaping up. She was quite surprised with how easy this move had been compared to times past.

The thirty days, which had at first seemed as though it would be an eternity, had flown by, with all of the preparations, packing, and details that had to be sorted out to make the move across town. It felt like they had moved to another county!

Until that first day of loading their belongings into boxes, and satisfying the curiosity of friends and neighbors who had dropped by, Louise hadn't thought about the fact that they were leaving the familiar West End of Louisville. It was there that she had been born and raised – where she knew all of the best meat and produce markets, drug stores, and everything else. Louisville was a big city, and yet the neighborhood seemed like a small town, where she walked the familiar streets, met friends and neighbors going about their day, window-shopped on Fourth, hopped on the streetcar or the bus, or caught a cab. The boys had to pull up roots and would be starting at new schools come Monday morning – a fact that made none of them happy. And their beloved church, with their precious friends – and especially Doc – would now be so far away.

But, it's all for the good. Life out here in the suburbs will be easier, with Vic so much closer to the station. She gave a quick nod, pushing away any melancholy thoughts, especially since, except for Lilly, she was now farther away from the other members of her family. Her brother Sonny, his wife Sarah, and their two daughters, still lived in a large apartment on Breckinridge. Louise's younger brother, Billy, had rented a room in a boarding house nearby for a stint, before moving downtown to be closer to his work. Until then, both of her brothers had dropped in, at least for a few minutes, nearly every week at the old place.

Turning, she readjusted the new white and green ivy print curtains, and spied the little plant that Ruth had given her as a housewarming present, resting on the windowsill above the sink. Its pretty little bowl, white and decorated with a spray of ivy across the front, went perfectly with the room's décor. "I saw this and thought you'd love it," her friend had said when presenting the gift.

Ruth had been especially complimentary of everything Louise had done in regard to arranging and decorating the house, and it had gone a long way in helping Louise forget the biting comments she had made the night they had bought the house. Deep down, Louise knew Ruth hadn't meant anything hurtful by her words. She understood that it was simply a matter of her mouth working before her brain was engaged. At any rate, the two had, of course, remained friends.

Humming along with the tune on the small radio sitting on the counter – Elvis Presley's silly rockabilly song, *Baby Let's Play House* – Louise found herself moving her feet and hips to the fast beat of the music as she filled a glass with water and gave the plant a drink.

Glancing out the window to make sure Buddy and Jimmy were still playing in the back yard, she paused as a red cardinal landed on the sill outside the window and promptly turned its head to look through the glass at her.

Louise stopped all motion, watching to see what the beautiful little bird would do, as she remembered something her father, Willis, used to say. *When a red cardinal visits you or crosses your path, it's good luck, or a loved one in heaven is trying to say, "Hello! I'm with you!"* Her breath caught as she stared at the little bird, marveling that it seemed to see right into her spirit…and then one of its eyes seem to wink at her! Just like her father used to do! Almost immediately, it was as if she heard her father's gentle voice murmur, "I'm here, Sweet pea...I love you, baby girl...My pride and joy...My pretty Mary Louise..."

Tears sprang to her eyes and she closed them, shutting out the world, the song on the radio, and everything else, just to bask for a moment in her father's love as she whispered, "I love you too, Daddy." *Oh Daddy...I wish you hadn't been taken from us so soon. I wasn't ready to lose you.*

Memories floated down like leaves on a sunny Autumn day...of her father's beloved face, with his wire rim glasses, eyes crinkled in a chuckle as he laughed... of his big, gnarled hand, firm, but gentle as he calmed her or meted out some sort of discipline...of him trying valiantly to stem the influx of water into the apartment house during the flood, and then when he realized it was hopeless, how he set about an orderly evacuation of their home... but mostly of the feeling of his arms around her as he pressed her to his chest in a warm, firm hug, and his voice murmuring that she was his precious girl...

All too soon, however, reality intruded on her memories.

"Hey Mom, I don't think this is gonna work," Tommy complained as he made his way into the kitchen, stepping over empty boxes in the hallway.

Louise opened her eyes with a sigh and raised her hands to her face. Noticing the redbird took one more look inside before flitting away out of sight, she turned to confront the problem. "What's not working, Tommy?"

"Me and Buddy's furniture in that little bitty bedroom. No matter how I rearrange the beds and the dressers, something doesn't fit. And there's no basement, no place to store anything, except the carport," he grumbled, huffing a sigh as he came into the kitchen and flopped down in a chair. "I wish Dad were here. He can always figure out stuff like this."

Louise smiled lovingly and walked over to him, laying one hand on his head and running her fingers lightly through his thick, wavy, light brown locks. Although his features resembled his biological father, Louise thanked the Lord that he had not inherited his personality. It wasn't like Tommy to whine and complain, but he had been a trifle moody about the whole situation of the move. She knew that part of the problem was he was having separation anxieties from his latest girlfriend – a cute little number named Betty, who was a cheerleader at his old school, Shawnee High.

"At least you two have a room now," Louise reminded him, referring to the fact that they had carved out a portion of the living room at the old house to make a sleeping area for he and Buddy. "What if all of us had to live in one room?"

He gave her a shocked look, as if he couldn't imagine such a thing.

Louise nodded with a chuckle. "When I was young, there were six of us, Grandma and Grandpa, your Uncle Sonny, Aunt Edna, me, and Uncle Billy. For years, after Daddy lost his job at the mill, we had to all live in one room. It was on the first floor of a big apartment house and the only bathroom was on the second floor – and we had to share it with the other tenants. Compared to that, this is a castle," she admonished.

"How in the world could six people live in one room?" he asked incredulously, trying to picture such a scene and wondering if his mother was exaggerating. His earliest memories placed him, his mother, and his beloved stepfather in a nice apartment with a large living room, a big dining room, their own bathroom, and even a little room of his own. He remembered when the hateful landlord divided the apartment and gave half of it to a mean old woman who always seemed to be in a bad mood. It hadn't been very long at all before Mom and Chief had looked around for a bigger place.

"I don't know, but we did," his mother answered, her eyes staring straight ahead for a moment as she pictured the situation. "It was all we had, so we had to make do. And if *we* could do it then, you can do this now, when circumstances are so much better. Hmm?" She gazed into his eyes, brows arched.

He dipped his head with a sigh and nodded, accepting the chastisement.

Louise softened again, leaning to wrap an arm around his shoulder. "Don't worry, everything will work out. Maybe Vic will come home a little early again tonight. Floyd and Oscar can close up. I'll give him a call and see… oh, I forgot, the phone's still not hooked up," she murmured, once again feeling frustration at knowing that they would have to wait two weeks for a telephone, since the previous owner had never bothered to have one installed in the house and wires would have to be run.

Then with an encouraging smile, she added, "In the meantime, why don't you gather up the boxes…" she paused as the doorbell rang, followed by raucous knocking on the front door.

Glancing at the clock on the wall by the refrigerator, she murmured, "I wonder who that could be," even as she made her way over boxes and crushed newspaper to the door.

Wishing for the sidelights surrounding the front door at the old house, through which she could always take a peek to identify a visitor, she swung the door open. There stood Ruth, Fleet with little Alexa on her hip, and two ladies she didn't know, one of which was holding a pie while the other held an overflowing basket.

"Surprise!" Fleet hollered in her customary boisterous manner. Louise opened the screen door to let them in.

"I hope we're not coming at a bad time," one of the other ladies offered as the four filed inside. The tall woman with jet black hair styled in a bun, a long face, and black-rimmed glasses, held out one hand for Louise to shake. "My name is Elizabeth Ross, and this is Barbara Dixon," she gestured to the fourth woman, a petite, pretty lady with wavy, light brown hair and gorgeous green eyes who was smiling a greeting. "She lives three doors down, and I live at the head of the street," the larger woman continued. "We wanted to come and welcome you to the neighborhood."

"And just as they were walking up your sidewalk, me and Ruth pulled up for a visit and to see if we could help you get settled. Party time!" Fleet added jokingly. Mrs. Ross and Mrs. Dixon gave her a sidelong glance, but Louise was used to her wacky friend's sense of humor.

Laughing, she answered, "I would love the help, although there isn't much left to do…"

"Well, this is for you," Mrs. Ross offered, handing the basket to Louise with a friendly smile. Tommy stepped up behind his mother to see what was in the basket, and she introduced him to their new neighbors.

The shorter lady handed him the pie. With a twinkle in his eyes, he licked his lips and said, "Mmm, apple, my favorite!" before taking it to the kitchen with a grin that said there wouldn't be much left for the others when he was through.

Taken by surprise at the unexpected visit, Louise hesitatingly took the basket, perusing its contents, which included baked goods, coffee and tea, cleaning products, and even a set of hand towels for the bathroom. Mrs. Dixon removed a small bottle of apple wine from underneath her arm and handed it to Louise with a friendly smile.

"Thank you very much, ladies," Louise gushed, truly over-whelmed by their thoughtfulness. No one had ever welcomed her to a new place before, and she was momentarily rendered speechless. The thought sprang to her mind about the first day they moved into Mrs. Despaine's apartment house, and what a horrible "welcome" that had been. *What a nice thing for these ladies to do…and just another good thing about moving here…*

"So we bring you a little bit of help, a basketful of fun, and a barrel full of laughs," Fleet announced with a snort, causing all of the ladies to laugh as she produced, with a flourish, a frilly white-ruffled apron with a green ivy motif. "Ruth here told me about you decorating with ivy in the kitchen. I had to go to three stores to find that gem," Fleet announced to the group, adding with a dramatic swipe of her hand against her forehead, "Thought I was going to have to break down and make you something, heaven forbid!" She punctuated that bit with a shudder.

Good old Fleet, always the life of the party. She and that husband of hers were sure made for one another, Louise mused as she gestured for the chuckling ladies to have a seat on the couch.

Making themselves comfortable, they shared small talk for a while, with Louise telling her new neighbors a bit about the family and that her husband managed a Phillips 66 station for a living; the ladies shared about their own homes and families. Louise took note that the pretty Mrs. Dixon's husband was in the military and stationed overseas, so she lived alone with their two school-aged children.

Finally, the taller of the two, Mrs. Ross, stood to her feet and proclaimed that they should be running along. Louise politely asked them to stay longer and offered to make them a glass of tea.

"Oh no, we don't want to keep you from what ever you were doing," Mrs. Dixon remarked kindly as she declined the offer. "We just wanted to come by and welcome you to the neighborhood, and to tell you that we are just down the way should you need anything. Liz is at two twenty-two, and I'm three doors down the other way at two forty-three."

"Thank you so much. I'll remember," Louise nodded as the two made their way to the door. With a few more words and a promise to see them soon, the ladies departed.

Louise closed the door and turned to her friends with a smile. "Well don't that beat all? A welcome committee. I think I'm going to like living here."

"Two ladies welcomed us like that when we first moved here, too," Ruth grinned.

"Yeah, that's swell," Fleet agreed. "So, show me around the place," she added, adjusting Alexa on her hip as the little girl began to fuss. Although Alec had helped the day of the move, Fleet had stayed home with a sick Alexa; thus, she hadn't had the opportunity to see her friends' new house. Louise automatically reached out and took the child from Fleet's arms, relieving the mother for a few moments. Alexa quieted immediately and stared up at Louise with that expression babies always get – something akin to fascination.

"Well, this is the living room…and right through here is the kitchen and dinette…" she began as Lilly came in the kitchen door from the back yard, where she had been hanging up a large load of laundry. She greeted the ladies as she walked through with a large basket of freshly dried towels.

When the tour ended in the back yard and the ladies were watching Jimmy and Buddy kick a ball back and forth, Fleet turned to Louise with a twinkle in her eyes and a toss of her head.

"Think I'll see if I can talk my man into moving out here. It'd be like old times again, huh? I sure don't want to be left downtown with everybody moving to the burbs!"

And that's just what she did. Within a month, the house right next door became available and the Alders' snapped it up.

The gang was together again!

ଯୀ୧

CHAPTER 7

The Robbery

V IC HANDED THE customer his change and the required number of green trading stamps, and stepped back to allow the car to roll past him from its place at the gas pumps. Seconds later, its tires caused the driveway bell to sound its twin dings.

Taking a small wad of bills from his shirt pocket, Vic added the single dollar and refolded the paper before slipping the roll back in his pocket.

Vic watched the customer drive away, the vehicle's motor emitting a loud knocking sound. *The poor schnook…his car's about to go on the fritz, right here at Christmas, and he don't have the money to pay me to fix it. Maybe I could let him make payments…* The man had told him he would be back after the first of the year to get the motor worked on. *Maybe he will…maybe he won't. From the sound of it, it might just seize up before then…*

Glancing up at the cloud cover, he zipped his jacket up a little higher and involuntarily shivered, thinking the weatherman might be right for a change and they were in for a snow. *The kids would love that. It might be a White Christmas after all.*

With no vehicles to work on and no other customers wheeling in, he stood for a few moments at the center island, his hands deep in the pockets of his tan uniform trousers as he surveyed his domain. His station was still the last vestige of civilization before acres and acres of cornfields stretched out on the road to

Shelbyville. Only the East Drive-In Theater, which was so far up the road one couldn't see it from the station, interrupted the fields. He had heard a rumor that the owners of the farm had been thinking about selling off some acreage for a big 'mall', but so far nothing definite had been decided. Until then, Matthews Service Station was the last stop, a driver's last chance to get gas if they wanted to cruise to Shelbyville on a Sunday afternoon. Thus far, that had worked just fine for Vic and his small crew.

The contract with U-Haul had infused some much-needed cash into Vic's coffers, and the bonus of having his trusted friend Floyd there to oversee that part of the operation was a godsend. Only one U-Haul trailer was parked on the smooth concrete of his station's lot at the moment, as the other two had been rented.

Just then, movement caught his attention and Vic glanced to the right, toward the Frisch's Big Boy Restaurant next door. He saw a little girl break away from her mother and run over to the small, newly built walking bridge that spanned the drainage ditch between the two properties, the mother hot on the little girl's heels. The woman grabbed the child's hand and fussed at her not to run off that way. Vic watched as the mother towed her little girl toward Shelbyville Road and the bus stop. It being past time for breakfast, but not quite the lunch hour, something made him wonder if she had been inside asking about a waitress job.

A cold gust of wind made the freestanding green and white *S & H Green Stamps* sign out front swing with a squeak, and Vic turned his gaze toward it while reaching to flip up his jacket collar against the wind. It didn't take long for him to decide he would be more comfortable inside his heated office.

Stepping down off the pump's concrete slab, he ambled over to the door and let himself in, closing it firmly against another cold gust.

He glanced at the clock on the back wall as he mentally went over the schedule for his employees, and he realized that it would be another hour before Oscar arrived for his shift. Floyd had taken off for the day, since he had manned the station the day before to allow Vic to spend Sunday with his family.

Walking over to the radio on the desk, he flipped it on and was immediately serenaded by Bing Crosby singing the last few bars of *White Christmas,* followed by the disc jockey saying that maybe this year it would happen. Vic gave a chuckle and sat down in the swivel chair at his desk, enjoying its familiar soft squeak.

Need to get busy and get the deposit together, he mused as he took out the cash box and began going through the motions of counting the receipts and money earned since Friday's trip to the bank. He thought again about Oscar, running late because he had to take his mother to a doctor's appointment, which meant Vic was alone at the station, counting money – something he wouldn't normally have done – and now would be going to the bank later than usual. *Can't be helped. It'll be okay this one time...*

He looked at the checks, stacked the bills in denominations, and began rolling the coins in their rappers. It had been a good weekend. Lots of gallons had been sold, leaving the big underground tanks down to barely a quarter full. There were three small repair projects, two brake-jobs and a dozen oil changes and lube jobs, which hadn't taken much time, but had netted a fair profit.

Focusing on a penny and reading the minting year as 1910, Vic knew Buddy would be excited to add this to the Lincoln Head penny collection he had started at the beginning of the school year. With a smile as he imagined his son's enthusiasm when he presented it to him that evening, Vic pocketed the coin and continued his calculations.

He smiled again as it occurred to him that this would be the biggest bank deposit he had made since opening the station, and he wondered if the teller at the bank would notice. *Nah. Probably not.* Even after Oscar and Floyd's salaries and meeting the bills, he would have a good pile for Christmas presents. He closed his eyes for a moment. *Thanks, Lord.* Things were looking up, and it sure felt good. He jogged his memory for a few things Louise had mentioned that she wanted to get the boys, plus a few items he had planned to get for her...like maybe a new coat, or earrings to match the amethyst necklace she still wore nearly every day...

As he counted and sorted, the thought occurred to him that since the bank he used was halfway between the station and home...maybe he could run home for an early lunch...*and maybe some dessert*, he chuckled, his eyes twinkling.

This brought his thoughts around to his wife and the fact that something seemed to be wrong, but he just couldn't put his finger on it. Somehow, she didn't seem...happy. It wore on him and tore at him, as he adored her and couldn't stand the thought of her being anything but blissful. But she wouldn't tell him what was wrong.

Turning his head to the left to stare through the glass window, he unconsciously brought one hand up to rub over his chin, still smooth from that morning's shave. He sighed, lamenting the fact that he and Louise, his precious wife, just didn't seem to be able to communicate like they used to do.

After all they'd been through together...loving one another and pining for each other through all those long years of separation...then their early years of marriage when she had slaved in the cigar factory and he had taken any job he could get...all of the hardships, disappointments, and heartaches they had weathered together...and then having their two precious boys and building a life with one another...by now, there should be no secrets between them.

In his mind, he ticked off reasons Louise should have been happy...they had bought and moved into the first house they owned vs. rented; lately he had purposely made time to be with her and the kids, taking off early every chance he had, and they had even gone out to dinner and a movie on several occasions; they had gone to the drive-in as a family before the cold weather had set in... He paused at that thought, his lips forming a half grin as he remembered them trying to decide between *Oklahoma* and *The Seven Year Itch*, but Louise had bristled at the poster of the latter one – with Marilyn Monroe's white dress furling up in the wind.

Shaking his head with a snicker, he went back to fitting the coins into rolls, still ticking items off the invisible list in his mind – she had purchased all kinds of things for the house, and although it had made his wallet scream bloody murder, he hadn't said a word. She had her friends nearby, since Fleet and Alec had moved next door, and Ruth and Earl lived just a few doors down. *But maybe she missed seein' her brothers on a daily basis. She's too young to be going through the change, isn't she? She mentioned in passing that it would be nice to hear the pitter patter of little feet again, now that our youngest is in school full time...* Could she be pining this much over wanting another baby? They had been trying toward that end...or at least, hadn't been trying to *prevent* it, but it hadn't happened yet.

He decided right then that he'd have to set her down and have a long talk. The thought had occurred to him more than once, but he'd been putting it off because it never seemed like the right time. He stacked the bills on top of the checks. *Tonight...after everybody's in bed...*

Suddenly, the office door opened and cold air rushed throughout the space. Surprised that he hadn't seen a car pull onto the lot, or heard the driveway bells, he looked up. His mouth went instantly dry and his heart dropped to his stomach, and then began galloping double time as he encountered the most unexpected sight he could have imagined. A tall man in a full ski mask and a beat up old army jacket stood in the doorway, pointing a silver, pearl-handled revolver directly at Vic.

Before Vic could move or even blink, the man growled, "Don't do anything stupid! All I want is that deposit on your desk there. Hand it over and I'll be on my way. Don't make me use this," he added, brandishing the gun and casting quick looks behind and around himself to make sure no customers were coming. Vic wondered if he was imagining that the gun pointed at him was trembling. Could the robber be nervous? *A nervous hand holding a gun…that ain't good…*

Vic ground his teeth together, silently cursing this jerk that dared to come in to *his station* to steal all of his hard-earned money. *Just my luck!* Anger bubbled up, threatening to boil over, but Vic controlled the monumental urge to do something foolish and get himself shot.

"Keep the checks. Just stuff the money in the bag and toss it here. Hurry up!" the bandit demanded. The man must have seen the rebellion in his eyes as Vic hesitated, because he extended his arm with the gun pointing toward Vic. "NOW!"

With a mumbled oath, Vic stuffed the bills and coin rolls inside the money pouch, yanked the drawstring closed, and tossed it to the man – deliberately short, so that it fell to the floor. The burglar stepped two paces closer and bent down to retrieve it, just as Vic had hoped he would. Vic reached for a tire iron that happened to be on the corner of the desk and stood up to edge around. He only made it two steps when the man straightened up and barked, "Stop right there! Put it down, turn around, and put your hands behind your head. Do it!"

Grumbling a few choice words, his mind racing as he tried to think of a way to stop this slime ball from taking off with his dough, Vic grudgingly obliged. The man grasped the back collar of Vic's jacket and with the gun jabbing his back, roughly propelled him over to the door of the storeroom. He shoved Vic inside and slammed the door, but finding no lock, reached for a heavy, metal-backed chair and dragged it over, wedging it under the doorknob.

Through the metal surface of the portal, Vic heard the robber say, "Sorry man…I hated to do it…but I been out of work…I got kids…it's Christmas…you just don't know what it's like. You're a business owner – you got plenty. You're living *your* dream… Anyway…Merry Christmas."

With that, all was silent. Vic strained his ears, hearing nothing but the faint sounds of a car's motor. *He must have parked over in the Frisch's lot and walked...*

Vic banged on the door, hollering, but no one came. He flipped on the small room's light switch, stewing and angry – at himself and at the thief – and then he began to pace. He should have taken more care, should have known something was afoot... Who was that guy? Did he seem familiar? Something about him teased the edges of Vic's memory. However, his irritation level rose another notch when he just couldn't place him.

Finally after about twenty minutes, Vic heard the faint *ding ding* of the driveway bells. He heard the customer beep his horn, and he prayed that the person would get out and come looking for him, rather than just driving off in a huff. *Lord, let them come find me.*

His prayers were answered. In under a minute, he heard the glass door to the office open and a man's voice called out, "Anybody here?"

Vic beat on the door. "I'm in here! Let me out!"

Almost immediately, he heard a scraping sound and the door was yanked open. There stood one of his regulars, Dave Madison. Boy, was he glad to see him!

"Matthews, what the heck?"

"I've been robbed."

₨₩

VIC'S LONGTIME FRIEND, Detective John Womack, nodded thoughtfully as he looked down at the items he had jotted in his notebook. Vic had called for him right away, and having been in the vicinity, headquarters had radioed and he had arrived on the scene within five minutes.

"Okay, can you think of anything else? Anything at all, no matter if it seems insignificant."

Vic thought for a moment, searching his mind as he tried to

figure out what was familiar about the thief. Could it have been someone he knew? One of his former employees that he'd had to fire? But, none of them had been as tall as the robber... Finally, he sighed and shook his head, running a hand back through his hair in frustration.

"What?" the detective queried.

"I don't know...there was just something about the guy that seemed familiar, but with that ski mask on and it muffling his voice...I just don't know."

"Familiar, huh?" Womack asked, a thoughtful look gracing his face. Then with a teasing snort, he asked off-handedly, "You got any enemies I don't know about? Somebody from your past life of crime?"

Vic shot him a look and got up to get himself a cup of hot coffee from the pot on a little table next to his desk. Holding the pot aloft, he gestured it toward Womack in silent question, but the man shook his head to indicate he didn't want a second cup. Vic knew his friend was just yanking his chain with that crack about his past life of crime – referring to his months as a 'bookie' before, and a little while into, his and Louise's marriage. It had become a source of good-natured baiting between them – since his one and only time of being arrested was how the two had met. That was *many* years ago. The detective was well aware that his friend intended never to dabble in anything like that again.

Vic took a sip of his coffee, hot and black, just like he liked it. With a sigh, he mumbled, "Aww, I dunno. Maybe I'm just imagining things. All I know is – that guy comin' in here stickin' me up and takin' my weekend receipts has really put a crimp in my operations. And right here at Christmas time, too, that's the rub!"

"Sir, do you need me for anything else?" a voice asked from the doorway. David Madison, the customer who had rescued Vic from his temporary holding cell, stood with his hat in his hands, unconsciously running the band around in his fingers. He had just come from the bathroom on the side of the building.

Womack turned to the man. "No, that's all, Mr. Madison. You're free to go. Thank you for sticking around and answering my questions."

"No problem. I just wish I'd seen something or someone. That I could give you something to go on, but, I just didn't see a thing..."

"I know, and thanks," the detective cut him off, not needing to hear it again.

"Well, uh, then I guess I'll be going. I hope you catch the man who did it. What's this world coming to, anyway? Just isn't right."

Vic smiled his thanks and the man placed his hat on his head, nodded a goodbye, and went on out the door. The two men inside watched as he got in his car and drove off the lot.

Vic's detective friend turned back to him. "And you're absolutely sure he's not the guy – that he didn't double back and let you out just to give himself an alibi?"

"Nope. The robber was a good six inches taller than Madison. His voice was deeper, too."

Womack flipped his notebook closed and stood up. "Well, okay then. I'll turn in a report and get right on it...but I got to tell ya, I don't have much to go on. I could get the lab boys out here to dust the office for prints, but there's probably a blue million on those doorknobs anyway..." Vic smirked, agreeing with that assessment as the detective continued, "If you'd just seen or heard the guy's car. Well, I'll go over to Frisch's and see if anybody over there saw anything."

Just then, something in Vic's mind clicked, like a piece in a puzzle fitting into place. He looked up at his friend and then held up one hand, first finger extended. "Wait...I just remembered something..."

෫〇෭

CHAPTER 8

A Little Nudging From Above

"*WHAT?*" LOUISE EXCLAIMED when Vic told her about the robbery a few hours later. Standing at the kitchen sink, she whirled around and faced him as he stood, relaxed, hands in pockets, in the center of the room.

"Oh Vic! The man had a *gun*? You could have been killed!" she stepped forward and touched his arm, her eyes searching his to try and get a handle on what he was feeling. Seeing what seemed to be peace in his warm brown eyes, she continued, "But what kind of a person robs a man of his hard-earned money right before Christmas?" Then, shifting gears in the middle of the stream, she almost snarled, "I don't believe he really has a wife and kids. The jerk," she fumed, stepping back and wrapping her arms around her middle, her emotions escalating like a roller coaster. "I hope they catch him and lock him up where he belongs!"

His expression revealing he wished he had broken the news to her in a different manner, Vic drew his wife into his arms, attempting to calm her.

She enveloped her arms around his back and wailed, "Why did this happen *now*? Just when things seemed like they were settling down and we might actually get ahead? Why do bad things always happen to us?" she lamented, fighting with feelings of frustration and concern. Her whole world seemed as if it were on the verge of collapse. All morning, she had been trying to push away a melancholy cloud that had seemed to be hovering over her every move. Once the excitement of the new house had worn off, for reasons even she couldn't seem to define, she had settled back into the old familiar mode of dissatisfaction and angst.

Vic's news had been like the straw that broke the camel's back.

"Ssshh honey," her husband soothed as he kept his arms tight about her. "Everything's going to be okay. John had some leads he was gonna follow. Said he'd get back to me soon."

Louise drew back, still agitated, but forcing herself to calm down. She reminded herself, it wasn't often that Vic took time out during the day to come home, and she had hardly registered the unexpected treat before the look on his face had sent her into orbit. Just the thought of her husband being held up by an armed assailant sent chills down her spine. Now, every time he was at work, she would be worrying if another armed hold-up man would take advantage – and maybe next time, actually shoot and not just threaten!

"I told Oscar to be extra careful while he's there alone," Vic went on, seeming to read her thoughts, "but I don't think the guy will come back…and it was like he knew I had the deposit there." Pausing for a moment, he confided, "I think I might know who it was…"

Louise's eyes opened wide in surprise as they met his. "You *knew* him? Who was it?" she demanded, bristling and puffing herself up to her full five-foot-two, as if she would get in the car and go confront the guy herself.

Vic pressed his lips together and gave one negative shake of his head. "I don't want to say just yet. We'll see what John finds out. In the meantime…all this excitement this mornin' has me starvin'. What's for lunch, babe?" This last he added with twinkling eyes. In truth, once his detective friend had arrived on the scene and they had hashed over the details, Vic had begun to relax and calm down. Matter of fact, he had a strong feeling that everything was going to work out, somehow, some way. He didn't know how, but he felt it, nonetheless. It might have had something to do with an unexpected visit by his friend and mentor, Doc Latham, who had prayed with Vic for a quick resolve of the situation. After one of Doc's Heaven-touching prayers, Vic always felt better.

Still ruffled, Louise turned toward the counter, as they were standing together in the middle of the kitchen. She knew it made her husband uncomfortable for her to continue on, haranguing about something in anger, so attempting to get a rein on her emotions, she asked resignedly, "What would you rather have…leftovers, or soup and grilled cheese?"

Vic drew near again and slipped his arms around her from the back, leaning down to whisper in her ear, "And maybe a little *dessert* after…"

Those words melted the fear and apprehension away, as he knew they would. It was their private code for stealing a little romantic time alone together. They'd had *dessert* after lunch many times in the early days of their marriage, but once the kids had come along and Lilly had moved in, those interludes had dwindled down to few and far between. In all of the years since the moment she had met Vic, it had only taken one touch or one whisper in her ear in that special way of his, for her to melt right into his arms. The potency of his allure had never waned.

She turned her head and snuggled against him for a moment, meeting his lips for a quick, but promising kiss. Pulling back, she met his eyes, and he was thrilled to see the sparkle in those beautiful hazel depths as she teasingly whispered, "Well, if you're wantin' dessert with this meal, I better get crackin'."

He chuckled and gave her a squeeze. "I'll help get the show on the road."

With that, he leaned in again and nuzzled her neck, giving her ear a soft nip before turning to the sink to wash his hands.

Leftovers were warmed up and placed on the table in record time.

ℰ◯ℛ

THE NEXT DAY, Vic looked over from adding oil to a customer's engine to find John Womack leaning against the doorpost of the office, grinning at him like the proverbial Cheshire cat.

Vic maneuvered out from under the hood of the '52 Ford Coupe he was working on for one of his regulars and reached for the ever-present shop rag in his back pocket. Eyeing his friend with a raised eyebrow as he wiped his hands, he observed, "From that grin on your face, I take it you come bearin' good news?"

The grin only got bigger as John milked the suspense a bit longer. His sense of humor at times reminded Vic of Alec's.

"Come on, man. You catch the guy already or what?"

Oscar looked over from his task of stocking oilcans on a shelf as Floyd moseyed in from serving a gas customer. The detective acknowledged the other two and then glanced back to Vic. "You could say that."

Vic's eyes narrowed as he studied his friend. "It was *him*, wasn't it?"

Womack gave a nod. "You pegged it. Ran his plates, got a search warrant, and bang, busted."

"It was *who*, Chief?" Floyd asked, looking from one man to the other.

Vic glanced at Floyd with a wry smile. "Remember that Hilliard fella last week – the '48 Rambler with the loud knock?"

Floyd nodded. "De one that sounded like it couldn't get outta its own way?"

"Yep," Vic acknowledged. "Hilliard picked it up yesterday, sayin' he didn't have the money for the repairs and he'd have to come back later. But he asked me all kind 'a questions, like what's the station's hours and when I made the deposit, and how much help I had. He said he was dreaming of trying to borrow the capital to open his own station – although at the moment, he couldn't even afford repairs to his own vehicle."

The detective took up the story, "So he pulls away in the car, but circles around a few minutes later and parks in Frisch's lot next door. He changes into an old jacket, walks over, ducks around the side of the building on the field side, slips on a ski mask, and proceeds to stick up what he figures is an easy mark."

Vic scowled at that, remembering that he had been deep in thought about his wife at the time. "I sure was. He caught me with my head in the clouds."

"But boss, I don't get how you knew it was him," Oscar asked, clearly confused.

Womack leaned into the doorjamb and gave his friend a nod of respect. "Vic had heard the guy's car pull away after he was barricaded in the storage room – and it was making a God-awful knocking noise. Coupled with that, he realized that the robber's voice was similar – and a few things he said, like that Vic here was *living his dream*. When I got to his house with the search warrant, I could hear a whale of an argument going on inside."

"A what?" Vic asked, moving on into the office. The others followed, hanging on to every word the detective said.

Womack laughed. "Seems your illustrious burglar was receiving a royal chewing-out by his wife. When I knocked on the door and I showed her my badge, she took me right into the kitchen and handed me the deposit bag, her husband standing there with his mouth open in shock. Don't that beat all?" he added, shaking his head at the craziness of how things had played out. "In eighteen years on the force, I've never run across anything like it."

"Wit' de money still in de bag?" Floyd asked as he shoved his U-Haul cap back and scratched his head with a laugh.

"Yep. Speaking of which…" John grinned again and reached inside his jacket. He pulled out said bag, with the First National Bank logo stamped on the front, and tossed it to Vic. "Count it, should be all there."

"I got a question," Floyd asked as he drew near Vic. "How'd you prove dis partic'ler bag belongs to Vic?"

John wiggled his eyebrows. "The magic of detective work." At Floyd and Oscar's blank looks, he laughed and admitted, "Along with the cash, there was a check inside, made out to Matthews Service Station. Seems like Vic overlooked that one...accidentally on purpose?"

Vic laughed and shook his head as he manipulated the drawstring on the canvas bank deposit bag and took out the bills. Taking a quick count, he nodded. "Yep, it's all there." Looking back up at his friend and shaking his head in amazement again, he asked, "Don't you need to keep this...for evidence or something?"

Womack shrugged. "Usually. But under extenuating circumstances, I have the authority to release an item if I feel like it. Extenuating as in – *Christmastime*."

Vic nodded, tossing the bag and money onto his desk. "So...now what happens?"

John turned to sit down in a chair in front of the desk and crossed one leg over the other as Floyd and Oscar gathered near. "He'll get at least six months. It was his first offense but..." he paused as he drew a smooth wooden pipe out of his inside pocket and readied it to light, before glancing at Vic. "But he didn't really have a gun, so it wasn't 'armed robbery', which is a felony."

"Yes he did, I saw it. He stuck it in my back when he was shovin' me in that closet," Vic insisted, but the detective grinned around the stem of the pipe and met his friend's eyes.

"It was a toy. Quite a realistic one, granted – pearl handle and all – but a toy, nonetheless. He never intended to shoot or harm you."

"Well I'll be..." Vic murmured. That gun had fooled him completely, and all the time, it was a toy cap gun. "Well, now I feel like a dang fool for allowing the jerk to make off with my money, when I could have just decked him and been done with it."

Womack lit the pipe and pulled in a deep draw, eyeing his friend. "Seems the guy's a veteran, but when he came back from the war, he couldn't get his old job back, and has had trouble finding work ever since. His wife had threatened to leave him and take their little girl. Matter of fact, she'd been right next door at Frisch's just minutes before he pulled his stunt, applying for a waitress job."

Vic's eyes widened, realizing he had stood and watched them, having no idea that her husband was about to stick him up.

"Mrs. Hilliard was really giving him the business about what a stupid stunt he had pulled when I knocked on the door. She'd been trying to get him to get in the car and take the money back to you – I just made it easier. She uh…" Vic's friend paused, "she said to tell you she was very sorry for what her husband did, and that she feels partly responsible, as her threat to leave him is what sent him over the edge of desperation. She said he's never done a dishonest thing like this before, and she's known him practically all their lives. She's hoping…"

Vic's eyes narrowed as he surveyed the smooth talking detective. "Hoping what?"

The man drew on the pipe again. "Well, she's kind of hoping that you'll see your way clear to dropping the charges."

"Drop the charges!" "Can Vic *do* that?" "After what he *did?*" the three men listening reacted simultaneously.

Womack nodded as he blew out a puff of smoke. "If he brought 'em, he can drop 'em."

Vic circled his desk and plopped into the chair at this totally unexpected development. Drop the charges…after he had been so all-fired angry at the man the day before, he would almost have wished him strung up to the nearest tree. Now, he sat looking into Womack's knowing eyes, and he couldn't help but relate. How many years had he, himself, gone jobless, no matter how hard he had tried. He knew just what the man had been feel-ing…well…*almost*. His own desperation had resulted in him taking a job that was less than legal, but it wasn't outright thievery. Although, he and Louise hadn't been married already, with a small child. What would he have done if Louise had given him such an ultimatum? He shuddered to imagine.

All three men were staring at him in wide-eyed concentration, waiting for what he would say. After a minute, he made his decision. How could he do anything less? It was Christmas-time…he had his money back…the guy was a family man… Vic already knew what Doc would say. He'd be quoting something Jesus said about forgiving seventy times seven.

"All right. I'll drop 'em," he nodded at John. "But first…do you happen to know what he did while in the service? Where he served? And…" he paused, looking directly into his friend's eyes. "What's his attitude like? Would you trust him?"

This time, the detective removed the pipe from his mouth and flashed his full grin, as he answered, "He said he'd worked in the motor pool. I believe he realizes what a stupid idea it was and I don't think he'll ever try something like that again, plus his wife said if he ever did, she'd leave him for sure. And yes, I'd trust him. I'd stake my reputation on it." Placing the pipe back in his mouth, he clamped it to the side and added with a wink, "Kind of like I did a few years back with another young fella who needed a break."

Vic nodded. "All right. That's good enough for me. Hang on, let me make a quick phone call." Floyd and Oscar glanced at one another, answering each other's silent queries with matching shrugs.

Vic picked up the phone and dialed a number. Waiting a few rings, he sat back in the chair as it emitted a soft squeak, smiling as a familiar voice answered.

"Hap?" he addressed his former boss, Horatio Alvin Pait, but no one called him that on threat of bodily harm. He went by his initials in everything but his marriage license and his business license. The man had been a good friend as well as employer, and had even helped Vic to start his own business – in spite of the fact that it meant losing his best employee. Now, they were contemporaries, as both owned and managed service stations. Hap's was a Gulf station, downtown near Fourth and Chestnut, although his biggest moneymaker was the large parking lot one block over, which Vic had managed for his intrepid boss.

The three interested males watching his face as he held the phone to his ear only heard one side of the conversation. "How's it goin'? Aw, I'm doin' just fine. Family's fine. Yep, the boys are growin' like weeds. Station's fine. Business is good. Yep. Hey listen…I wonder if you would do me a favor. See, it's like this…" he began, and spent the next few minutes filling his friend in on everything that had happened – and the opinion of their mutual friend, John "Law" Womack.

He listened as Hap responded pretty much as he had done – on the strength of Vic's word he would go out on a limb and give this guy a break.

"But," Hap stated emphatically. "You tell Womack, if Hilliard crosses me just one time, I'll string *him* up from the rafters…" adding just what body part he would use.

Vic laughed at that, and the relaxed detective let out a loud guffaw when he passed on the message.

By the time he got off the phone twenty minutes later, Vic was all smiles, and happy that all was right with the world again. He had his money back, he could proceed with his plans to infuse a little romance back into his marriage, and he had been instrumental in seeing that another family had a happy Christmas.

Hap had agreed to take on the repentant robber as an employee at his newest venture – a Gulf Station farther up Shelbyville Road. It was even on the bus line, so Hilliard could get to work and back while saving up the money to have his car repaired.

Sometimes things just worked out…with a little bit of nudging from above and little bit of obeying here below.

ℰᏩℭᏫ

CHAPTER 9

Christmas in Buechel

V IC HAD BEEN blessed with an extra heavy string of customers at the station, and as soon as school let out, Tommy was back to work, helping Chief any way he could.

It was Friday, a week prior to Christmas, before Vic had an opportunity to take an evening off. He spent it with the family, picking out a Christmas tree at a nearby seller stand.

Louise had been cleaning, sprucing, and decorating to beat the band. On Saturday morning, she and the youngest boys tackled the job of putting up and decorating the tree.

"Put a little more right up there, on the left...see that shy spot?" Louise coached eight-and-a-half-year-old Buddy, who was helping put the final touches on their masterpiece.

Using a kitchen chair to reach the upper parts of the tree, Buddy moved it over a bit and climbed back up to try his best to follow her orders. "Here, Mama?" he asked as he tossed a handful of shiny tinsel at what he thought was the spot.

"No, not there, up a little more, and to the left. Don't you see that empty space?" Louise demanded, a bit abrasively. Buddy clamped his teeth on his bottom lip as he concentrated. Leaning toward the tree to grasp some of the last placed handful, he took careful aim and flung a good amount at the offending open area, filling it perfectly. "How's that?" he asked, turning his head eagerly to look down at his mother several feet back.

Louise squinted at the finished product, with her hands on her hips, and finally gave a nod. "It'll have to do, I guess. Climb on down."

The boy obeyed, feeling a bit let down when he couldn't seem to please his mom.

Lilly walked into the room from the kitchen, glancing around at the decorations while wiping her hands on a kitchen towel. Having heard the conversation, she examined the tree and nodded approval, her eyes sliding over to her daughter as she assessed Louise's mood.

Watching her daughter fussing with the garland strung on the tree, Lilly offered, "Everything looks fine, Louise. It's a beautiful tree." Pausing, she added, "Is something wrong?"

Louise briefly looked over at her mother, trying to tamp down her feelings of anxiety. For the life of her, she couldn't figure out why she felt so on edge. Every little thing seemed to agitate her, but she was ashamed of those emotions, as they made her feel selfish and ungrateful. "No, nothing's wrong," she denied, answering over her shoulder as she continued to fiddle with the tree. "I just want everything to be perfect for our first Christmas in our new house."

Lilly nodded, pursing her lips thoughtfully, her eyes narrowing as she continued to watch. Finally, she decided against trying to initiate a pep talk and with a shrug of one shoulder, she turned and went back into the kitchen to continue with her baking.

"Can I put the pointer on, Mama, can I?" Jimmy begged, as he eagerly removed the delicate Mercury Glass tree topper from its protective tissue paper-lined cardboard box. The turquoise and silver topper, with its round glittering base tapering up to a long cylindrical point, had become extremely fragile over the years. Purchased along with other beautiful ornaments the first Christmas that Vic and Louise were married in 1941, the topper was one of Louise's cherished possessions.

"Oh, be careful, honey!" she gasped as she hurried to his side and gently removed the breakable item from his hands.

"I am. I won't break it, Mama," he insisted. "Can I put it on?" he begged again, gazing up at her anxiously as he bounced with little-boy energy.

Holding it gingerly, Louise was momentarily taken back to the wonderful night she and Vic had brought it home to their apartment. Vic made her feel like a princess and he her knight on a white horse as he had bought nearly everything she asked for on their trip to purchase Christmas decorations. Now, every year as she removed the treasured ornaments from their box, sweet nostalgia hit her like a tidal wave. In her mind's eye, she relived the evening…Tommy so little Vic was holding him in his arms…both she and Vic so young and eager to make a good life for themselves and her little boy…Vic being such a sweet daddy to little Tommy…Vic being such a wonderful husband and provider to Louise…

"Please?" a sweet voice asked. She glanced down and her heart melted. Jimmy was such a lovable child, adorably cute with his big dark-hazel eyes and dimples like his father. As her youngest, he was nearly impossible to deny when he made a request in such an endearing manner.

She reached out a hand and lovingly smoothed the coal black hair back from his forehead as an impish smile lit his countenance. "All right, but we'll have to find the ladder. Mama can't pick you up that high, and we want to have the Christmas tree all decorated before Daddy and Tommy get home from work tonight."

"I'll get it!" Buddy yelled over his shoulder as he turned to run through the living room and kitchen, opening the back door to step out into the carport and retrieve said ladder. The wooden, paint-speckled ladder was quite heavy, but he managed to half carry, half drag it into the living room, with Lilly following along behind and fussing.

With much vigilant coaching, and instructions to Buddy to

help hold the ladder still, Louise guided Jimmy to climb up and secure the treasured item at the top of the tree.

As she and Buddy stepped back, she wrapped an arm across his shoulders and they smiled up at the precocious youngster and the finished product.

"How's that, Mama?" he asked with a huge grin.

"Just perfect, honey. Just perfect," she answered as both of her boys gazed at her lovingly.

At that moment, life was good.

ⅆ)℞

CHRISTMAS MORNING DAWNED cloudy and cold, with six inches of white powdery snow already on the ground and the air heavy with the promise of more.

Just as the sun was trying to peak over the horizon, two dark-haired, dark-eyed little boys sprang out of bed and raced into the living room of the house on Granvil Drive to see what Santa Claus had brought during the night. There in front of the sparkling Christmas tree stood a striking red and black Firestone Super Cruiser bicycle, with training wheels attached. A big tag hung from the handlebars that read, "For Buddy, From Santa." Buddy squealed with delight and ran toward it, while Jimmy eagerly looked around the room, hoping he had received one as well.

Vic and Louise awakened simultaneously as they heard the commotion. Their eyes met, each one smiling indulgently as they climbed out of bed and put on their robes for the start of an early day. Meeting Tommy in the hall, with Lilly stepping out of the other bedroom and tying the belt on her robe, they crept down the hall and peeked around the corner, watching the two youngest as they gleefully honked the bike's horn and marveled at all of its features. Jimmy was busy trying to get Buddy to allow him to sit on it.

"Looks like that was a good choice," Vic whispered in Louise's ear. She nodded against his cheek and gave his hands, which were wrapped around her middle, a squeeze.

Moving on into the room to join the festivities, Buddy looked over and exclaimed, "Look what Santa brought me!"

Jimmy, however, came toward his parents, lower lip sticking out sadly. "Santa brought Buddy a bicycle…but he didn't bring *me* one…"

"Oh Jimmy, honey," Louise crooned softly as she sat down on the couch and reached out to pull him into her arms. "Didn't you see what Santa brought *you*?" she asked as she gestured to the other side of the tree, where a large stuffed bear sat perched inside the back of a pedal car fashioned after a 1955 Volkswagen pickup truck. Like a Volkswagen microbus with the back end opened up as a truck bed, it was painted red and white, with the U-Haul Company logo emblazoned on the side.

Jimmy walked over to it and removed the bear. Tucking it under one arm, he reached to touch the top of the cab and pouted in disappointment. "But it's a *pedal car*. Don't Santa know I'm six and a half now? Pedal cars're for *babies*," he commented with a scowl.

Louise exchanged glances with Vic, and he gave her an I-told-you-so look. When he had told her about the U-Haul Dealer Incentive he had received from the company – a brand new, shiny, custom-made pedal car – she had begged him to bring it home for their youngest instead of raffling it off, the way most dealers would have. He had tried to talk her into getting Jimmy a bicycle, as they had for Buddy, but she had adamantly insisted that Jimmy was too little and she didn't want him to fall and get hurt. If Vic had one weakness, it was that he could never deny Louise anything she truly wanted and begged him for – if it was in his power to do it.

Vic knew his wife had never gotten over the fact that their youngest son had been born with a hernia, and had cried and screamed nearly every day of his life until he was a year old and the doctors had found the problem. As a result, from the time he had recovered from his surgery, Louise had handled him with kid gloves, so afraid that he would hurt himself. The problem, however, was that little Jimmy had a mind of his own and he was all boy – which meant he forged ahead to do rough and tumble things like all the other boys. The taut reins Louise tried to keep on him only seemed to cinch tighter and tighter as he grew. He had just begun to try his wings and squirm out from under her thumb a bit once he had started school.

Louise resisted this with all her strength, often jokingly lamenting to Vic that she wanted to keep her boys as babies forever. At times, he wondered if she were truly jesting or not.

Trying to smooth things over about the pedal car blunder, Vic moved to ruffle Jimmy's hair. "Maybe you'll get a bicycle for your birthday in July…providin' you behave till then…"

Jimmy's mood immediately lifted and he squeezed himself inside the brightly painted truck, one arm still holding the large stuffed bear. He pressed the horn button on the steering wheel and it emitted a *beep beep* sound. With a giggle, he worked the pedals to ride it around the living room. With the Christmas tree and other items now filling up the space, it was a chore for him to find room to maneuver.

"Whoa there, Tiger," Vic chuckled as he stepped out of the way just in time. He leaned to keep his balance as Jimmy squeezed past in the truck, accompanied by a rascally giggle.

Tommy held up one leg for Jimmy to 'drive' under, and then had to scramble to sidestep as Buddy came zooming by on his new bicycle on his way into the kitchen. The teen shook his head and chuckled, thinking, *what a day to be snowed in,* as his little brothers filled the house with joyous racket. *But I wouldn't trade them for the world,* he added silently, as happy giggles drifted in from a 'crash' in the kitchen.

Now that everyone was awake and up, they gathered around

the tree to begin opening their presents.

Sixteen-year-old Tommy received an RCA Victrola record player, inside its own carrying case, along with a nice supply of records, including *Rock Around the Clock* by Bill Haley and the Comets, and *Sixteen Tons* by Tennessee Ernie Ford. Pleased with his gift, he hugged his dad and gave his mom a kiss on the cheek before immediately putting one of the records on the turntable, a little ditty by an up-and-coming young singer named Elvis Presley.

As the rockabilly music of *Blue Moon of Kentucky* began, Tommy grinned mischievously and started moving his feet to the beat as he gyrated over to his grandmother, who had just settled herself on the couch. Taking her hands, he pulled her to her feet and danced her around the room, singing along with the record – and doing a fine imitation of Elvis' voice. After just a minute, Lilly laughed and pulled out of his grip. "That's enough dancing for me, young man," she huffed with a chuckle. She fanned herself and swished her hands to shoo him away as he tried to grab her again. "Get your Mama up there to dance with you."

Without missing a beat, Tommy wiggled his eyebrows and boogied over to Louise, taking his giggling mother by the hands and tugging her up to join him. Together they swished and sashayed to the music as Tommy serenaded. The boys and Vic clapped along in time to the music. Vic's eyes twinkled happily as he watched his ladylove laughing and dancing.

Louise joined Tommy on the chorus, and they finished out the song together.

"Oh, that was so good! Play that other one that we got you by him," Louise requested, and Tommy moved to the player and put on the next record, Elvis' rendition of *That's Alright Mama.* Once again, he matched the singer word for word, warble for warble, even pretending to hold a microphone as he belted out the lyrics. It was obvious that Tommy had inherited his mother's musical talents. The adults were all convinced that Tommy Blankenbaker could someday have a singing career; he sure had the talent and charisma.

A little later, Vic smiled at his wife and leaned in to give her a kiss, thanking her for the nice leather three-fold wallet she had given him. Lilly and Louise both opened gifts from the boys – a bottle of perfume, a pair of fuzzy house slippers for each, one in blue and the other in green, and a Perry Como record that Lilly could play on Tommy's phonograph. It was a wonderful Christmas.

When everyone had finished opening their gifts, Vic went over and hunkered down by the tree to retrieve a small wrapped box he had been saving for last. Turning, he sidled up next to Louise as she sat on the couch and laid it in her hands.

"What's this?" she asked, a little breathlessly.

He shrugged teasingly. "I dunno. It's got your name on it. Open it."

Louise gazed into his eyes for a moment, and then carefully began to loosen the tape, always mindful to try and save the paper to use another time.

"Aww, come on, just rip the dang thing open," Vic teased, making like he would take it from her hands and do it for her.

She laughed and finally got the box unwrapped. A small black velvet box. Meeting his eyes, she opened the top and looked down, gasping in pleasure at what was inside.

Vic smiled broadly. "Hope you like 'em…I'm just sorry it took me so long ta get 'em for ya," he added softly as he watched her take the pair of amethyst earrings out of the box and hold them up to her ears. The others gathered around with ooo's and ahhh's. Vic reached to gently grasp the necklace she still wore nearly every day and held it up; the new earrings a near perfect match.

"Oh Vic, I love them! Thank you so much, honey," Louise gushed as she quickly clipped them on.

"Lemme see," Vic requested softly, leaning back to get the full effect of his beautiful wife wearing his gift. The lights on the

Christmas tree made the necklace and the new earrings sparkle –
almost as much as her eyes as she gazed at him. "Perfect. Just like
you, babe."

At that, tears stung Louise's eyes and she leaned toward him,
offering her lips for a kiss. He didn't disappoint her. Matter of
fact, their lips lingered for an extra few moments – only stopping
when a teasing little voice sang from across the room, "Daddy's
kissing Mama. Daddy's kissing Mama!"

They broke apart laughing and Vic took Louise into his arms
for a hug.

Neither one could remember a better, happier Christmas.

„∞›

"HEY GUYS, COME on in here outta the cold," Vic encouraged
later in the day as he stepped aside and held the front door open
for Alec, Earl, and their families.

"Oh, let me hold her," Louise said to Fleet as the latter handed over her baby girl, warmly bundled in layers of pink – pink
booties, pink knit cap, and a frilly pink dress, covered over in a
soft pink blanket.

Louise walked over to the couch carrying the precious little
girl, speaking in the singsong voice everyone used with babies as
she settled on the seat and began to remove the outerwear.
Quickly becoming too warm in the comfortably heated house,
little Alexa began to fuss.

"Oh goo'ness, goo'ness, I'm 'a hurryin'," Louise chattered to
the baby as she worked at removing the layers.

Alec grinned proudly as Fleet looked on with a loving smile.
"She's got a temper, that's for sure. If she don't get her way *right
now*, look out."

Fleet laughed and nodded, "Ain't *that* the truth."

"She gets that from *you*, my fiery-tempered wife," he cracked,
laughing when Fleet playfully stuck her tongue out at him.

Louise carefully removed the knit cap and readjusted the tiny pink bow atop the short, fine honey-colored hair. Feeling better now that the restricting garments were removed, ten-month-old Alexa looked up, her chestnut brown eyes with those long black lashes opened wide at Louise as she cooed adorably.

"Oh Fleet, her eyes are turning more the color of yours all the time – and her hair, too! She's you made over," Louise mused, bouncing the baby on her lap and making silly faces at her to get her to giggle.

"Yep, that's what I've been saying," Alec agreed, slipping an arm around his wife as he reached past her with his other hand to allow the baby to grasp on to one of his fingers. "Looks like she's gonna be the spitting image of her mama, which means, I'm gonna need a big ol' bat to keep the boys away when she turns around sixteen or so."

"Oh you," Fleet murmured, pressing a shoulder against her husband's chest as if to scold him, even as her eyes met his in loving thanks for his comment.

Just then, Alexa clapped her little hands together joyfully, and then spread her arms and reached up to Louise, practically climbing up her body to give her a hug before settling down comfortably on her lap as if she never wanted to move from that spot. Fleet laughed, "She's such a cuddle bug; so different from AJ. Once he began crawling, he never wanted to stay on my lap for more that five seconds – and cuddling was out of the question!"

"Oh, that's just boys for you," Ruth piped up from across the room. "My Terry is the same way, never any time for his Mama. But Gina's still a Mama's girl – aren't you sweetie," she directed at her nine-year-old daughter, perched on the arm of her chair. The girl smiled shyly as all attention from the adults in the room suddenly turned to her.

"Little girls sure can be cute," Vic agreed, thinking of something that had happened the day before. "John Hilliard came by the station yesterday and brought his wife and little girl," he began, but Earl interrupted, "You mean, the guy that held you up? I still can't believe you dropped the charges."

Vic gave a small shrug, knowing his friend probably wouldn't understand. Earl had always been the kind to hold a grudge for extended periods. "It just seemed like the right thing to do," he explained – again – before continuing, "and I'm glad I did. Hilliard's wife and child don't deserve the hardship of him bein' locked up for months. But, anyway, he apologized and thanked me…" he paused as Jimmy, Buddy, Terry, and AJ raised their voices in competition over something in the other room. Remembering the Hilliard's little girl, he mused without thinking, "Their little girl was so sweet. She's about five, I think…dark hair and dark eyes, like her mother…she came up to me and crooked a finger at me, and when I bent down to her level, she whispered, 'Thank you for being nice to my Daddy,' and then gave me a big kiss on the cheek. I tell ya, my heart just melted." A tad choked up, he added with a laugh, "If I hadn't already decided to drop the charges, I probably would have, then. She sure is a cute little thing."

The others in the room nodded, making observations about the differences between little boys and little girls…but no one noticed that Louise had settled back against the cushions of the couch, the expression on her face anything but joyful.

A weird kind of jealousy had swept over her as her husband extolled the virtues of that child. Her arms tightened around the baby girl in her lap as her countenance reflected her thoughts. *Maybe that's what I'm missing…all we have is boys running around, Tommy, Buddy, Jimmy…what we need is a little girl to balance everything out.*

Yes…if I just had a little girl to cuddle…make clothes for…dress up in frilly outfits…buy dolls for…then I'd be content. Then, we'd have everything…

From that moment on, it became Louise's mission in life to have a little girl of her own.

ℰ ℭ

CHAPTER 10

The Longing

J ANUARY STARTED OFF with a bang.

Just when things at the station seemed to be running like a well-oiled machine, Oscar quit to move back to Tennessee with his ailing mother. This he announced at a moment when the station was full up on customers – a line at the pumps, cars parked willy-nilly waiting for oil changes, and car wash customers waiting in line to get the winter sludge washed off. With Tommy back at school, it was everything Vic, Floyd and Oscar could do to keep up.

"You're *what*?" Vic ground out as his third man announced that this would be his last day. They were both working the pumps.

"I'm s…sorry, Mr. Matthews," the young man had stammered, "But Ma needs me – I'm all she's got. I hope you can find somebody real quick like," he added sheepishly as he topped off a customer's gas tank and reached for the payment from the hand sticking out the partially opened window.

Vic took his cap off his head and swept a hand back through his hair, wondering how in the world he and Floyd were going to be able to handle things until they could bring a new man on board. He shook his head as the wry thought ran through his mind that he was almost wishing for fewer customers.

Glancing at Oscar and noticing the cowed look on his face,

Vic instantly felt bad for allowing his temper to flare.

"It's all right, Oscar. You go and take care of your mother. God'll bring help along," he added, surprised when the words came out of his mouth. Feeling guilty that he hadn't immediately thought of asking God's aid, he shut his eyes and prayed as he stood with his hand on the pump handle, *Father in Heaven...I always seem to complain, gripe, worry, and pace, rather than ask Your help. I'm askin' now, Lord...bring us somebody. Bring us the right somebody. In Jesus' Name...Amen.*

"Hey Chief, tel'phone!" Floyd called from the office. Vic waved acknowledgment and took the payment from his customer before trotting over to take the call, thinking, *Man, when it rains, it pours. But...guess I gotta make hay while the sun shines.*

JUST A FEW days later, God answered that prayer in an unexpected way. Vic and Floyd were finishing up a quick lunch in the office before getting back to their repair work. Chuckling over something funny that had happened while they were serving together in the CCC's, Vic looked out the window and noticed a rather diminutive, older black man, hesitatingly walking across the concrete lot as a Trailways bus pulled away.

"Who's this comin'?" Vic mumbled as he stuffed the last bite of his sandwich in his mouth, prompting Floyd to turn from his perched position on a stool by the window, and gaze outside.

"Oh hey, dat's Pasta' Duke," Floyd murmured as he got up and opened the glass door, motioning the man in out of the cold.

The little man scurried inside, rubbing his bare hands together in an attempt to ward off the cold as Floyd shut the door behind him.

Turning, Floyd flashed his gleaming smile at his friend-turned-boss and made the introductions.

"Chief, dis here's Pasta' Duke I was tellin' you about. Pasta' Duke, dis here's Vic Matthews."

Vic rose from the chair as he wiped his mouth on a napkin

and stepped forward with his right hand extended, meeting the man halfway across the room. Indeed, Floyd had been telling him about the pastor of the fledgling church in the West End, which he'd begun attending not long after his time in the service was up and he had settled in Louisville. Floyd had said the preacher was a feisty 'character,' who was in need of making some extra money to live on, since the congregants at the little church could barely give enough to keep the utilities paid.

"Pastor Duke, good to meet ya."

The short-statured, ebony-skinned man had a surprisingly strong grip, a big, white, happy-go-lucky grin, a wide nose, and receding wiry black hair liberally sprinkled with silver. He immediately reminded Vic of his favorite musician, Louie "Satchmo" Armstrong. However, the resemblance ended when the man spoke, as rather than a raspy voice like Satchmo, this man's tone was several octaves higher.

"Aw, jus' calls me Duke. M'real name's Eustis Brown, but I gots bone tired 'a people callin' me *Useless Brown*, so's I copped de' name Duke and it jus' kinda stucks ta me," he explained with a chuckle.

Vic nodded, liking the man straight away. It was hard not to, as he had an infectious, cheerful air about him that immediately put you at ease, as if you'd known him all your life. "So, Floyd tells me you're a preacher…"

Duke nodded animatedly, flashing his big smile at Floyd. "Dat's right, dat's right. Gots me a lil' chu'ch down in Po'tland," he explained, referring to a neighborhood in the west end of the city. "Gots me a room at de' back," he added, cackling as if what he said had been funny. Vic would soon realize that old Duke cackled all the time. His explanation for that was, *It's jus' de joy of de Lawd slippin' outta me.*

Vic nodded, but his brows drew together a bit. He gauged the man to be in his sixties, or maybe older. It was hard to tell. "Floyd says you might wanna come work for me…but Portland, man that'd be a long trip every day…you got transportation?"

Old Duke shoved his hands in his pants' pockets, rocked back on his heels, and cackled. "Long trip. Yezza, that it is. Ain't got no auto-mobeel, but de bus does me jus' fine. An' I's make good use a' de' time. Prac'tis m'sermons on a…captive aud'ence!"

The three of them laughed together at that.

And so, Old Duke the preacher became a bona fide member of the crew at Matthews' Service Station. He quickly became a solid wheel in the cog, performing any task that Vic told him to do. No matter what it was, sweeping the floor, stocking a shelf, changing oil in a car, pumping gas, or any of a dozen other duties, Duke always completed it with his big grin flashing. His cackling chuckle accompanied anything he said, and with a profusion of "Praise de' Lawd's" at every turn.

By the start of February, it seemed as if Duke had always been part of the team. Maybe a rag-tag team at first observation, but between the three, they got the job done – and what was most important to Vic, his employees were men he could trust.

Vic was exceedingly thankful for the station – a place where he could control the outcome and know that his hard work would result in a job well done.

His home life, on the other hand, had him scrambling for answers and wishing for things to be the way they used to be…

ℰℬ

LOUISE STOOD GAZING out the large front window at a heart-tugging scene as she clutched a forgotten dust rag in one hand, as her other hand formed a fist pressed against her chest. As it was an unseasonably warm February day, the next-door neighbor was out front taking a walk; her little girl was pushing a pink and white baby stroller and happily following along behind her mother.

The child's sweet laughter found its way to Louise's ears.

Jerry and Sue Bridges, the couple that occupied the house to the Matthews' left, had bought their house new four years before, so Louise had been told. Sue Bridges had confided over the fence one day, about a month after the Matthews had moved in, that when she and Jerry had been married ten years with no babies, she feared she would never get pregnant – then not long after the move, it suddenly happened. Now, they had an adorable three-year-old little girl named Debbie and Sue was pregnant again. The two women had laughed together that maybe it was the water in the neighborhood, as there seemed to be an ever-increasing number of children being born. Sue had smilingly 'warned' Louise that she might be next…

Now, it had become Louise's silent obsession.

Five months…we've been trying five months to have another baby. It had always happened so quickly before…what if I can't get pregnant again?

The longings plagued her night and day, with the result being that everyone in the family had begun to suffer. She snapped at the boys, argued with Lilly, and worst of all, her relationship with Vic had degenerated to "testy" at best. When they made love now, it was with the desperate objective of procreation. Although she hadn't realized it, unconsciously, Louise blamed Vic for her barren situation, citing the fact that on their fifth anniversary, when *he* had decided they would start having kids, it had happened almost immediately. Then later, when they had talked about Buddy needing a companion closer to his age, *whalah*, she found herself in the family way again.

But now…five months they had been trying, with no success.

Doubts, regrets, fears, and torments swirled in her mind and filled her thoughts – and in these last few days she had found herself lamenting over the baby she had lost on the shores of the Ohio nearly fifteen years prior. Although the baby had been the product of an extremely unhappy first marriage, Louise had grieved its loss until she became pre-occupied with the happy fact of Vic being back in her life.

Now, she wondered…what if that baby had been a girl? What

if that baby had been the *only* girl she would ever have? The fear of that twisted her heart into a tight knot, so much so that at times she could barely breathe.

Just then, Sue turned and knelt down to tie Debbie's shoelaces, and happening to glance over, she spotted Louise in the window. Smiling widely, the neighbor waved, before saying something to the child and pointed to the house. Little Debbie turned and flapped her hands with innocent joy up at Louise. Reaching into the stroller, she grasped the baby doll Louise had given her for her birthday, and clasped it to her chest in a fierce hug. *Sue told me just the other day that Debbie took that doll everywhere; that it was her most prized possession.* Tears sprang to Louise's eyes as she waved in return, and she closed them tightly, swallowing back the sadness and dread.

You should be grateful for what you have, her conscience whispered as she turned from the achingly sweet scene out front. Picking up a framed family photo from an end table, she gazed down at the images while gently wiping the dust rag over the glass. The photo had been taken the year before, and everyone was smiling brightly. She blinked away the tears as she softly ran a finger around the sweet faces of her two youngest children...they were growing up too soon! No longer babies; each had very strong personalities and were most decidedly *male.* And sixteen-year-old Tommy – he was so handsome, and very nearly a man now.

Her three sons...

But no girl.

Oh, why am I feeling this way? Why can't I just be satisfied with what I have? Why do I feel such loss, such a hole in my heart for someone I've never even met? What if...what if God doesn't allow me to have my longed-for little girl. What will I do...? I have to get HOLD of myself!

A moment later, Lilly came in with a load of laundry and sat on the couch to fold it.

"It's such a nice day today, Louise – you really should go out and get some fresh air. We've been cooped up here in the house for months," Lilly observed as she folded one of Jimmy's shirts. "With that nice breeze, these dried in no time. Why, a body would think its springtime, and not the first week of February." Pausing for a moment, she shook her head as a thought occurred. "My my, so different from twenty years ago...all that rain and water...then all that wet, miserable snow, and then all the mud. My lands, I thought we'd never get the musty, damp smell out of everything once the flood receded. You remember?" she added, casting an eye at her daughter, who was listlessly wiping at a table that was already dust-free.

Lilly studied her for a moment. "What's wrong, Louise? You've been moping around like this for weeks."

Knowing her mother would probably give her a lecture on being ungrateful for the good things she already had, and knowing she would deserve it if she did, Louise drew in a breath and then let it out slowly. "Nothing. I'm all right."

Stepping over to the basket on the couch, she reached down and picked up a pair of Jimmy's pajamas. Starting to fold them, she paused, and then brought them to her chest as she pictured him wearing them. He needed new ones; these were inches too short, as he'd been going through another growth spurt as of late. That wasn't the only change – her 'baby' had told her the previous night that he was a big boy now and she didn't need to tuck him in and kiss him goodnight anymore. She felt a twinge of hurt again as the thought ran through her mind. She couldn't help but wonder how things would be if Jimmy had been a girl.

She glanced at her mother, who had gone back to folding.

"Mama?" she began as she wondered how to phrase the burning questions in her heart. "Which of us did you feel closer to?" At Lilly's puzzled look, she added, "Did you feel closer to the boys, or to us girls?"

Lilly wavered for a moment, searching her memory. Then with a shrug, she reached for another article of clothing.

"Oh, I wouldn't say I felt closer to..." she delayed a second and shot Louise a look before continuing. "Well…I was always a bit partial to Sonny…because he was my first with your father after all the trouble I had about Edna." Rushing on, she added, "But when all of you were young, we were just trying to survive and I had many things on my mind, like where I would get food to feed everyone once your father couldn't keep a job after the Crash."

Louise nodded, images from her childhood running through her mind. "And, now that we're all grown?"

"Well…I guess because I live with you, I feel closer to you. I never felt especially close to Edna…but Billy and I share a close bond…and of course, Sonny."

Louise stayed silent for a few minutes as they finished folding the load of clothes. Finally, she picked up the basket to take it to the boys' bedroom, when she suddenly halted in her tracks to look into her mother's pale blue eyes. "Mama…how come you never lived with Sonny? I mean…do you live with me because I'm your daughter and you feel a closer kinship because of that…or…"

Lilly rose and headed into the kitchen to begin preparations for that night's dinner, saying over her shoulder, "That might be one reason." Then stopping in the doorway, she turned back and added, "Another might be that Sonny's wife never offered me a spare bed." Meeting Louise's eyes to let her meaning sink in, namely that Louise's spouse was a much more accommodating person than Sonny's, she went on through the doorway.

Louise thought for a moment about that. Vic was, indeed, a good son-in-law. *And a good husband. You'd do well to remember that, young lady,* her conscience, sounding suspiciously like her mother's voice, whispered.

Yes Ma'am, she answered as she followed her mother into the kitchen.

ഇാൟ

CHAPTER 11

The Flirt, The Bigot, and The Fight

F EBRUARY MARCHED ON.
Louise's birthday came and went, celebrating with just the family. It was pleasant, but Vic worked at the station all day on several big repair jobs. He apologized profusely when he got home, and promised to make it up to her the following weekend as he handed her a hastily purchased birthday card. She forced a smile and thanked him with a kiss. Obviously relieved, he kissed her back, and then went on down the hall to take a nice, long, hot shower. She stuffed her disappointment back into a closet in her heart and locked the door.

Valentine's Day came on a Tuesday, and between Louise's responsibilities at the boys' schools, as she had volunteered to bake cupcakes for each of their classes, and Vic being busy at the station, they didn't do anything special. He did get her a card, that he signed, "To my lil' babe, from your Honeybabe," which normally would have melted her heart, but this time it seemed to sour her stomach just a bit when she read the words.

Louise spent her days in deep contemplation over the problem of her not getting pregnant. She told herself she should just give up and go on with her life, but the more she tried to do just that, the more she seemed to long for another baby. Not just another baby – a little girl she could dress up in pink. She thought about it every waking moment, and dreamed about it at night.

And with each passing day, the relationship between herself and Vic grew just a tad bit cooler.

ℰↃℭℛ

AT THE STATION one unseasonably warm day in early March, Vic backed out from under the hood of the '47 Mercury he was working on just as a decidedly feminine voice called out, "Yoo-hoo, Vic!"

He leaned around the car's fender to see his neighbor from three doors down, Barbara Dixon, waving at him from the open bay door. He could see her yellow, '53 Chevrolet convertible behind her, the engine still running.

Reaching for the shop rag in his back pocket, he walked toward her as he wiped his hands. "What can I do for you, Mrs. Dixon?"

The attractive and shapely woman, wearing a yellow and white plaid dress with a pleated skirt and buttons up the form-fitting bodice, stood with one hand fluttering at the neck of her dress, looking up at him with that helpless female gaze that always hooks a man to want to help. A soft white sweater surrounded her shoulders, and he absently noticed that she had left a few of the top buttons on her dress undone. The thought went through his mind that his neighbor in the service, Tyler Dixon, sure had him one heck of a wife waiting at home. She knew just how to accentuate her "assets" and seemed to enjoy getting attention, especially from all of the male neighbors on Granvil Drive. It seemed there was always one at her house doing something or another for the "helpless" military stay-at-home wife. He wondered idly how the wives in the neighborhood felt about her – and in particular – how *his* wife felt, since he'd not heard Louise mention the woman's name since the welcome committee the first week they moved in.

"Oh, call me Barbara, since we're neighbors and all," she

corrected, batting her eyelashes at him. "But I don't want to take you away from what you're doing," she smiled innocently.

He smiled back and gave her a nod. "That's okay, Barbara. It'll keep. What can I do for you?" he asked again. "Do you have a problem with your car?"

"Oh yes, I do. With Tyler gone, it seems like there's always something I can't do. It's just so aggravating sometimes," she purred, touching Vic's arm as he edged past her through the doorway to get out to the car.

He listened for a moment. "Sounds like it's runnin' okay…"

The woman laughed and fanned her face with a white lace hanky. "Oh, silly me! It's not the engine, it's the top."

"The top?" Vic repeated, walking closer and running his hands over the convertible top, which seemed in A-1 shape.

"Yes. It's such a nice, warm day…I was going to take a drive out to see my mother, and I wanted to put the top down – but I can't for the life of me get the silly thing to work! I've never put it down by myself…Tyler always took care of that," she added with a helpless shrug.

Vic smiled absently at the woman, thinking the last time he had talked to her, she hadn't seemed quite so…clueless. "Aw, there's nothin' to it," he explained, opening the driver's door and leaning inside. Feeling for the levers above the windshield, he moved them to the open position, and then reached down to push the button on the dashboard. Immediately, the mechanism's motor started humming and the top began to fold slowly back just like it should. "See? Easy as pie. You just flip those levers there, push the button, and it does the rest. Then later, when you want to put the top up, you push the button again and let it come all the way forward, then lock the levers back in place. No problem," he explained, as if he were teaching a child.

"Oh Vic, thank you! You make everything seem so easy!" the woman simpered, pushing up a little too close to the back of him in the guise of looking where he was pointing.

He cleared his throat and maneuvered out of her grasp.

"No problem at all. Do you need some gas for your drive?" he asked, gesturing toward the pumps.

"Oh no, thank you. The tank is still full from when I came yesterday…" she answered as he nodded with a small, polite smile. She seemed to be waiting for him to say more, but he looked around at the car he was working on, his mind already back under the hood. Just then, a car came onto the lot, making both driveway bells ding.

"Well, you have a good drive out to your mother's, then. Bye now," he ended, hoping she would go on about her business. Something about the way she was gazing at him, kind of like looking through the glass case at the butcher's at a slab of prime beef, made him uncomfortable.

She seemed to take the hint and climbed into her car, moving the gearshift into drive and waving at him. "Thanks again!"

He watched her go with a return wave.

A raised voice floated over from the direction of the gas pumps, attracting his attention immediately.

"I'm sor'y, suh. I'll jus' go get Floyd tah pump yo gas fo yah," Duke was saying to a man in a brand new, bright red 1956 Lincoln Premiere with a gleaming white top and wide white wall tires.

The man looked over Duke's shoulder and saw Floyd headed their way, having also heard the raised voices. "Another darkie? What *is* this, a station run by coloreds?" he sneered just as Vic came striding up.

"What's the problem, mister? You got something personal against my men, here?" he asked in a tight voice as he stopped at the man's door.

"I don't want no colored putting his filthy hands on my car, chipping the paint when they try to get the pump nozzle in the slot, and anything else they can think of to mess up," the man fumed self-righteously.

It was all Vic could do to keep from hauling the insolent man through the car's window, and he had a mighty urge to plant his fist in the man's mouth. Gritting his teeth instead, he growled, "You get out of here, mister. We don't need your business."

"And you won't get it!" the bigot sputtered. "I've got friends and I'll spread the word to skip your place. There are plenty of other gas stations, you know! I can make trouble for you and your ni****-loving kind!"

In a heartbeat, Vic reached in and grabbed the creep's shirt-front in his fist. The coward's eyes immediately bugged out in fright. "Listen you scumbag, I don't need your business, nor theirs' neither. We've got more than enough to keep us busy," Vic barely got his hand out of the way as the man gunned his motor and sped away, shouting over his shoulder several racial insults.

Vic was livid. Heart pounding like the banging of a bass drum, palms sweating, he took a ragged breath and then turned to his men. Placing a hand on their shoulders, they began to walk together back toward the office.

"My, my, my. I'm sor'y, boss. I..." Duke began, but Vic cut him off.

"You ain't got anything to be sorry about, Duke. We don't need his kind," he countered, with a few insults of his own thrown in the direction of the rude customer.

Floyd said nothing, but the look in his eyes bothered Vic. It was a look of resignation instead of righteous anger, and spoke volumes about hurts and insults from his past. His friend's expression made Vic's heart ache.

Suddenly, Duke started cackling that laugh of his. "Well, I's tell ya what I'sa gonna do. I's gonna pray fo' dat man ta get saved, and let de' Good Lawd spank his be-hind."

Floyd and Vic burst out laughing.

"You do that, Duke. And I just might join ya – once I get over wantin' to beat the slimeball's head in," Vic added with a chuckle.

၈၁ၥ၃

WHEN VIC ARRIVED home that evening, leaving Floyd and Duke there to close up, he felt the frosty atmosphere as soon as he walked in the front door. His family was seated at the kitchen table, but no one was talking. Unbeknownst to him, Louise had been fussing at everyone before he'd gotten there. Even Jimmy and Buddy were quiet, trying to stay out of range of her radar.

Vic washed his hands at the sink, walked over and sat down, picked up his fork, and took a bite of the chicken and dumplings he scooped onto his plate. Without thinking, he dropped his fork on the table and griped, "This ain't even warm!"

One comment was all it took.

Like a covered pot that had suddenly reached its boiling point, Louise shot up out of her chair, grabbed his plate, scraped the food back into the bowl, stomped over to the stove, and shoved the concoction back into the pot without even a pause. Then with more force than needed, she twisted the knob on the burner to high, grumbling under her breath something about slaving over a hot stove all day – which of course, she hadn't, but it felt good to say it, anyway.

Tommy, Jimmy, Buddy, and Lilly all looked at one another, startled and unsure what to do or say, their forks frozen in mid air.

Vic, however, had reached his limit. He'd suffered frustrations all day with missing or wrong parts, the Phillips' company tanker delivering a short order, and he had smashed his knuckle with a wrench. The incident with the ignorant bigot had been the icing on the cake. Now this.

Muttering a curse word, he swung around in his chair to glare at his wife's profile as she stood at the stove, too vigorously stirring the food in the pot. He could see her lips were clamped shut. "Louise, what the *he*…" he paused, fighting valiantly to tamp down his temper. "What is your *problem*? You've been like a cat that got its tail mashed by a rockin' chair for weeks, and I've had just about all I can stan…"

She whirled around, stopping him mid word. "What's my *problem*? I'll tell you what my problem is! My problem is my *husband* is too busy working and flirting with the neighbor women to bother himself to care about what *I* need! That's my *problem*, Mr. Matthews!"

The collective jaws of everyone else in the room dropped. Lilly pushed back her chair and reached to grasp Jimmy and Buddy by the hands, nearly dragging them up from their seats as she ushered them out of the room and down the hall to the room she shared with Jimmy. Before she could get them inside and get the door shut, the occupants in the kitchen could hear Jimmy's little voice ask, "What's wrong with Mama, Grandma?"

Tommy didn't know what to do. He'd never seen his parents so angry at one another, and he was torn between wanting to flee the premises, and wondering if he should somehow try to referee. Neither prospect seemed ideal.

Louise was so angry, she was trembling, and Vic was equally mad. Hearts pounding, they were breathing as hard as if they had just finished a 10K run. Before Lilly had gotten the boys to the doorway, he snarled, "*Flirting* with the neighbor women? Just what is *that* supposed to mean? And *how* am I not carin' about what you need?"

Somewhere in the back of Louise's mind, she knew the accusations she had thrown at him were unreasonable and totally ridiculous, but reason and sanity had somehow taken a flying leap off the Second Street Bridge. Turning fully toward him, she rammed her fists onto her hips and stared him down.

"Mrs. Barbara Dixon, our neighbor three doors down? You know – the one with the wavy, light brown hair and gorgeous green eyes?" She paused for him to react in some way, but he sat silent, as if he were waiting for her to make her point. She continued sarcastically, "The one built like *Jayne Mansfield*? The one you stopped everything for today to work on her car, as a *special favor* to her?" He opened his mouth to protest that he had not *stopped* everything, but had merely helped her with a problem as he would any other customer, but Louise forged right on, "The one who's *husband* is serving in the military somewhere overseas and she's all alone with two little kids and needs *big, strong, wonderful Vic*...to be her knight on a white horse?" she added that last bit as a barb, knowing the point would slice deep. Vic had always called himself her knight, and as a sweet reminder of his promise, on their dresser, she kept the figurine of a knight on a steed he had won her at Fontaine Ferry all those years ago.

Vic shook his head and ran a hand back through his hair. "That's the most ridiculous thing you've ever said to me. How'd you know I worked on her car earlier, anyway?" he added, not realizing how that would sound.

Louise's eyes flared even more as she immediately deduced that he meant he hadn't wanted her to find out. "I *saw* her at the A & P after she left you and she told me *all about it*," she snapped, flinging a hand in the general direction of the grocery store. Then placing a hand on one hip again, she propped her other elbow on her waist, let her wrist go slack, and tilted her head to one side, batting her eyelashes and smiling in a good imitation of the woman. "Your husband is just the *most wonderful* man to put everything aside to help me like that," she simpered as she mocked the woman in an embellished Southern Belle accent. "He's just the nicest, sweetest, kindest man I've ever met. Why, you're the luckiest woman in the whole world to have a man like him," she exaggerated her performance.

For a crazy moment, he almost laughed at the comical way she had mimicked the neighbor, but aggravation and anger still simmered too close to the surface. Closing his eyes, he drew in a deep breath, battling with the urge to stand up and shout his anger and hurt back in her face. To yell that he wanted the old Louise back, the one who used to be sweet and loving, instead of this shrew that now occupied her body. Instead, he clamped his mouth shut; knowing words like that would only make things worse.

He couldn't believe Louise would be jealous of that woman – didn't she know he only had eyes for *her*, no matter what? Not to mention that crack about him being the woman's knight. It was a low blow. He considered it a sweet, sentimental private thing between them, that he was Louise's Knight on a white steed. The way she had thrown it out there like that felt as if she had thrown the figurine in the dirt and stomped on it, and on his heart in the process.

Pressing his lips firmly together, he reminded himself what her real frustration was – the fact that she wanted another baby so badly and it hadn't happened yet. But was that *his* fault?

Slowly, he enunciated his words, "I don't care what she implied, all I did was help her put her convertible top down. Took all of about a minute. She thanked me and left. Period."

Vexing tears clouded Louise's eyes as she turned back to the now boiling chicken and dumplings, realizing just in time to take it off the fire before it scorched. She turned the burner off and stood with her back to her husband, her hands curled in tight fists as she made herself draw in deep, slow breaths. *What's wrong with me? Why did I let that counterfeit southern belle get under my skin like that? I haven't felt this jealous since I found out about Alex's sister Rose making a play for Vic. I know he loves me…* Shaking her head with a soft groan, she silently fumed, "*What's wrong with you, stupid woman?*"

Across the room, Tommy opened his mouth several times to try and insert something that would defuse the tension, but nothing seemed appropriate. He'd seen the woman they were fighting about flirt with several of the neighbor men before, and he rightly figured that *she* had been the one doing the flirting. Not to mention, he had spent a great deal of time with his dad, away from his mom, and he'd never seen his father *flirt* with another woman. That didn't mean he hadn't, but Tommy just couldn't bring himself to believe that of his beloved Chief. Finally, wisely, he closed his mouth and decided to let them work things out between themselves.

A full, uncomfortably silent minute went by, and finally, Louise drew one last deep breath and let it out in a resigned huff, mumbling, "Well, no use letting this food go to waste. Might as well sit down and eat." Without turning, she called over her shoulder as she grabbed the pot's handle, "Tommy, go tell Grandma and your brothers to come back and finish their supper." The teen didn't hesitate a second, but stood right up and disappeared down the hall.

Louise turned then, and Vic turned around in his chair to face the table again, both relieved that the tension in the room had somewhat dissipated. Drawing near Vic's chair, Louise spooned out a good portion of chicken and dumplings onto his plate, mumbling softly, "Careful...it's hot."

He murmured his thanks as the others filed back into the room, their eyes darting between the two previously combating adults.

The skirmish was over, but both of them wondered why they suddenly seemed to be in a war.

ཉོ ལྷ

CHAPTER 12

The Reconciliation

THE REST OF the evening went smoothly, as the family
finished up supper and retired to the living room to watch a
few shows on the television. A difference was noticeable,
however, in that Vic and Louise seated themselves at opposite
ends of the couch, instead of side by side. Jimmy stationed
himself between his parents, with his head on his mother's lap
and his feet propped on his father's thigh.

Lilly sat in the family's 1920's art deco cocktail armchair that
Sonny had given them several years before when he and Sarah
had bought new furniture. Quickly becoming *Grandma's chair,* it
was covered in a soft beige material with a design of small brown
flowers and its wide, wing-style arms were perfect for reading to
children – with one draped over the arm and leaning into the
reader – or for mending. Just then, she was doing the latter. Every
few minutes, she kept glancing over at her daughter and son-in-
law, trying to gauge if the argument from earlier was truly
resolved.

Buddy lounged on one of the other chairs, his attention divided between one of the family's favorite television programs – *I
love Lucy* – and a copy of *The Public Defender in Action* comic book
that had arrived in the mail that day.

Tommy had left immediately after dinner to go hang out at a
friend's house. Guiltily, Louise wondered if the young man had

taken the first opportunity to flee the tension in the household.

For once, as the family watched the Ricardos weather a typical Lucy-inspired fiasco, Louise seemed to see the TV couple in a new light. Lucy was in rare form, outrageously jealous over something innocent and refusing to speak to Ricky, except for scathing remarks and wild accusations. Normally, everyone in the room would have laughed along with the audience the viewers could hear off camera. That night, however, Louise cringed; the plot too closely mirrored real life for comfort.

Vic and Louise both lapsed into silence, both of them deep in their own private thoughts.

He sat staring at the framed photograph of the family, on the table directly across from his seat on the couch, wondering how things in their life had changed so drastically. Thinking back over the years of their marriage, he couldn't remember them ever having such heated words before, and his conscience smarted for his part in the proceedings.

Louise stared unseeingly at the screen, the fingers of one hand absently combing through her youngest son's short black hair as he snuggled on her lap. She didn't like herself very much at that moment. It had been a long time since she had felt such deep dissatisfaction and frustration – not since the years she had spent in her miserable first marriage with TJ Blankenbaker, Tommy's real father. Part of her brain knew she should "stop and smell the roses" and be grateful for all of the many blessings in her life…and she wondered why that seemed to be so difficult to do.

Deep in thought, neither realized when the show ended and *December Bride* had come on. However, it did signal to Lilly that it was 9:30 and time for the boys to get to bed. With a glance at the parents, Lilly pushed her mending aside and stood to her feet, shepherding the youngsters down the hall for their nightly bedtime regimen. It didn't take long, since they had already had their baths earlier.

Minutes later, after kissing the boys goodnight and unable to find interest in the program, Vic and Louise finally rose and turned off the television. She paused next to the set, uncertain. They had not moved from their positions on opposite ends of the couch. Knowing they would soon have to break the silence between them and go into their room together, Vic glanced at his wife and mumbled, "I'll be back in a while...I'm goin' for a walk," and slipped into a jacket as he headed out the door.

Louise watched him go, and then with a sigh, dragged herself down the hall to the bedroom. She slowly removed her light blue striped dress and tossed it into the hamper in the corner. Glancing up at the mirror over the dresser, she stared at her reflection, her amethyst necklace glinting in the soft light of the lamp on the nightstand. Reaching up with one hand, she caressed the stone with her fingers as she let her memories float back to that magical day at Fontaine Ferry Park, nineteen years before...

Arriving at the huge carousel just in time to step onto its ground level surface for its next cycle, Vic tugged Louise through the maze of majestic, beautifully carved and painted horses to one of the stationary seats.

"But...aren't we going to ride a horse...? Louise began, but the intense look in his eyes stopped her protest and she followed him onto the seat. Music played and children laughed and talked as Louise felt Vic take her hand and turn her toward him while he reached into his shirt pocket and retrieved a small, velvet covered box. Her heart jumped as she thought he was about to present her with a ring.

With a shy smile, Vic explained, "I wanted to get ya something nice, and especially since I didn't have any money to get ya anything for your birthday...so...well...I hope you like it."

Opening the box and finding the lovely pendant on a simple silver chain, she gasped, "Oh Vic! An amethyst necklace! It's beautiful!"

Never had she felt so cherished. It was as if all of her childhood dreams of finding her 'Prince Charming' had culminated in that moment.

"Here, lemme put it on ya," he whispered, undoing the clasp and reaching around behind her head to fasten it. She turned then, gazing into his eyes

as he sat back to view the pendant as it sparkled against her skin. She smiled lovingly and he reached for one of her hands, bringing it up to his lips and grazing the surface of her knuckles with a soft kiss as she told him she felt bad that he had spent so much money on her.

"You're worth it. You're an angel. The sweetest, truest, most beautiful angel I've ever known," he softly declared.

Angel, Louise unconsciously winced as reality came rushing back with a jolt. Right then, with her harsh words and anger fresh in her mind, she felt quite the opposite. Remorse seemed to fill her belly and overflow into her veins like liquid fire. And now…Vic had gone out for a walk, too uncomfortable around her to come to bed. With a touch of melancholy, she remembered her father, Willis, doing the same thing many times after arguments with her mother. *Was she becoming like her mother?*

Sighing dejectedly, she gathered her things to take a bath.

ℰᏩᏬ

DEEP IN THOUGHT, Vic walked along Granvil Drive – in the opposite direction from Barbara Dixon's house. His emotions were tied up in knots and he had been afraid that he and Louise would have words again, so he had skipped out to walk and think. Part of him hoped she would be asleep by the time he returned.

Although it had been a pleasant day weather-wise, cooler temperatures had arrived with the setting of the sun. Now, he was thankful he had thought to grab his tan uniform jacket before he left the house as he walked along with his hands stuck into his pockets. The environment around him was silent, since it was early spring and no crickets or night bugs were out yet. A full, bright moon lit his way along the sidewalk.

As he strode along, he could see into the windows of other houses along the street as families settled down for the night. He heard laughter from one house as he passed by; from the next, the clear sounds of a program on a television set. From somewhere nearby, he heard a backdoor open as a female voice encouraged, "Go on, now," and he figured she had let her cat out before turning in for the night.

The street curved to the left and he aimlessly followed it around, his rubber-soled work shoes making no sound on the concrete sidewalk. Shoving his hands deeper into his jacket pockets, a few minutes later, he raised his head and saw the barricade at the end of the street. Beyond were acres and acres of empty land that had been covered in row after row of corn stalks when they'd first moved in. He kept going, easily stepping over the barricade and stopping at the base of a large oak tree at the edge of the field.

Tiredly, he lowered himself down and placed his back against the sturdy trunk. Adeptly removing a cigarette from the pack in his shirt pocket and retrieving his lighter from his pants, he quickly lit up. Then he just sat, staring straight ahead as he blew the smoke out to one side, his wrists resting on his up-drawn knees. One hand held the lit cigarette between two fingers while the thumb of the other hand unconsciously rubbed the smooth surface of his father's lighter.

With all of the stress and tension of his normal days at the station, plus the confrontation with the racist jerk that afternoon, he surely didn't need to come home to a shrewish wife. *She never used to be that way...she was always even-tempered, and so good with the kids. She always knew just what to say to make everything seem all right...* Shaking his head in frustration, he brought the cigarette up to his mouth and took a long drag, then leaned his head back against the trunk to gaze upward at the deep blue night sky filled with thousands of stars and a big round moon. *I've been tryin' and tryin' to be patient with this obsession she has about wanting another baby...but I don't know...how much is a man supposed to take without explodin'?*

Vic closed his eyes, moving the cigarette to his mouth and taking another long draw, blowing it out slowly as he felt the nicotine begin to have a calming effect. He let his mind drift back over the years that he and Louise had been together; as far back as their idyllic summer of dating immediately after the waters of the Flood receded. She had been just a girl then…but he hadn't known just how *much* of a girl she actually was – and his thoughts touched on the heated words they'd had the night he had found out. The accusations he had flung in her face, and her resulting tears. He had stormed off, enraged, having no clue that would be the last sight he would have of her sweet face and breathtaking hazel eyes for four miserably long, lonely years.

But since their reunion, followed six months later by their marriage, they had lived a blissful, contented life…at least he *thought* they had. Had she not been as pleased with him as she had seemed? He shook his head against the thought. No, she had only begun showing signs of dissatisfaction around the time that their youngest had started school. Lilly had told him Louise was suffering a bit of 'empty nest' syndrome, and that things would smooth out once a schedule became established. However, to his way of thinking, they hadn't. She seemed to have slipped from that right into wanting another baby – and not just a baby – a girl. It had to be a *girl*.

Heaven knows he had tried to fulfill her request, but so far, it hadn't happened. Even when she *did* get pregnant, how could he guarantee that the child would be female? It was almost as if she expected him to make sure! How in blazes could he do that? He wasn't God, for cripes sake!

Shaking his head again, he let it drop, and then lowered his hand and stubbed the cigarette out into the hard-packed dirt. He knew he should get up and go home, but he dreaded the potential of another scene between them. Becoming conscious of the smooth feel of the lighter in his left hand, he wished, for the thousandth time, that his father were still alive so that he could talk over with him this puzzle in his relationship with his wife. *Did Pop and Mama have a good relationship? I don't have a clue. The only couples I've watched much of is Jack and Liz – but they almost made me want to swear off being married myself. Al and Goldie…they've got a pretty good marriage…* he nodded in response to his thoughts. *I wonder if they ever fight…*

Finally, the thought occurred to him that he should pray about the problem. Slipping his lighter back into his pocket, he threaded his fingers together and lifted a silent prayer to God – for his wife, for their relationship, for her happiness and contentment – and for good measure, he asked that the Almighty grant the blessing of another baby. *God…it don't matter to me whether it's a boy or a girl…I love all my boys, You know that. But God…she seems to want a little girl real bad, so if You can see fit, will You make it happen?* He sat for a few minutes, but nothing more came to him, so he quietly ended the prayer.

A few minutes later, with the evening breeze picking up, Vic realized he was beginning to feel a bit chilled. *Well, gotta go back sometime,* he sighed as he pushed his way to his feet and began to retrace his steps.

In minutes, he was standing on the front porch of the darkened house.

$$\mathcal{SO}\mathcal{GR}$$

VIC STILL WASN'T back by the time Louise settled in on her side of the bed. She lay there in the quiet darkness, keenly feeling his absence. With a pang, she realized this was the first time in their marriage, other than when she'd had their babies, and that one awful night he had spent in jail, that she had gone to bed alone. It wasn't a nice feeling.

All through the motions of taking a leisurely bath, brushing out her hair, and performing her nightly routine, her thoughts had been on her husband and their earlier fight.

Back and forth her emotions seemed to swing, first one way, and then the other. She had felt shame at her outburst, followed by thoughts of blaming him for her feelings. Then, once she was in bed waiting for his return, she began to feel anger that he had gone for a walk instead of talking things out with her. It felt too much like what her father used to do after a row with her mother.

For the first time, she realized her father, Willis, had never really engaged in an argument with Lilly. He had merely sat there, hardly saying anything beyond an occasional grunt, just letting her vociferate on and on until finally he had stood, put aside his newspaper, and left the apartment. Her mother had always muttered and grumbled when he did – but by the time Willis had returned, Lilly had always been in a better frame of mind. *I guess that's what Vic is hoping, too…*

Feeling aggravation, but with no specific point of origin, Louise flopped over in the bed facing the wall, and punched her pillow – several times for good measure. *Let him stay out there and freeze, see if I care.*

Deliberately closing her eyes, she tried her best to go to sleep.

Minutes later, she heard a soft sound on the porch and she stiffened, listening. She heard the front door open softly, close, and then heard the sound of his rubber soles on the hardwood floor of the hallway. She stayed perfectly still, striving to make her breathing steady as if she were asleep.

More sounds…the rustle of clothing on the other side of the room, and then the whispered sound of him padding into the bathroom and softly shutting the door. As quietly as he could, he took his shower and finished his preparations for bed.

Her mind had never ceased its pendulum of thoughts, and when he finally emerged from the bath and gently eased himself into the bed, the pleasant scent of his aftershave and deodorant wafted her way as he settled under the covers. He lay perfectly still, and she knew he was trying to ascertain if she were asleep or not.

Finally, he whispered, "You awake?"

For a moment, she debated over whether or not to give him

the silent treatment, but ultimately reason won out and she whispered back, "Yes," although she didn't turn around.

He waited, but she made no move to engage with him. At length, he muttered, "You still mad?"

For some reason, him asking her the question stirred the coals of her anger, and she ground her teeth together, feeling her heart speed up. He took her silence as affirmation.

Sighing softly, he murmured, "Babe, you *know* I didn't flirt with that woman. She was just tryin' to push your buttons, is all. You oughta know that," he added, his voice leaning toward firm.

In response to that she flounced over, but stared up at the ceiling rather than at him. Her mind was thinking to say, "Yes, I know that," but for reasons unclear even to her, she exclaimed, "How am I supposed to know that? I don't know what you do all day at the station! For all I know, you could have a string of women coming in for you to 'stop what you're doing and work on their cars'!" Her voice had gone from whispering to speaking, louder and louder with each word.

"Aw, don't be stupid!" he fired back. Immediately, he regretted his choice of words when she shot straight up in bed and glared down at him.

"Oh, so now I'm *stupid?*"

Swearing under his breath as his frustration level zoomed through the roof again, he sprang up next to her and whisper-yelled, "That ain't what I meant, and you know it!"

"I'm not going to stay here and be insulted," she flung back, not bothering to lower her voice, and trying desperately to disentangle her legs from the suddenly clinging covers.

"Quiet!" he hissed. "You wanna wake everybody up? And where do you think you're going? We need to talk this thing out."

"Well, I don't *feel* like talking now!" she countered as she started to flee, but he gently grasped her arm and held fast as she carried on, "Maybe I would have before you went out to take your *long-walk-to-cool-off,* like Daddy always did to get away from

Mama when they had a fight, but now, I just don't *care* anymore!"

"Aw Mary Lou...don't leave the bed...stay and talk to me," he requested, his voice deep.

Something about the husky tone of his voice and that special way he uttered her name made her breath catch. This was her *husband*, her wonderful Vic, her soul mate...her best friend. Why had all those old insecurities from the hurts of her past suddenly decided to reincarnate out of thin air to torment her? They were dead, gone, and buried years ago. *Why am I acting like this?*

Suddenly feeling decidedly ashamed of herself again, she turned her head away and started to cry.

The anger that had ramped up so quickly in Vic had taken a nosedive, then immediately flew out the window, and now he felt like the biggest heel in the world. He'd never been able to stand hearing her cry; it always tore at his insides. Now, knowing *he* was the reason for her tears, he felt even worse – something akin to garage floor grime on the bottom of his work shoes.

He gently tugged on her arm, wanting desperately to explain, and what's more, to stem the tide of her tears. "I'm sorry, babe. I didn't mean to upset you. This has been a crazy day. I shouldn't 'a brought the station's problems home..."

After a few moments, Louise sniffed and wiped her cheeks with the back of one hand. Turning her head, she looked over her shoulder at him. "Problems? What problems?"

He rifled his other hand back through his damp hair as he told her of the encounter with the rude, racist customer. By the time he finished, Louise had turned toward him, tears stopped and all thoughts of their silly argument forgotten.

"Oh Vic! That's terrible!" she responded. "I hope you told him not to ever come back!"

"You bet I did," he answered with a nod. "Dirtbags like him need to be tied up and horsewhipped." Then with a snort, he shook his head in wonder. "But good old Duke...he'd fuss at me if he heard me say that. He said he'd pray for the man and *Let the*

Good Lawd spank his be-hind."

They chuckled softly together.

Turning toward her, he reached out and gently clasped her hands. With a small smile, he mumbled, "Are we okay now?" and was relieved when she nodded and leaned over to brush his lips with hers. He took her into his arms and they sat rocking in one another's embrace for quite some time, thankful for the restored tranquility between them.

Finally, they lay back down and she settled against his side.

"Let's get some sleep, huh?" he whispered, pressing a kiss against her hair.

She nodded, feeling more relaxed and at peace than she had in months. *I've got so much to be thankful for...especially for this man who loves me so unconditionally. Forgive me, God, for wanting more...* After a few moments, she tilted her head back for him to kiss her, and he complied – a long, warm, wonderful meeting of lips.

When their eyes opened, each one smiled softly, and Louise brought up a hand to caress her husband's smooth, whisker-free cheek.

"I love you so much, Vic."

He turned his head slightly and pressed a kiss to her palm. "I love you too, babe. You mean the world to me. You know that, don't ya?"

She smiled dreamily and gently ran a thumb over his smooth, warm lips, whispering as he kissed it. "I'm sorry I've been so...hard to live with lately...I'm surprised you didn't put me over your knee."

He grinned and wiggled his eyebrows at her. "I thought about it a few times."

She chuckled and leaned forward to kiss him again.

His lips covered hers as his hands leisurely roamed and squeezed in all the right places. Finally, he pulled back and nuzzled noses with her, murmuring, "I'm sorry, too...I shoulda been more understanding. I don't ever want you to even *think* I'd look at another woman."

"I know you wouldn't," she answered, but his lips muffled her response, as he suddenly wanted to make sure she truly understood that fact.

One kiss led to two and then three. Then as he deepened the kiss, they became thoroughly engrossed in one another.

As natural as a spring rain, they continued on for the next long while, immersing themselves in deep, utterly satisfying lovemaking – with no 'agenda' in mind.

Finally, in the early hours of the morning, they fell asleep in one another's arms.

ဆဝၕ

CHAPTER 13

Duke and The Wasp Nest

O N A BRIGHT Saturday in May, which also happened to be Derby Day, Louise stood looking at herself in the bedroom mirror. Turning to the side, she eyed her figure for a moment, and her still-flat stomach, before closing her eyes and gratefully laying a hand against her belly.

The words of her obstetrician, Dr. Clarence Denton, floated back to her memory from the day before.

"I put it around the second week of December, the 11th or so," he had said. *"Now, I want you to take it easy, it's been almost seven years since your last baby, Mrs. Matthews. Rest often, and no picking up heavy items or working too hard – let some of that passel of boys help you,"* he had cautioned as he ushered her out of his office.

"Oh, don't you worry, Dr. Denton. I don't plan on letting *anything* interfere with this pregnancy," Louise had assured him.

She had driven home so blissfully happy, she could hardly concentrate on the road.

Vic had been ecstatic and relieved when she had told him that night. Waiting until he arrived home from work to tell him instead of calling him on the phone had taken an extraordinary amount of patience. But, when he had walked in the front door, she had been standing in the kitchen doorway with such a dazzling smile, at first he didn't notice the item dangling from her fingers. When it finally registered, he laughed, knowing she was harking back to what he had done on their fifth anniversary – she was holding a pair of baby booties, only this time they were pink.

He stepped toward her and swung her into his arms, asking when he finally stepped back, "When?"

"Dr. Denton says December 11."

He gave a nod of satisfaction, and quickly figuring in his head, his eyes sparkled as he realized they had probably conceived on the night of their big fight. *I guess that got things stirred up in more ways than one.*

Indeed, everyone in the family seemed relieved...well, all except the youngest member, Jimmy. He had taken the news with a stoic face and once the congratulations and excitement had died down, he grumbled, "Whatta we need some ol' baby for?" With that, the young boy had stomped out the back door and spent a good while kicking a ball around the back yard.

Gazing at her image in the mirror and picturing herself once again big with child, Louise patted the space where the tiny baby resided as she mused, "Oh, he'll change his mind once the baby is here...once his little *sister* is here," she added as a spoken wish.

With a happy sigh, she left the bedroom and made her way to the kitchen. Lunch dishes had been cleared away and now Lilly was busy working on a project, making homemade Concord grape jam, using a large pressure cooker and glass jars to be sealed with paraffin wax.

"Oh, Louise, we don't have enough wax," Lilly commented as her daughter walked in the room. "We had plenty of fabric and rubber bands, so I thought we had enough wax left from last time we canned, but there was only one bar in that box," she added, gesturing over her shoulder to an open box of Gulfwax sitting on the table.

"All right, Mama, I'll drive up to the grocery and get..." she paused as shrieks sounded from the direction of the carport. "What on earth?" she asked as she headed toward the door.

Before she reached it, Jimmy and Buddy came barreling

through, Jimmy's face wet with tears as he held one arm in pain, and Buddy's eyes wide with fear.

"What happened?" Louise asked, startled and concerned, trying to figure out the problem amidst the crying. "Did you hurt yourself? Let me see…" she directed, trying to pry Jimmy's hand from his arm.

"He got stung by a wasp, Mama," Buddy explained, out of breath. "We were trying to get my bicycle out, it got pushed back behind lots of other stuff, and a wasp landed on him. I told him not to swat at it, but he did anyway," he added with a pointed, *I-told-you-so* look at his brother. Jimmy, meanwhile, kept up his crying and squealing.

"It hurts, Mama! It hurts!"

"Mama, I kept hearing a buzzing sound, and we saw a couple more flying around. It's so dark in there, we couldn't tell, but I think there's a wasp nest in the carport!" Buddy reported, his big brown eyes open wide with alarm.

Louise shivered as she imagined trying to deal with the situation at hand; she absolutely *hated* wasps. *Oh, I wish Vic were here! Or even Tommy!* She lamented, but her oldest had gone to an all-day Derby party at one of his friends' homes.

Sitting down in a kitchen chair, Louise pulled her distraught youngster into her arms to try and stem his tears.

Lilly wiped her hands on a towel and went to the refrigerator. Grabbing two ice cubes from a tray in the freezer, she wrapped them in a soft, clean towel. "Here, hold this on it while I make up a baking soda poultice," she advised. Louise nodded and took the towel as she pried Jimmy's hand off the area, making sure the stinger had not remained.

"Here, sweetheart, let Mama put this ice on it. It'll help. Hush now, you'll be all right," she crooned. Jimmy sniffled and whined in pain as his grandmother scurried around the kitchen gathering what she needed.

Soon Lilly was back with a small bowl, stirring the thick paste with one finger. "Now here, let me see…" Louise moved the towel away and Lilly spread a good amount of paste onto the affected area. Pulling another chair away from the table, she directed, "Now honey, you sit still, right here, and let that paste dry. That'll pull some of the poison out and make it stop hurting. Once it's dry, we'll put on another batch."

Once they got the boy settled and he seemed to be calming down, Louise stood and gathered her courage. "Buddy, come with me and we'll see if we can see a nest. We'll go in the front way."

Finding a flashlight in a kitchen drawer, the two made their way out the front door and over to the wide opening to the three-sided carport. With no windows, the further back you went, the darker it got. From the front, they couldn't even see the back wall. They never kept the car inside, as the structure was too full of boxes and all kinds of things they had stored there. There was only a path to the kitchen door.

Peeking inside, they saw no wasps flying around, but they could now hear a constant buzzing noise. Steadying her nerve, Louise exchanged glances with her son, turned the flashlight on and aimed it at the top of the back wall, moving the beam slowly toward the house. Nothing. Then she moved it to the right, and when it reached the corner, both she and Buddy sucked in shocked gasps when their eyes landed on their worst fear – the biggest wasp nest Louise had ever seen – as big around as a dinner plate. There were so many wasps on the paper-like comb; they were scrambling to find room, and even falling off of it. She estimated at least a hundred of the insects vying for space!

"Good Lord!" Louise squealed, nearly dropping the light. Without further adieu, she hurriedly ushered her son back toward the front of the house and they ran inside, slamming the door behind them as if the whole colony was on their heels.

"I told ya! I told ya! Dang, did you see the size of that thing?" Buddy gushed as they hurried into the kitchen.

"Jimmy, there's a nest all right – *this big*!" he exclaimed as he held his arms wide. Although he was exaggerating, the size was still monstrous. Jimmy started to cry again.

Exchanging looks with her mother, Louise muttered, "I'm calling Vic," as she moved toward the phone on the kitchen wall. *Absolutely no way am I dealing with that!*

℘℧

THE PHONE RANG in the station's glass-sided office. Vic picked it up on the third ring and rattled off his greeting by rote, "Matthews Phillips 66 and U-Haul Rental, can I help you?" Listening for a moment as his flustered wife poured out her fear and frustration about what she termed a *huge* wasp nest in the corner of the carport, Vic's face relaxed into his dimpled grin, thinking this was probably one of those "pregnancy exaggerations."

Nodding, although she couldn't see the action, he murmured, "Okay baby, I'll take care of it, don't you worry. And don't go back out there, you hear?" He grinned again when she emphatically assured him she would *not* go anywhere *near* the monstrosity.

When he hung up the phone, he shook his head with a soft chuckle.

Floyd came through the door from the bay area and reached up on the shelf to grasp a few canisters of oil. He looked over at his boss and smiled when he heard him laugh.

"Who was dat, Chief?"

Vic stood up from the desk and looked across at his employee and friend. Quickly, Vic told Floyd about the situation.

"I gotta get Mr. Dickerson's DeSoto finished, though. Do me a favor and run over to the house, and take care of it for Louise, all right?" Vic asked, but Floyd immediately began shaking his head.

"Can't do that, Chief. Remember when we was at the CC camp and I almost died that time from gettin' stung? The doc tol' me I was a-ler...how you say dat...?"

"Allergic?" Vic supplied.

"Yep, dat's the word. He said I was a-ler-gic and if I get's stung again, dat be all she wrote. Sorry, Chief..." he added.

"No, that's all right, Floyd. I forgot all about that, and I sure don't want you to take a chance," Vic conceded as he smiled at his friend.

Duke walked through the door just then, handing Vic the money for a full tank of gas and two quarts of oil he'd just sold to a customer.

Turning his attention to his other employee, Vic began, "Duke, the missus just called. Somethin' about a wasp nest. My youngest boy got stung. But you know how women are, they blow everything outta proportion," he gave a soft snicker. "I want you to take the pickup and go over to my house and take care of it, okay? That is...you ever been stung by a wasp?" he asked, glancing at Floyd.

"Yessah, when I was jus' a tad pole. Hurt like the dickens. Sho' made me re-spec them creatures. Sho' made me wonder what de good Lawd made such a thang fo', too...but I's guess He gots His reasons."

"Well, I'd 'preciate it if you'll go take care of it for me. She shouldn't get upset right now, and I sure don't want her to get stung," Vic added, knowing Duke would understand, as both of his men knew that his wife was expecting.

"Yessah, yessah, I sho' will," Duke replied, catching the keys to Vic's old pickup as his boss tossed them his way and told him the address and how to get there. "Yessah. Be back showt'ly."

So, the little man with a face and physique like Louis Armstrong, but a voice like Andy Divine, clambered up into the truck and headed toward Granvil Drive, singing an old negro spiritual. As he backed up the truck and put it in gear, Vic heard him sing, "Joshua fit de battle a' Jerico, Jerico, Jerico. Joshua fit de battle a' Jerico...an' de wasper nest come a tumblin' down." This he followed with his trademark cackle.

Vic and Floyd both shook their heads, chuckling, and went on back to the cars they were repairing.

Fifteen minutes later, Duke pulled into the driveway of the house, and Louise, Lilly, Buddy, and Jimmy came spilling out of the front door, headed his way. He put the truck in gear and turned off the motor as they converged on him at the driver's door. All of them were talking at once and his eyes were as round as saucers as he tried to make sense out of what they were saying.

"Ho now, ho now, one'ta time. Miz Matt'ews, why don' you tell me," he encouraged as he eased his way out of the vehicle and into their midst.

Louise proceeded to tell him where the nest was and how big it was, as she handed him the flashlight. "Go on, take a look if you don't believe me," she encouraged as she saw the doubting expression on his face. She pointed toward the yawning opening to the three-sided structure.

Duke, feeling just a bit hesitant, took the light and headed up the concrete driveway as the four scurried toward the front door of the house. Lilly went on inside, taking Jimmy with her. The boy hollered from the doorway, "Be careful, Mr. Duke! Don't let 'em get ya! It hurts!"

Swallowing, his heart beginning to hammer, the old man crept near the opening and snapped on the light. Louise knew the instant he saw the nest, as his eyes nearly bugged out of his head and he began to stammer, "Oh my my my my my. My my my my my my," his head shaking back and forth as if he couldn't believe his eyes.

"See what I mean?" Louise called, as he headed her way, his expression revealing his shock. She knew he was wondering how in the world he would be able to knock that thing down without getting the life stung out of him.

"What are you going to do?" Louise asked, her arms crossed over her chest, feeling a shiver of fear even though it was a warm spring day and she was totally out of sight of the buzzing menace.

"Lawd Jesus, I gots ta do some studyin' on dis, now. Yess'm. Lawd hep' us all," he mumbled, pacing back and forth. He walked back over, peeped around the corner and shined the light on the nest again, shook his head, and then retraced his steps.

Louise watched him, but truly she had no ideas to even toss his way. She was just glad she wasn't the one faced with the task. However, she didn't want the little man to get stung, either.

Finally, he muttered, "Ma'am...I think I's gonna go over to da haw'dware sto' and get somethin' to take care 'a dis. I be back," he assured. "Now ma'am, Chief said fo' you ta stay way away from 'dere, alright?"

She nodded and watched him walk to the truck, looking over his shoulder every few steps and muttering to himself in his sing-song voice that he'd never seen nothing like that in all his live long days.

Thirty minutes later, he was back.

The men at the hardware store had listened to his problem and said the best thing they could recommend would be to saturate the nest with turpentine. Lots of turpentine. They cautioned him to take careful aim, let it fly, and then run for the hills.

Out at the street, he poured the liquid from the containers into a metal bucket, nearly filling it to the top. Louise could hear from the doorway that he was mumbling prayers as he worked. She was saying a few as well. Then, once he was ready, he hollered for them to go inside and shut the door. The four inside the house ran to the kitchen door and Louise pushed the curtain aside and snapped on the outside light. The glow didn't even reach halfway to the corner, which was why they had never noticed the threat before, but it helped some.

From inside, they watched as little gray-haired Duke, who seemed half scared out of his wits, but steadfast and determined nonetheless, inched his way inside. His lips were moving in what Louise figured was continuous prayers sent up to God. The watchers all held their breath. Louise prayed for Duke's safety, and for a miracle, half wishing Vic had come himself or sent Floyd, as she wondered how this wiry little man could handle such a job. *Goodness, I hope it doesn't give him a heart attack!*

He got as close as he dared, the flashlight trained on the menace. The buzzing of the predators nearly dissolved his courage. His hands were shaking as he hummed the Joshua tune. Then suddenly, he squared his shoulders, positioned the flashlight on a box so it was pointed at the structure, and began to take his aim. He eyed the nest, and with both hands firmly on the bucket, carefully swung it up and back…once…twice…three times…and then with a shout as if he pictured the walls of Jericho falling down, he let the turpentine fly.

Louise couldn't believe it – a direct hit! As if guided by the Hand of God like David's Goliath-felling rock, the gargantuan nest was instantly saturated with the potent solution, along with every single wasp on it except one! The lone survivor zoomed toward the man with the bucket, but he knocked it out of the air and stepped on it, squishing it with his shoe.

The four inside the house erupted with shouts of triumph.

His grin and swagger returning in full force, old Duke cackled and stopped outside of the carport just as the others spilled out the front door again.

Buddy ran up to him, "Wow, what a shot! That was sure something, Mr. Duke!"

"I wouldn't have believed it without seeing that for myself. That was amazing," Lilly complimented.

"Oh Duke, thank you!" Louise gushed, reaching out to lay a hand on the man's arm. "You couldn't have done a more perfect job. One whoosh! I've never seen anything like it. How'd you DO that?"

He laughed as he set the bucket down on the sidewalk and took a rag out of his back pocket, using it to wipe the sweat off his face and neck.

"Ma'am, I do b'lieve de good Lawd had His hand on mine. Shucks, you know'd I was ready ta run fo' de hills if'n I missed." He grinned and cackled again. "But, de Lawd is faithful. I figga'd if'n He could help David kill ol' Go-liath with jus' one little rock, dis here wouldn't be too hawd. Yes, indeed. De Lawd is faithful."

"Yes He is," Louise agreed, looking toward the opening to the carport and shaking her head in wonder.

"I'd say, Ma'am, dis'll be a story you'll be a tellin' yo grand chil'un someday. Fo' sho, fo' sho. I'd say you won't forget dis day."

"That I will, Duke. That I will." Looking back at the friendly little man with the big wide, gleaming smile, she opened her mouth to add something else, when they heard through the screen door an ominous hissing sound coming from the inside of the house. Wide-eyed, Louise met Lilly's eyes, and then the older woman let out a screech.

"The pressure cooker!" she exclaimed, and turned to hurry to the door.

"Oh no!" Louise gasped. As one, they all began to run, trying to fit through the front door at one time, Duke right on their heels.

When they reached the kitchen doorway, the five stood still, looking like the cast of an Abbott & Costello movie, mouths open, eyes round as golf balls.

Little Jimmy was the first to utter a word. "Ewwww!"

Indeed, it was the pressure cooker. In all the excitement about the wasp sting, and then the huge nest, and the turpentine adventure, Lilly had failed to secure the top on the device and hadn't realized she had turned on the burner. Dark blue goo had spilled out from the pot and onto the stove, running down the front and pooling onto the floor in an ever-widening puddle. Drops had also splashed on nearby surfaces, and the air was full of heavy purple steam.

It was actually only seconds before the two women rushed

forward to corral the mess, and Duke reached for the boiling pot, managing to move it off the fire and into the kitchen sink out of harm's way.

Staring at the mess on the floor and contemplating how best to start the cleanup, Louise placed her fists on her hips with a frustrated sigh.

"You're so right, Duke. This will be a day I'll never forget!"

෨෨

CHAPTER 14

We'll Be Seeing You, Billy Boy

THE WHOPPER OF a wasp nest became the fodder for many jokes and comments. Duke told the story to anyone who would listen, and each time Vic overheard a telling, the nest got bigger...and bigger...and bigger.

The task, of course, had fallen to Vic to get the dead nest down to toss in the garbage can. What a monster! Privately, he conceded that if he'd been the one to sling the turpentine, he might embellish the tale a bit himself, although the reality was frightening enough on its own.

That summer wasn't all fun and games, however.

Two months later, on what promised to be a hot day in July, judging by the temperature during the night, Louise awoke with a deep feeling of dread. She tried to look around, but the room was pitch dark except for a tiny sliver of light seeping past the edge of the curtain, owing to the streetlight out front.

Lying in bed beside a sleeping Vic, she pressed one hand to her chest, and laid the other arm over her eyes as another wave of fear swept through her. *What is wrong? Something bad is going to happen today...I just know it. Oh, please God, don't let anything happen to the baby...or Vic, or the kids, or Mama...* She lay there for several minutes with her heart pounding triple time before finally deciding to get up and go splash cold water on her face. *Maybe I'm just too hot. Or that fish we had for supper last night was bad...*

Swinging her legs out of bed, she padded out to the hall and across to the bathroom.

Moments later, toweling her face dry, an image of her brother, Billy, came into her mind so clear, it was as if he was standing right beside her. He gave her a tiny smile, but his eyes looked sad and sort of empty.

Billy? Louise stood still, wondering if something might be wrong with her brother. Could he be in some kind of danger? Searching her mind, she realized it had been quite a while since she had seen him. She knew he rented a tiny room somewhere downtown and had been getting by playing drums and sometimes piano – which he had taught himself – in a little joint in the West End. She smiled at that thought, wondering from whom she and Billy had gotten their musical talents, because neither one of their parents could carry a tune in a bucket.

However, with a cringe, she thought about the fact that Billy had been drinking...whiskey...*a lot*...ever since he had returned from serving in the Army during the Korean War. She had remained very concerned about him after his discharge, when the family found out about an incident on board the ship returning from overseas. He had been minding his own business, standing at the rail, when a fellow soldier on the deck above dropped a helmet – and it had hit Billy in the head, knocking him out! He had been unconscious for several minutes and suffered a mild concussion. Louise suspected the injury probably caused him recurring pain, although for reasons of his own, he never mentioned it.

Between that and his horrific experiences in a cold, wet fox-hole in Korea, Louise felt that her dear brother had turned to the bottle for solace he couldn't seem to find elsewhere. All the family knew of his time in Korea was from a photo he had shown them of him and his foxhole mate, a large black man by the name of John Barrow. She had a feeling his war memories were worse than anyone could imagine, but he would never tell them any specifics of what he'd gone through during those dreadful months.

Thinking back, she tried to remember the last time she had seen her youngest brother. Her older brother, Sonny, had been out to their Buechel house at least a dozen times since they had moved in, but Billy hadn't. Come to think of it, not even during the holidays, as he'd been working and couldn't get off, but he had called and wished everyone a Merry Christmas. *So, how long has it been since I saw him... Oh yes...that time he came to the house on 38th...in a taxi...and asked if he could borrow some money.* Pressing her lips together, Louise remembered how bad she had felt telling him she didn't have any to give him. Lilly had searched her purse and come up with a lone quarter, which she had handed to him. Dejected, he had looked at the coin, then back up at the two of them and mumbled a soft, "Thanks," kissed each one on the cheek, and went back out to the waiting cab. She hadn't seen him since.

I hope he's all right... Louise returned to the bedroom and focused on the clock on Vic's side of the bed. *4 A.M. When I get up, I'll try to call down to where he works and see if I can find out if he's okay. What was the name of the place? Mmm, I can't remember. I'll ask Mama, she'll know.*

With that, she said a small prayer for her brother's safety, and then lay back down to try and go back to sleep. The feeling of dread, however, wouldn't subside.

೮ଓ

ONCE EVERYONE WAS up, ate breakfast, and Vic and Tommy had left for the station, Louise found herself standing at the kitchen sink, washing the dishes. The phone on the wall by the door started ringing and a shiver of fear ran down her back. *Billy!*

Drying her hands on her apron, she walked over and picked up the receiver.

"H...hello?"

A man on the other end cleared his throat and began, "This is Chaplain McDaniel at Veteran's Hospital...I'm calling to try and locate Mrs. Willis Hoskins..."

"Yes, that's my mother...hold on a minute," Louise answered, her voice a bit shaky. *Oh please...don't let this be something bad about Billy!* Somehow, however, she knew deep down that it was.

Her hand quivering, her mouth suddenly dry with trepidation, Louise nervously set the receiver down on the counter and brought both hands to her face trying to bring her emotions under control. Walking back through the house, she found her mother making her bed in the room she shared with Jimmy.

"Mama?" Louise began, hesitating for a moment as Lilly turned to meet her gaze. "You're wanted on the phone...it's a chaplain at the Veteran's Hospital."

"Veteran's Hospital? My lands, I hope nothing is wrong with one of the boys," she exclaimed as she followed her daughter out the door and down the hall. Both of them, however, knew it must be something bad – why else would a chaplain at a hospital be calling?

Lilly picked up the receiver and addressed the man on the phone, listened a moment, then nodded. "Yes, certainly. I'll be there as soon as I can."

When Lilly hung up the phone, she turned to Louise. "Your brother, Billy, showed up at the hospital yesterday and they kept him overnight. They want me to come...said Billy listed me as who to call in an emergency."

"I wonder what's wrong? Did he get in an accident? What did the chaplain say?" Louise queried, trying to ignore the niggling suspicion that it had something to do with his drinking.

"He didn't say, just said to come," Lilly responded, but Louise could tell by the look on her mother's face that she didn't feel good about the situation.

"Come on, I'll drive you. We'll take the boys up to the station and let Vic know what's going on."

They did just that, and within the hour, they walked through the main doors of the Veteran's Hospital on Zorn Avenue – the newer, seven-story, red brick, 494-bed facility that had opened just several years prior. Louise had heard about it and seen pictures, but she had never had the need to go there...until now.

Stopping at the front desk and inquiring after the chaplain who had called, a man standing to the side turned and introduced himself – as if he had been waiting for them. Louise swallowed down her apprehension and reached over to grasp her mother's hand as she and Lilly followed him down a short hall to his office.

After they were seated and the chaplain had offered to get them something to drink, which they declined, he began, "Mrs. Hoskins, your son, Billy, arrived here to the hospital in a taxi at around 7:30 last night. He was complaining of abdominal pain, nausea, vomiting, fever, chills...a general malaise..." he paused, clearing his throat. Louise tried to imagine what would be wrong with her brother...Influenza? Appendicitis? Absently, she also wondered if this chaplain had been on the job very long, as he seemed to be uncomfortable speaking with a patient's family members. As he continued, she pushed that thought away and tried to concentrate on what he was saying.

"The surgeon on duty took him right in and performed a procedure...they were, however, unable to...they tried their best..." he paused again, this time meeting her eyes.

Suddenly, Lilly realized the truth. Perhaps she had felt it the moment she got the phone call, but she sat forward and looked the chaplain in the eye. "Are you trying to tell us that...he *died?*"

With a reluctant nod, he whispered, "Yes. I'm so sorry."

Louise felt the room tilt; she couldn't believe her ears! Her little brother? Dark haired, blue-eyed, handsome Billy Hoskins? The baby she had taken care of and dressed like he was her own doll? The boy who had loved to ride the rides at Fontaine Ferry? The youngster who had followed her and her friends around everywhere she went, driving her crazy? The young man who had been such a part of her life from the time she could remember? How could he be *dead*? He was too young! Why, he was...he was...only twenty-eight!

Images came rushing in, Billy as a toddler, learning to walk and talk...Billy on his first day of school...Billy grinning around a missing front tooth and excitedly asking her if she thought the tooth fairy would come...Billy in the middle of the boat as Vic rescued the family during the Flood...Billy running in fear from the nurse who wanted to give him a smallpox shot. More images swam through...Billy as a handsome, lanky teen, dancing with pretty Bernice Grant to the silly song, "Boogie Woogie Bugle Boy of Company B"...Billy crying in Sonny's arms at their father's funeral...on and on the memories came. This couldn't be real.

When the room righted itself again, Louise slowly realized she was holding a small glass of water that the chaplain had obviously provided, and that he was kneeling at her chair, patting her hand. She turned her head and saw her mother in the next chair, using a handkerchief to wipe at a continuous flow of tears.

Now, Louise realized she had tears on her own cheeks. *Oh Billy! My sweet Billy boy, my little brother! I...I didn't even get to say goodbye!*

Reaching over to place a hand on her mother's arm in an attempt to comfort, Louise opened her mouth to speak, but no words came. Clearing her throat, she tried again. "You okay, Mama?" Lilly answered with a small nod.

Louise turned to the chaplain, asking softly, "What...what was wrong with him?"

"The doctors ruled that he suffered a pancreatic hemorrhage. It had progressed too far and they were unable to stop it in time," he answered gently, gripping her hand, obviously worried whether she would be all right or not.

Louise didn't know what to do or say. She felt numb and confused. The kind chaplain seemed to understand, and he murmured softly, "We've called your husband. He's on his way."

At that moment, Louise centered all her thoughts on that piece of information. Vic…she'd hold on until he arrived, then everything would be all right…

ℴ¢

"OH BABE, I'M so sorry," Vic whispered as he rocked her gently in his arms. Although the thought of Louise's younger brother dead came as a blow to him, as he had truly loved his brother-in-law, he knew the news had hit his wife hard, and he was especially concerned because of her condition.

"I…I can't believe it…" she sniffled, burrowing her face into his uniform shirt and clutching his sides tightly. Her heart felt compressed, to the point of pain, and it was hard to draw in a deep breath. However, she managed to squeak, "My sweet Billy!"

"I know, babe. It's a shock…we didn't even know he was sick…"

Louise nodded against him. "It was probably the drinking. But…some people drink for years and years and nothing happens…Billy was still young…" she whined softly.

"Sometimes that happens…" he murmured, not really knowing what to say to make her feel better. He glanced over, watching Louise's other brother, Sonny, doing his best to comfort a distraught Lilly. Only, how does one comfort a mother who just lost her son?

After a few minutes, Louise sniffled again and turned her face, speaking softly, "I woke up early this morning, feeling scared, so I got up and got a drink of water, washed my face…and I saw him just as clear…like he was standing right there looking at me. He kind of smiled…but his eyes were so sad. It was about four o'clock…"

Vic stiffened for a moment, and then tightened his arms around her. "That chaplain said Billy passed away at 3:55…"

Louise gasped and leaned back enough to see her husband's face. "He...he came to see me...to tell me goodbye," she whispered in awe, the knowledge swept over her in a huge wave of emotion, which helped just a bit to relieve her sadness.

Vic smiled tenderly and bringing up a hand holding a dry handkerchief, he dabbed at her tears. "Yeah, seems he did."

Louise nodded, staring at nothing. "I wish I...could have helped him not be so sad...after he came back from the war..."

"Well...the chaplain told me that he spoke to Billy when he first arrived...he said he got right with the Lord. Your brother's not in pain anymore, honey. Try to hang on that... Some day you'll see him again."

ഇ)(R

MUCH LIKE WHEN Willis had died; Sonny and Vic took care of all the arrangements. They made sure Billy had a nice gravesite at Calvary Cemetery, in the Veteran's section. It was under a pleasant shade tree, right alongside a walking path.

Lilly held up well, only breaking down in tears once during the service. Sonny stayed right by his mother's side, slipping an arm around her when he thought she needed the comfort. Edna and her husband Gene couldn't make it, as they didn't have money for train fare from New York – or so Edna had said when she had answered Sonny's phone call. Vic had his own thoughts about the validity of that, since Edna's husband worked for New York Central Railroad and could get tickets any time he wanted. However, he kept his opinions to himself, so as not to upset Lilly and Louise.

For the most part, the funeral was a somber affair, one in which Louise would later remember very few details. The one bit that stood out in her memory was the remarks made by her son, Tommy. No one else wished to or felt like getting up to say anything about the life of the deceased. Louise was too distraught, plus she'd had the fear of a superstitious old wives' tale spoken over her by her friend, Ruth, who had blatantly and with much conviction, declared that Louise would lose the baby if she attended her brother's funeral. "Everybody knows it's bad luck, Louise – it just is!"

"Well, I don't believe that!" Louise had shot back. "I'm going to my little brother's funeral and that's *that*. Nothing's going to happen to the baby because of it." Deep down, however, a seed of fear had been planted and she had to fight hard against it.

Sonny, who used to have a go-getter personality and was always ready with a joke, had changed dramatically after his marriage to the soft-spoken Sarah. Now a man of few words, he had gone completely mute regarding his feelings for his younger brother. Louise understood – Sonny was too afraid that he would get up there in front of everyone and get choked up, and to his way of thinking, make himself look the "fool".

Doc Latham had agreed to officiate the service, but as he was gathering his notes to begin, seventeen-year-old Tommy signaled that he would like to speak. With a gentle smile, the pastor nodded.

Tom stood, walked to the small podium, and cleared his throat.

"Um…I thought somebody should say something about Uncle Billy, so I guess I will. He um…he was the best kind of uncle a kid could have, because most of the time, he was kind of a kid himself," he paused and looked around at his teary-eyed family, the confused faces of his little brothers, and the friends that had made the trip to the funeral home, namely Alec, Earl, and their families. He noticed Bernice Grant wiping tears.

All eyes on him, he hesitatingly continued. "From my…my earliest memories when I was just a kid, Uncle Billy was always around, always laughing and joking, kind of happy-go-lucky. He's the one who taught me how to tie my shoestrings…he showed me how to blow a big bubble with a wad of chewing gum, without letting it pop all over my face...he taught me how to shoot marbles, and beat all the neighbor kids out of their pennies," he paused and smiled as some in the small audience chuckled. Gathering his thoughts, he glanced down at Louise, watching her wipe away tears as Vic tightened his arm a little closer around her shoulders.

"But my best memory of him was one night when he took me with him to see some friends downtown, and we ended up singing with them and goofing around. Before that, I didn't even know he knew how to play music, but he sure did. He told me that night that I had the knack, too, after me and him sang a song together. He said I had real talent. I'll never forget it...it meant a lot to me that he thought so."

He stopped again, pressing his lips together as if he were thinking whether or not he should mention his next thoughts. Glancing around again, he went on, "He was different after he came back from the war. He didn't laugh and joke like he used to...he didn't come around much. I asked him once after that if being a soldier was exciting, and he looked me in the eye, real serious, and said, 'Nephew, you better pray to the Almighty that you *never* have to find out.' I never asked him again, but I knew that whatever he'd been through over there must have been pretty bad to change him that much. Anyway...that's about all," he finished with a shrug and a sniffle as he stepped down to take his seat, surreptitiously swiping at his eyes.

Several of Billy's friends from Paddy's, the small bar where he had made a few bucks playing drums or piano late at night, had come to pay their respects. At that point, they solemnly got up and made their way to the front of the small assembly. In honor of their friend, they brought their instruments and played a slow version of, "I'll Be Seeing You." It was one of the songs, they said, that Billy could play on the piano so well that patrons requested it all the time.

When they finished, one of the musicians saluted toward the

coffin, mumbling, "We'll be seein' you, Billy Boy." Then, he and the other band members respectfully inclined their heads to the family and shuffled quietly to the back of the small sanctuary.

There wasn't a dry eye in the room when Doc stood to deliver the funeral sermon.

Billy would have been happy to know that through his death, two of his fellow musicians, who had also served with him in the war, gave their hearts, burdens, and torments to the Lord – bringing something good from something bad.

It was a memory Louise would ponder in her heart, always.

ഇൗ൜

CHAPTER 15

The Scare at the Fair

"MAMA, DADDY SAID to ask you if you want to go to the fair," Jimmy announced as he ran out into the backyard and over to where she stood hanging a wet towel on the clothesline. It was a Monday afternoon in late August, and the boy had secured the help of his older brother to telephone the station.

Louise turned toward him, clothespins in her mouth, and mumbled around them, "De Fai?" At his confused expression, she reached up to take the pins from her mouth and restated, "The Fair?"

He nodded vigorously. "Yep. He says it's up to you!"

She eyed him, wondering how the boy had even heard of it. The Kentucky State Fair wasn't something they had gone to as a family.

As if he read her mind, he expounded, "Me and Buddy saw about it on the television! They got rides, and ice cream, and cotton candy, and horses, and all kinds of stuff. Oh Mama, can we go, please, please, please?" By this point, seven-year-old Jimmy knew just how to charm his mother, knowing she could seldom resist his big hazel eyes trained on her so imploringly.

Louise had seen the commercials for the Fair as well, and knew that the city was pushing it this year as THE event for families – before school started again and lives settled back down into routine. The Kentucky Fair and Exposition Center, which was celebrating its grand opening that year, was supposed to be the most modern, multipurpose facility of its kind in the world. She had heard that NBC's *TODAY Show* would broadcast live from the grounds. It was shaping up to be a big deal.

Just that morning, she had read in the paper that they were predicting attendance to top 500,000 during the nine-day event, and break many records. With a new stadium for football games, a large coliseum for rodeos, ice shows and horse shows, dozens of exhibits under twenty-two acres of roof, and scores of rides and midway concessionaires, it seemed to have something for everyone. Louise figured she wouldn't be able to get out of going, although at five months pregnant, the prospect of all of that walking had her feet already aching.

With a sigh, she smiled down at her son and ran a hand back through his thick, dark hair, idly thinking he was due for his start-of-the-school-year haircut. Gently gripping his chin, she asked, "Is your father still on the phone?"

"No ma'am, he said he was busy, but he would see if he can take off early."

The hopeful, expectant look on his face was too much to ignore. With a chuckle, she agreed. "Alright, call him back and see if he can take off before supper. Tell him we'll pack a picnic basket and take it with us."

"Yippee!" he hollered as he spun around and raced back to the house, yelling on the way, "Buddy! Buddy! We're goin'! She said yes!"

Louise shook her head, laughing, as she finished hanging out the load of towels. *It might be fun at that...Vic and I haven't been to anything like that since the last time we went to Fountain Ferry...*

ℰᴣᏩ

"I CAN'T BELIEVE all these cars," Vic mumbled as he obediently followed the orders of a red-vested parking attendant with flags pointing which direction to go to find overflow parking. "We'll be lucky to find a spot – and remember where it is to come back to eat."

Louise nodded, biting her lip as she tried to decide what would be best. In the back seat of their dark green Oldsmobile, Buddy and Jimmy were perched on the edge of the seat, barely containing their excitement. Next to them sat Tommy and his date, a cute blonde by the name of Jennifer. She was shy and about all you could get out of her was a giggle in answer to just about any question. Louise turned around and spoke to them all, "I think it'd be best if we go ahead and eat, then we won't have to worry about taking time out to find our way back…"

They all agreed, and soon Vic found a spot to park the car. It was far from any shade trees, but it couldn't be helped. They piled out and Vic opened the trunk to retrieve the basket. Lilly, who had stayed home to enjoy a rare night alone in the house, had packed a load of delicious food for them to take, including fried chicken, potato salad, pickles, a glass bottle of milk, and various other treats. It didn't take the family long to eat their fill, as the boys were champing at the bit to get going.

Finally, with a twinkle in his eye, Vic put away his plate and reached into his pocket, producing four quarters. He made a show of splitting them between Buddy and Jimmy. "Now here's you some spending money – but be careful how you spend it, cause once it's gone, it's gone. And don't let nobody steal it from ya, neither. There's pickpockets everywhere," he added with a nod to each one. Their eyes rounding, each nodded in return and carefully pocketed the coins.

"Okay, let's go fairin'," he addressed the group, and the family, including Tommy's date, took off together for the main entrance. Weaving their way through the sea of parked cars, Vic held Louise's hand as they neared other fairgoers and the crowd started to thicken. "Boys, stay with us," Vic instructed.

Minutes later, they stood at the feet of one of the most unusual sights they had ever seen. Buddy and Jimmy were awed as they all stared up at a giant doll, or overgrown mannequin, wearing an oversized blue denim shirt and pants, and sitting on a large bale of hay inside a picket fence. One arm was extended as if he were pointing straight ahead. The sign at the base said it was, "Freddy Farm Bureau," and that he was 18 feet tall, with a shoe size of 31, and fingers 11 inches long! The semblance of light brown hair was painted on his large head, and he had the biggest, bluest eyes you could ever imagine.

"Gosh…he's *big!*" Jimmy murmured, jumping a bit when a voice came from the direction of the huge figurine.

"Hi there, young man. My name's Freddy. What's yours?"

Jimmy giggled, "Hey, can you see me?" while the rest of the family laughed out loud.

"It must be a recording," Tommy chuckled, glancing at the girl at his side. She blushed and nodded.

"No, young man, I'm not a recording," it answered, then clarified when Tom's mouth dropped open and he looked back at the unmoving mouth. "Yes, you, young man in the blue shirt, with the wavy brown hair and blue eyes. That's quite a cute blonde you have with you. Is she your girlfriend?"

"Hey! How the heck…?" Tommy sputtered, glancing around to see if someone was playing a trick on them, but there was no evidence of how the phenomenon was occurring.

"And sir," the motionless human figure addressed Vic, "you and your lovely wife…may I inquire as to when the addition to your happy family will arrive?"

Louise blinked, mouth open, and turned to look up at Vic. This was getting a bit eerie. "Um…in December," she answered the overgrown doll's question.

"Ahh, December. A Christmas baby, perhaps. That's nice," the mannequin continued. The mouth on the large face wasn't moving, but the voice seemed to be coming from inside of the head; although none of them could figure out how in the world it was happening, and how he could see and hear them so clearly. "I'm the official greeter for the Kentucky State Fair. I know everything there is to know about it. Is there anything you want to ask me?" Freddy inquired.

Buddy looked around, and then back again at the doll. "Um...do you know which way to go for the rides on the midway?" feeling a bit silly to be asking a lifelike, albeit non-moving, gargantuan toy. But, could you call something that big a toy? *Maybe it's a toy for King Kong,* the boy inwardly joked.

"Certainly...what's your name, young man?"

"Uhh, Buddy..."

"Well, Buddy, that's a happy name. And I bet you're the apple of your Mama's eye." Buddy turned his head and smiled up at Louise, but she was looking at Freddy and missed the connection.

"I'm pleased to make your acquaintance," Freddy continued. "Now, to answer your question, you go to the left from here and the midway with the rides is over on that side of the exposition center. You can't miss it."

"Th...thank you," Buddy answered, glancing up at his father.

"Have a wonderful time at the Kentucky State Fair!" the doll encouraged. "Come back to see me before you leave. Ride the double Ferris Wheel one time for me...I'm too big, they won't let me on it."

Vic had had enough and nodding to the odd spectacle, he took his family in hand. 'Freddy' added, "Goodbye, sir," as they moved on toward the main doors of the building.

Louise shuddered and stole a peek back over her shoulder. "That gave me the heebie jeebies. If a body didn't know better, you'd think it's alive."

"Yeah," Vic scanned the area again, but still couldn't see any evidence of how the doll operated. Surely there was a man nearby speaking into a microphone, but for the life of him, he couldn't see where – and the chest of the doll didn't appear to be large enough for a man to fit inside comfortably. With a shrug, Vic decided to let it remain a mystery, just as they all heard Freddy begin a conversation with another family that had walked up to his base. "It's just something fun for the kids, though. Wherever the guy doin' the talking is, he's sure hidden good. Quite the novelty," he added with a dimpled grin.

Once inside the massive building, they took stock of where the different exhibits were and made plans on where they should go first. Tommy and Jennifer decided they wanted to explore on their own, and soon ambled off in search of excitement. Vic watched them go with a knowing smile, remembering his and Louise's date at Fontaine Ferry...and their time in the tunnel of love. Before the teens took off, Vic made sure they knew to meet the family back at Freddy by closing time.

"I think Buddy and Jimmy should stay with us," Louise insisted. "This is much larger than Fountain Ferry. Many more people...I don't want the boys to get lost from us..."

"Good idea. We'll just wander around and see the sights," Vic agreed, so the family moved forward into the crowd, shuffling along the many aisles of displays and vendors hawking their wares. It was big, loud, busy, and full of all kinds of amazing sights and unusual smells. Every booth had a seller who called out for your patronage which, of course, had *the best* whatever it was at the fair, and "well worth your money." Everything you could want seemed to be offered, from corn dogs to fresh fudge, cotton candy to hamburgers, pork rinds to barbeque, and finally to something called *funnel cakes*, which were fried dough sprinkled with powdered sugar – ugly, but delicious.

Before long, wandering down one of the large aisles and munching on various treats, they came upon a fenced-off area with a large sign that read, "Come to Safety Town," and depicted a kneeling police officer with one hand held up as if he were swearing an oath to something, facing two small children in pedal cars who were smiling and holding up their hands as well. There was a long line of kids waiting to climb aboard one of a large number of pedal cars and tricycles. An officer in uniform was speaking, informing the kids that if they followed all of the safety rules and navigated the course correctly, they would be given their own, genuine driver's licenses.

"What's this?" Vic murmured, as Jimmy hollered, "Oh neat! Look Daddy – I want a driver's license. Can I do this?" he asked, even as he was heading that way, powdered sugar from the large bites he had taken of a funnel cake still dusting his cheeks.

Vic took one look at the kids in the line, and a sign at the entrance that declared the cut off age was four, and realized with regret that his son was already past the age limit.

He reached out and laid a hand on Jimmy's shoulder. "I'm sorry, sport. You're too old for this. It's for little kids. We'll go find something else, okay?"

"But, I want to get my license," Jimmy insisted.

"It's *pedal cars*," Buddy pointed out. "You pitched a fit when you got one for Christmas."

"I don't care, I want a *license!*" he insisted, even louder. One of the officers looked over at the family and sent Vic a look of understanding with a small wave. He had obviously seen this reaction before.

Vic and Louise managed to coax their disappointed son on down the aisle away from the area, heading for other things that were more age appropriate, but they knew their son was *not* happy.

They managed, however, to find exhibits to keep him occupied, along with promises of riding the many rides out on the midway.

The pedal cars and licenses were soon forgotten…

ℰℭ

"WELL, SON-OF-A-GUN, HOW'S it goin', Vic ol' buddy?" a voice called thirty minutes later. Vic looked up to see the smiling grin of his old friend from the Flood days, Gerald Comstock, coming toward them with his wife and the youngest four of their eight kids. Tall and lanky, Gerald hardly looked a day older than he did back when Vic had met him, with just a bit of graying at the temples of his slightly thinner hair. His wife, Delores, was considerably heavier, but with eight kids…and what looked to be one in the oven…one couldn't fault her.

"Doin' fine, Ger. How's things with you?"

"Oh fine, fine," Gerald answered.

"Delores," Vic acknowledged the blonde at his friend's side. She smiled in greeting before she moved nearer Louise to strike up a conversation.

"Dee's in the family way, again. Gotta find out what's causin' that," Gerald joked with his trademark snicker. "I see you haven't figured that out yourself, yet, huh?" he added with a bawdy wink and a nod toward Louise, her condition obvious in her light-weight summer maternity dress. Vic chuckled and shook his head at his friend's antics.

"How's the station goin'?" Gerald asked as he reached out to corral several of his kids.

"Doin' well. Got me some good help. Things are workin' out," Vic answered, assuming a comfortable stance with his feet spread, and arms crossed on his chest.

"That's good," Gerald glanced over and snickered to see Louise and Delores comparing belly sizes and deep in a "woman-ly" conversation. Then the kids began to fidget as their parents spent several minutes chatting. The two men began to talk about the price of gas, which was the better candidate for the '56 presidential election between Eisenhower and Stevenson, and the latest movies they had seen at the theater. Minutes went by as the kids became more and more restless, waiting for their parents.

Suddenly, Louise's voice sent shivers down Vic's spine. "Jimmy!" she shrieked.

Vic whirled around, his eyes immediately focusing on the spot he had last seen their youngest – only to find it empty. His heart immediately jack hammered into high gear as he looked in all four directions, but among such a large crowd, all jostling and squeezing by, Jimmy was nowhere to be seen.

He spun back to his other son. "Buddy, where's your brother?"

The boy's big brown eyes wide with concern, he squawked, "I don't know, he was right over there a minute ago!"

Then Delores let out a screech. "Harold!"

Vic's stomach dropped. One of theirs was missing, as well. He turned toward Louise, whose eyes were wide and filling with tears, and he immediately strode over to put his arms around her as she squealed, "My baby, where *is* he? Oh Vic, *find* him!"

Vic swallowed back his panic and tried to think logically. *Where could he be? Are the two boys together? Which direction to start looking?*

Turning to Gerald and automatically assuming his *Chief* persona, he ordered, "You go north and east and I'll take south and west."

"Right, Chief," Gerald immediately answered.

Then glancing at the now crying women, Vic added, "You two stay here with the other kids so we'll know where to find you after we find *them*." Then reaching to cup Louise's cheek for a second, he added, "Don't worry. We'll find them." He hoped he was projecting more confidence than he felt at that moment.

"Daddy, can I come with you?" Buddy asked, taking a step toward his father.

Vic turned and met his namesake's eyes with a quick smile. "No son, I need you to stay here and protect your mother. Don't let me down."

At once, the boy's expression reflected pride that his father trusted him for such an important job. He nodded and moved close to Louise, wrapping an arm around her waist.

Then the two men took off at a trot, dodging people and strollers, eyes peeled for any sight of their sons.

Louise and Delores stood in the center of an intersection of aisles, holding on to one another and the other kids. Tears streaming, they both mumbled prayers for God to help their husbands find their boys.

Twenty agonizing minutes went by for the ladies before Delores turned her head and squealed, "They found them! Oh thank God!"

Louise swung around to see their husbands making their way back to them through the crowd of jostling people; the boys perched upon their shoulders. Each boy had drying tears on their faces, and the women figured they'd had their britches tanned once their fathers' found them.

As Vic reached the quite shaken mothers and the remaining kids, he lifted Jimmy off his shoulders, setting him firmly in front of his distraught mother. Vic met her eyes, explaining, "Found him back at the license place. Shoulda looked there first. Me and Gerald met up there and saw 'em. They were sitting on the hood of a police car, talkin' to one of the officers just as bold as you please, like they hadn't a care in the world."

Louise bent over and gave her youngest a fierce hug, then leaned back and grasped his arms. "James Alan Matthews, don't you *ever* do anything like that again. I was worried sick!"

Tears filled his hazel eyes and his bottom lip trembled. "I won't, Mama." Then, he glanced up at his stern-faced father and added, "I just wanted to get a license so I could help you drive and I could help work at the station…but Daddy said they ain't for the big cars."

The parents met one another's eyes, both of them feeling a mixture of pride and anguish over the incident. Their little boy was growing up, and soon wouldn't be a baby – or even *the* baby – anymore.

With another hug and a stern instruction to the boys to stay with them and not wander off, Vic and Louise parted from their friends and continued on with their evening at the Fair.

Several hours later, having ridden nearly every ride on the midway, two worn out parents and two tired little boys, the youngest nearly asleep on his father's shoulder, made their way back to the giant talking Freddy doll to meet up with Tommy and his date.

Louise, her feet swollen and aching, was nevertheless very glad they had come as she switched her stuffed animal prize to the other arm. Her prince charming had used up all of his change shooting at wooden ducks – and winning – until the proprietor grabbed his largest stuffed bear and thrust it in Vic's hands, begging him to move on so someone else could try.

With a laugh, Vic had handed the prize to his 'date' and they had wandered on together, nibbling on roasted peanuts. It was the first time he had won something for her since the knight statue that summer so long ago.

The evening netted several items for her cherished memories' box, and a warm, lovely memory to add to Louise's collection.

හ ශ

CHAPTER 16

The Beginnings of Obsession

S CHOOL STARTED AGAIN and life settled back into the familiar.
As she lowered her seven-months-pregnant self down to
her knees to scrub the floor around the commode one morning in
the second week of October, Louise allowed her mind to wander.
To her way of thinking, each day her boys were growing a little
more independent and farther away from her control. Little
Jimmy had made friends in school that she didn't know, neither
did she know their parents – and he had started keeping secrets
from her, something he had never done before. Buddy, as well,
had developed interests that he no longer shared with her. She
couldn't remember the last time either of them had run to her to
show off their newest discovery, or to ask her opinion or
permission for anything.

Straightening her back for a moment, she brushed her left
arm across her brow, her face red from the awkward exertion.
Thinking of the boys, she smiled as she pictured each one.

At seventeen, her oldest son Tommy was nearly an adult. He
had surpassed Vic in height, was strong, athletic and popular in
school, and had turned out to be quite handsome, as Louise had
always known he would. He was definitely not her sweet little
Tommykins that she could carry around on one hip anymore. He
was always busy going and doing – and he seemed to be squiring
a different girl around every few weeks.

At Vic's offhand comment on that subject the week before, Tommy had grinned that mischievous smile of his, and with a teasing chuckle, drawled, "Chief, ain't you never heard the saying about wanting to try every doughnut in the bakery window? Besides," he paused, with a wink of his twinkling blue eyes, "Can I help it if I'm irresistible?" With that, he had shrugged into his jacket and ran a hand back through his hair as he launched into an impromptu rendition of Ricky Nelson's new song, *I'm Walkin'*. Sounding amazingly like the young TV star, Tommy bee-bopped out the door as he sang, whirling the keys to the car around one finger. Louise snickered softly and shook her head at the memory.

Leaning back into her work, she next pictured Buddy, Vic's namesake. The boy had seemingly grown up overnight, and he had proven to be a studious young man, exhibiting a talent for music, and creating things with his hands. He was insatiably curious, always asking questions and forever wishing to know how things worked, or why *this* was *this* way, or *that* was *that* way.

Jimmy, on the other hand, was a rough and tough little boy – despite the fact that he was small for his age – and it had become plain for everyone but Louise to see that he resented the apron strings holding him back. If Louise wanted to dress him up in a cute little outfit and snap a picture of him with her Brownie camera, he found a way to go stomping through a mud puddle, or climb a tree and tear his pants. Or his latest desire – to go to the station with his father and help out in any way he could. He was a "Daddy's Boy" through and through.

Vic tried to tell his wife it was all part of nature's way, that their sons were growing up and she needed to relax her grip; after all, they were just being boys. Nothing he said, however, seemed to get through. Her memories of Jimmy as a tiny baby, in so much pain that he would scream, always seemed to be hovering at the back of her mind. She just couldn't let go of the need to protect, coddle, and mother him.

Each day it became more apparent that she could barely keep

up with the changes in either of her younger boys' personalities.

The situation, coupled with the on-going reality of her husband still working so many hours – in spite of the fact that he had more help – made her feel as if her life was missing some key element. There was a void deep inside that she couldn't seem to fill. This thought made Louise's expression harden and she leaned forward more, scrubbing harder at her task.

She often felt a nudge in her spirit, subtly reminding her that they had drifted from weekly attendance at church since their move to the east end of town. At that moment, she felt the prompting again, but she pushed the thoughts away. *I know, I know. We should start going again…but it's such a long drive now and the weather will be turning colder. Besides, I don't like to make the drive without Vic, and he's usually at the station.*

Even as that thought spun through her mind, she knew she was just making excuses. Vic had purposely made time on Sunday mornings to take the family to church. However, except for a handful of Sundays since August, Louise had found a reason not to go. She knew their friend, Irene, would be disappointed that she hadn't been praying like she used to…hadn't been thinking about the Lord or looking to Him for help with the constant feelings of lack and dissatisfaction, but stubbornly, she refused to acknowledge the fact – even in her own heart.

Instead, she convinced herself that if she could just have a girl, it would make everything complete. This new baby would be the key to her happiness. Everything would be balanced, and she wouldn't feel the emptiness that had become entrenched in her soul. Surely a little girl would bond with her in ways that the boys never had, and a daughter would never feel the need to grow up and be on her own.

It was the one thing about which she and Vic could not seem to be on the same page. She knew that he felt complete – with her and the boys – living out his dream. She also suspected that deep down it hurt him that his wife didn't think it was enough. That *he* was enough…

Still, she insistently pressed on in the same mode. Each morning, once Vic and the kids were out the door, Louise would walk back into the bedroom to tidy up and make the bed. Then, she would stand at the mirror caressing her burgeoning belly, murmuring to it, "Oh you in there…please be a girl. If you're not a girl, I just don't know what I'm going to do! You've *got* to be a girl!"

That morning, on her way down the hall, Lilly paused at the door and caught her doing just that, causing her to shake head in disapproval. "Louise, you've got to let go of this obsession. That baby could very well be another boy and you *know* it. It would be much better if you would just resign yourself to that fact. What are you going to do if it's not a girl – send it back?" she added derisively.

Louise whirled in anger. "Well, I don't *want* to resign myself! I've just *got* to have a girl this time! And I'm going to name her Anita Louise!"

Lilly's brows furrowed for a moment. "Have you discussed this with Vic?"

Louise turned back to the bed, fussing with covers that were already straight. "Yes…but he says we'll pick the name to match the child, the way we did with Jimmy."

The wise older woman pursed her lips and nodded, her eyes narrowing as she studied the different expressions chasing one another across her daughter's face. "Why *that* name?

Louise smoothed her hair and attempted to calm herself. "Well…I've always liked the actress Anita Louise, she's so beautiful…and I've always liked the name Anita. And…and I like *my* name too…" She glanced at her mother's expression and snapped, "*Well* – T.J. and Vic both have boys named after *them!* Why can't I have a girl partly named after *me?*"

Lilly merely shook her head with a sigh and continued on down the hall, muttering, "As I said, nothing guarantees this won't be another boy…"

"Oh, shut up," Louise mumbled, feeling decidedly petulant. Inwardly, she hated to admit, even to herself, that her mother was right – as usual. *Nobody understands…this baby just has to be a girl!* With a nod of determination, she headed out the door and to the kitchen to wash the breakfast dishes.

That afternoon when the boys got home from school, Louise could tell by the looks on their faces that they were hiding something.

Wiping flour from her hands, she turned toward them as they stood in the center of the kitchen, both heads of dark hair angled toward the floor.

"Boys? What is it?" she asked, placing her hands on her hips and bestowing upon them *the look*.

They glanced at one another, as if to say, "You go first." Jimmy pressed his lips together in a stubborn pout and shook his head once, sharply.

Finally, with a sigh, Buddy reached into his jacket pocket and withdrew a folded sheet of paper. He hesitantly handed it to his mom.

"What's this?" she asked as she took the paper and unfolded it. It was a note from Buddy's teacher, requesting a teacher/parent conference.

She looked up from the paper and opened her mouth to reprimand him, but he squawked in defense, "Jimmy got one, too!"

Louise closed her mouth and turned her gaze on her youngest, raising one eyebrow at him in question. He looked down and sighed, then slowly unzipped his jacket and took out an identical folded sheet of paper. With a grimace, he handed it over.

ℰᏻℭℛ

LOUISE SHOOK HER head in disbelief. Having just come from a

frustrating visit with Jimmy's teacher, in which the woman all but came out and said that her son wasn't getting enough attention at home, now Buddy's teacher seemed to be implying the same thing.

"He gets plenty of attention," Louise insisted, pinning the teacher with a glare as the woman uncomfortably shuffled papers and grading records.

"Mrs. Matthews..." the woman began. "As you know, I was Buddy's teacher last year for third grade and now I switched to teaching fourth. All through third grade, Buddy was attentive, polite, quiet, and always had his work finished on time. Now, I'm afraid the situation is quite the opposite – he seems distracted in class, moody, even brooding. He's been arguing with the other children, and on more than one occasion, he failed to turn in even a partially finished homework sheet. He, um…he says that he isn't getting any help at home…"

Louise sputtered and her heart began to pound. She cast about for something to say as guilt rose up within. Too many times lately, she *had* turned Buddy away when he had asked for help on his arithmetic or spelling. She had never been the best speller, since she, herself, hadn't finished high school, but she was pretty good at math. Vic had always helped quiz the boys on their spelling words, but now he was usually too tired when he came home from the station. Tommy used to sometimes help, as well, so she explained in halting terms that Buddy's older brother had become quite busy this school season since he had made the football team at Fern Creek, and no longer had the time to help his younger brothers after school as he once did. She said all of that while carefully avoiding the real issue – that she herself had all but stopped helping with homework.

The teacher, Mrs. Barnes, gave her a knowing look. "Buddy indicated that…you had become quite…preoccupied with um…" she paused, indicating with a flick of one hand Louise's obviously pregnant state.

Louise again blustered, "Well, I admit I am looking forward to having this baby…I'm hoping for a girl this time…but that doesn't mean that I've been neglecting Buddy and Jimmy. I resent you implying that I have," she insisted, although privately she wondered just what Buddy had said to his teacher. Did he really think that?

Mrs. Barnes met Louise's eyes and pursed her lips thoughtfully, obviously trying to decide what to say and what not to say. Finally, she opted for, "I see. Well, Buddy is a very bright boy and a good student. He has a keen mind and a flare for learning. I'm sure everything will smooth out once the baby comes and things get back to normal," she added on a positive note, but her expression seemed to indicate that she truly felt the opposite.

Feeling as if she had been thoroughly chastened, Louise stood and gathered her purse and jacket before extending her arm to shake hands with the teacher. "Thank you, Mrs. Barnes. My husband and I will have a talk with him."

Then, before the teacher could say anything else, Louise turned and fled the room.

ℰℭ

THAT EVENING, SHE and Vic sat down with the boys and tried to have a parent-to-child talk. However, both boys, for the most part, sat nearly mute – only mumbling one word answers to direct questions. They kept glancing at one another as they sat side by side on the couch in the living room. The more Vic questioned the reason for their actions, the more they clammed up, only peering furtively at their mother. Neither boy seemed to want to be the one to volunteer anything specific.

In frustration, Vic sent both boys to their rooms with instructions to finish their homework and to *darn well do a perfect job of it.* Once they left the living room, Vic stood and leaned down, brushing a kiss upon Louise's lips as he informed her that he needed to run back to the station and finish up an emergency repair on a regular customer's car.

"But Vic! What...what about us spending time together...watching television or something..." Louise whined.

"I'm sorry, babe," Vic apologized. "I'll try not to be long. Wait up for me, okay?" he added with what he hoped was sufficient charm as he leaned down once more and gave her a substantial kiss.

She didn't like that he was leaving, but she said no more, merely watched him remove from his pocket the keys to the truck and aim one more smile her way before he closed the door.

Sulking, Louise levered herself up off the over-stuffed chair and flipped on the television set. *Another evening spent alone.*

After spending only a few minutes watching the end of the news show, *The Huntley-Brinkley Report,* the next show to come on was *The Price is Right.* Normally she enjoyed it, but that night, sitting alone, it just didn't hold her interest. The house seemed empty, with Vic back at the station, Tommy out with friends, and Lilly visiting her sister, Leona, and her husband, Frank, who had recently moved back to Louisville from California. Louise had turned down the invitation to go with them, as she wasn't in the mood for celebrations.

With a sigh, Louise leaned over to grasp the small pile of baby furniture catalogs laying on the coffee table. In no time, she was immersed in plans and dreams for her oft longed-for little girl's bedroom – full of pink frills and lace. If truth be told, they were dreams that she'd had for a bedroom of her own while growing up. Back then, the thought of having her own room to do with whatever she wanted had been like wishing for the moon. Now, in doing that very thing for her own little girl, it would provide her with a bit of vicarious joy.

Minutes later, deep in concentration over different baby beds and their prices, and wondering how she could talk Vic into such an investment, Louise felt a hand gently tap her shoulder. She glanced up only long enough to see it was her son, Buddy.

"Mom? I'm stuck on a problem in my arithmetic home-work…" he hesitantly explained.

Completely forgetting the conference she'd had with his teacher earlier, Louise waved a hand in a vague motion, shooing him toward the hallway and the room he shared with his older brother. "Just keep trying on it, honey, you'll figure it out."

As she reached for a scrap piece of paper to add up the purchase price of several items for the dream room, she didn't see his downcast expression, nor did she notice when he turned in a defeated manner and retraced his steps to his room.

ॐ

TWO WEEKS LATER, the boys brought home their report cards, but were loathe to show them, as they both had ended up with a glaring D in one subject. Buddy still wasn't doing well in mathematics, and Jimmy was still having trouble with his spelling. After supper, Vic sat them both down with the intention of giving them a strong lecture.

"I just don't know what to think about this, you two. Seems like we've had a talk about your schoolwork before. I've a good mind to tell you both that you can't go trick-or-treating on Halloween. You know that?"

Suddenly breaking his silence, Buddy blurted, "But Mom promised she'd help, but she's not! It don't even seem like she loves us anymore – she's always thinking about baby stuff!" he added, obviously fighting to hold back tears. It was easy to see in his expressive eyes that he wanted to please his parents and make them proud, but was quite frustrated by the unavoidable circumstances.

Louise's heart began to thump as the guilt surged. She looked up from the small pink dress she had been stitching, first to Buddy's hurt look, then her husband's accusing stare, and then to

Jimmy's solemn hazel gaze. She moistened suddenly dry lips and opened her mouth to deny the accusation, but stopped, drawing the unfinished dress up to her chest. Embarrassed, she looked down at the item, and then back up at Buddy.

"Oh honey...you're right...I've been so pre-occupied with trying to get everything ready for the new baby, that I..." she paused, floundering. "I'm sorry..."

Vic continued to stare at his wife, at a loss about how to deal with the situation. He had truly thought things had gotten better – or at least, he had told himself they had. However, a memory of overhearing a conversation earlier in the week between all three of their boys, surfaced. The door to Tommy and Buddy's room had been ajar as Vic had made his way down the hall and he had overheard Tommy say, "Yeah, I know what you're saying, Bro. She's a lot different than she used to be." Then he had emitted a soft snort and added, "Last week, I thought she'd blow a gasket when she saw the newspaper article where I got arrested for drag racing, but she didn't say a word about it..."

Vic had continued on down the hall, telling himself that he needed to have a talk with their oldest about obeying traffic laws, but the comment, for some reason, had quickly left his mind.

Now, as he watched his wife hemming and hawing, Vic knew he had not realized the extent of the family's problem. Clearing his throat, he murmured, "Boys, go on down to your room. Your Mama and me are gonna talk about this. We'll call you in a few minutes."

Neither boy hesitated, but shot up off the couch as one and made tracks to vacate the room.

Once they were gone, Louise met her husband's eyes, obviously guilt-ridden. "Vic...we shouldn't punish them and not let them go trick-or-treating. It's my fault more than theirs."

Vic huffed out a breath, leaning forward, elbows on his knees and rubbing the back of his neck with one hand as he shook his head. "Babe...what's goin' on? I ain't ever seen you like this before. Why are you so hung up about this baby? You weren't like this with the others…"

She pressed her lips together and met his gaze, striving to put her feelings into words.

"I just…I want a little girl so bad…it's all I think about. I'm so tired of being in a house with nothing but messy boys!" she burst out, but then clamped her teeth on her bottom lip as she waited for his reaction to such a statement.

Vic stared at her, a myriad of emotions and thoughts rolling through his consciousness. He felt shocked and hurt that his normally sweet, loving wife now seemed so different – almost as if she didn't love him and the boys anymore. For a moment, he wondered if she was even losing her hold on reality. Images and memories ticked by of instances in the past year – things that he had swept under the rug, but now he reached under and pulled them back out to examine – his wife snapping at him and the boys, which was something she never used to do in the early days of their marriage. He sensed a feeling of deep dissatisfaction lurking within his normally even-tempered wife, but he couldn't put his finger on the root cause – and he certainly didn't want to believe that she was dissatisfied with *him*. Of all the marriages he'd witnessed, he would have wagered that theirs was one of, if not *the* strongest, most loving. Recollections of his brother Jack's wife Liz came to mind, but he steadfastly pushed them away. *No, my Louise would never turn into such a shrew.*

He'd looked away from her as the thoughts sailed through, but now he looked back and met her eyes – those lovely hazel eyes that always made him melt like a chocolate bar on a hot day. *No, she's still my sweet Mary Lou. We'll get through this, just like everything else that has happened since we got together. Flood, arguments, separation, ex-husbands, job problems, crazy landlords, live-in mother in laws…even deaths, haven't put a damper on our feelings for each other.*

Unbidden, several occurrences of the boys leaving messes or Tommy stuffing smelly gym clothes under his bed instead of putting them in the hamper came to mind, just then, and he began to chuckle. "Yeah, I guess us guys do make a lot of extra work for you ladies. Them tracking in dirt and leaves...me dragging in oil and grease from the station. I guess that's just the nature of the beast," he teased with a wink.

Louise laughed softly, relieved that he wasn't angry. She reached out and clasped his hand.

"I promise I'll try to pay more attention to them, like I should. I...I guess I just expected everyone to be as excited about the new baby as I am."

Vic smiled and tugged on her hand, drawing her over to the couch with him. Cuddling her against his firm chest, he kissed her soundly – and then kissed her again. Settling together in a warm snuggle, he murmured, "I guess the rest of us don't know how you're feelin'...the baby's part of you, so it's more real to ya, and on your mind all the time..."

"*She's* more real," Louise interrupted, teasingly insistent, her eyes twinkling under raised eyebrows.

He chuckled and shook his head. "Okay. *She*. I hope you're right about that. What' you gonna do with another boy runnin' around messin' things up if it's not a girl?" he asked, squeezing her a little as he tightened his embrace.

Louise just smiled and shook her head in denial as she lovingly rubbed a hand over her extended lap. "I know she's in there. I can't explain it. I just do."

"Well okay, then. A girl, it is," Vic returned obligingly. "In the meantime, those rascal boys of ours are waiting to hear the verdict."

Her smile widened as she looked up at him and leaned in for one more kiss. Then bending around his head, she called out, "Boys! Come here, please."

In seconds, Buddy and Jimmy came running, stopping at attention like little soldiers in front of the united parents. Each boy searched their parents' faces, feeling as if something had changed. They exchanged quick looks.

Louise sat up and took a hand from each boy. "Boys, I ask your forgiveness for being so absorbed in…other things…lately. I promise, from now on I'll try to do better. Forgive me?" she asked softly, tilting her head a bit to one side as she met each pair of eyes.

At once, they broke out with grins and launched themselves into her arms. She laughed and caught them, all three crashing against Vic's side as a chuckle left his lips. It was the most joyous moment the family had experienced in quite a while.

After a few kisses and squeezes, Louise murmured, "Now, what do you say we figure out what you two are going to dress up as for Halloween?"

She shook her head fondly as they began talking over each other, one idea after another tumbling willy-nilly as they extracted themselves from her grasp and plopped down onto the coffee table.

FRIDAY EVENING, JUST as the sun was going down, Louise finished gathering the elements of Halloween costumes for two excited boys. It was to be the first year Buddy and Jimmy would be allowed to go out trick-or-treating on their own, without their older brother or parents as escorts. Secretly, they planned not to return until their sacks were so full they could barely carry them.

Jimmy was decked out as the Lone Ranger, courtesy of his older brother, Tommy, who had dug into the back of his closet for an old costume he'd had from his days as the TV character's biggest fan. The doorbell rang as Tommy fixed the white cowboy hat on Jimmy's head over the black facemask and handed him an old pillowcase that they saved for candy gathering every year.

"We need to go! We're missing out!" Buddy exclaimed as Louise tried to finish fixing his costume.

"Well, hold still, young man. I've about got this…"

Vic glanced over from finishing up his annual task of carving the jack-o-lantern and grinned at his son's outfit.

The family had pulled together to accomplish the youngster's idea of dressing as a space-age robot, using two cardboard boxes covered with aluminum foil. A smaller box on his head with holes for eyes was topped with a beat up Chevy hubcap, and two bells out of an old telephone served as the ears. Kitchen cabinet knobs applied to the headpiece cleverly resembled bolts holding the 'body' together. Vic had scrounged around at the station and found some broken voltage regulators and various other automobile-related items to use as dials and controls for the front. Louise had affixed the foil-covered cardboard arms onto the body with a few spots of thread. In addition, a pair of Vic's old boots adorned the boy's feet, so big he had to clomp along in them, but he wasn't going to let that stop him.

"Got it," Louise mumbled as she finished securing the hubcap.

Finished with the carving, Vic washed his hands and turned back to survey the end product, which he approved with a nod and a pat on the cardboard back. "Okay, son, here's your sack. And Buddy, take this flashlight," he added as he pressed the metal item into his son's grasp. "You be careful and make sure your little brother is okay. Don't run off and leave him."

"I won't, Daddy," Buddy assured him, taking the job of older brother seriously as he gripped the light in one hand and the sack in the other. "Come on, Jimmy! Let's get going before all of the good stuff's gone!"

Lilly stepped aside from the task of giving out candy to the first arrivals and let the two boys pass by, with Louise following and fixing even as they scurried. "Okay, now you two *be careful* — and be sure to say thank you every time!" she called as they made their exit.

"Okay, Mama," Jimmy called as the two hurried down the walk to join the other kids.

Vic placed the lit pumpkin next to the door and then stood

with his wife and wrapped an arm around her shoulders.

Tired from the hustle and bustle, Louise rubbed her lower back with one hand. She and Vic stood with their arms around one another, watching their boys make their way down the street with the neighborhood kids, flashlight bobbing up and down as Buddy shuffled along.

"Are you sure they'll be all right…without one of us watching over them?" she murmured as the group headed up Fleet and Alec's sidewalk next door.

"Yeah, they'll be fine," Vic assured. "They're growin' up. We gotta let 'em stretch their wings some time."

The parents both smiled proudly as they heard a familiar voice say, "Hey, look at that keen robot suit!" They watched as their friend's porch light illuminated Alec as he dropped large handfuls of candy into first Buddy's sack and then Jimmy's.

"Thank you!" the boys chirped in succession.

Fleet looked over and spotted her friends standing outside and began to wander over, holding a bundled Alexa in her arms. She had told Louise earlier in the day that Alexa had come down with a cold, so she wasn't going to take her out trick-or-treating – although the little girl was too young to know the difference yet, anyway.

"Hey guys. That's a great suit Buddy has. When you first told me about it, I couldn't imagine how you'd pull it off, but you sure did. It looked amazing," she complimented.

"Thanks," Vic grinned as he reached in the bowl for a hand-ful of candy to drop in a ballerina's open bag. "Louise did most of it, but we all kind of helped. It was Buddy's idea mostly, though. He thought of the design. That boy of mine's got real talent. I think he's gonna grow up to be an engineer or something," he added with his *Proud Daddy* smile.

"I can't believe you're letting them go by themselves this year, though," Fleet observed as she looked down the street past her house, watching the waddling robot and the bobbing light, with the outline of the Lone Ranger skipping along beside him in the darkness.

"Don't remind me. I'm holding myself back from following," Louise admitted, catching Lilly's glance and hearing her mutter, "Pshaw. They don't need a mother hen shadowing their every move. They're good boys."

"Alas, like my husband and my mother keep reminding me – my little boys aren't so little anymore...which is all the more reason to be excited about the newest member of the Matthews' family that will arrive in a few months..." Louise added, purposely keeping her gaze on the costumed little people she was dealing with at the moment, and not on the two people she could see in her peripheral vision who were meeting one another's gazes.

Fleet missed the exchange as she cuddled a softly fussing Alexa. "I miss the days when AJ used to go out. Can't believe that boy is fifteen already. Would you believe he's got a girlfriend and he's over at her house tonight? Time sure flies."

"It sure does," Louise murmured as she thought about the years when they'd only had cute, precocious Tommy, who would charm all of the neighbors on three different streets, until his candy bag eventually became so full he couldn't drag it home. *I can't believe he's going on eighteen...* she mused, picturing him as she had seen him a few minutes before, dressed in his full football uniform in preparation of attending a Halloween party with some of his friends in the Fern Creek High senior class. *Now, Vic doesn't even think twice of tossing him the keys to the car...*

As Louise dipped a hand into the big bowl of candy to dole out some to each of a group of five kids who were jockeying for position, she heard a voice to her left yell, "Hey woman! I'm covered up in goblins, princesses, clowns, and ghosts over here! Get back here and help!" It was Alec, yelling from amidst a large group of kids, each holding a wide-open bag or paper sack in expectation.

Fleet laughed and called back, "Hold your horses!" Then turning, she rolled her eyes at her friends and groused, "Duty calls. Later gators. And Vic – hold on to this mother hen, here, and don't let her chase after her chicks tonight," she added, receiving a rumbling chuckle in response.

"*Bye*, Fleet," Louise called over her shoulder as she finished up another group of adorable small visitors.

When the evening finally came to an end, the boys had stayed out later than they had promised and Vic, at the urging of his wife, had to resort to taking the truck out to go look for them. He found them one street over, both trying to drag bulging sacks of candy down the sidewalk. Buddy had removed his robot costume's head at some point and stuffed it under one arm.

With a chuckle, Vic pulled over and helped them climb onto the tailgate, depositing their sacks in the back.

It was an exhausted, but satisfied and proud pair of boys that trudged into the house. Both were brimming with tales of the houses they had visited and the excitement they'd had that night, and they couldn't wait to share them with their mother.

She took it all in stride, to Vic's immense relief.

എ൭

CHAPTER 17

Elvis, Thanksgiving, and The Close Call

"A ND THE GIRLS were just going crazy. I've never seen anything like it in all my born days," Tommy commented as the family sat eating dinner at the kitchen table. "I couldn't see very well, but I think there were a couple of girls in front of the stage that even fainted. Some men carried 'em out."

Shaking his head as he thought about the sheer chaos he, several friends, and their girlfriends had experienced the evening before at Elvis Presley's much publicized second Louisville appearance, he went on, "The Armory was jam-packed – I doubt they could have gotten one more person in there. We were crammed in like sardines." Then, he thought about Peggy, the girl he had been dating since they had met at a Halloween party. "And man, I thought Peggy was gonna lose her mind. She screamed herself hoarse. Dang, all the girls around us were screaming and crying – I couldn't even hear Elvis up there singing."

"My goodness, why would anyone pay money to see a singer, and then scream so loudly they couldn't even hear him sing?" Lilly asked, frowning. "That's simply ridiculous."

Tommy shrugged, agreeing. "Don't know. But they sure did." Then with a snort, he admitted with an embarrassed grin, "I got caught up in it a bit myself. It was like...like the air was charged with electricity or something – and our seats were right down there on the floor level, in the middle of it all." He took a bite of his meal as he gathered his thoughts, wishing he could articulate the phenomena in a better way, but the words to justify the sensations and emotions of experiencing Elvis in person stubbornly eluded him. Truly, there seemed to be no words to adequately describe it.

"But anyway… Elvis was wearing a bright green jacket, and when he came up on the stage, he raised one arm to greet the audience and the place erupted in this big *roar* – I thought sure it was gonna blast the walls right out of that old building. Flash bulbs were popping everywhere, like a dang lightning storm. I'm tellin' you, the hair on the back of my neck stood right up." He glanced around at his captivated listeners, his blue eyes glittering with exhilaration. "Then, he turned his head and the crowd screamed again. He walked over and blew into the microphone, like he was checking if it was on, and the people roared even louder. Then he started singing the first song, but we couldn't hear much because of the noise of the crowd. He was all over the stage, but he didn't get nasty or anything – I'd heard they told him to keep it clean," he smirked. "But several times he did this thing where he would grind his hips or come up on the balls of his feet, and everybody went berserk."

"Sounds shameful," Lilly declared, her sharp eyes peering at her grandson as if she wondered if she should give him a lecture on the evils of lewd behavior.

Tommy gave a slight shrug, knowing his grandmother was a bit of a straight-laced prude. He glanced over at his father, and Vic sent him an amused wink.

Louise frowned in disgust. "I can't imagine such goings on. I've been to many swing concerts in my day, and although we were excited to see the bands, we were respectful enough to let them be heard. You paid to see a concert and then couldn't even hear it. Sounds like you wasted your money, Tommy."

"Oh, I dunno," the young man remarked, a forkful of mashed potatoes poised before his mouth as he considered the experience. "I'm glad I went. I have a feeling Elvis Presley is gonna be *big*, you know? Like maybe the biggest singing star ever. Heck, they're already calling him the *King of Rock and Roll* – and I'll be able to say I saw him in *person*."

He shoved the fork into his mouth and allowed the food to slide down his throat before shaking his head as if he were still under the intoxicating influence of the previous night's events. "There's just something...well, almost *magnetic* about the guy. When he's up there on the stage, you just can't take your eyes off him." He paused a moment as he pictured all of the things he had seen at the concert, then went on with a shrug, "I don't know, he's just...there's something special about him. That's all there is to it."

"Well, all I gotta say is – there's no way he will be a bigger star than Satchmo, or Cab Calloway, or *Sinatra*," Vic declared with a smirk before taking a large bite of his meatloaf.

"We'll see," Tommy grinned across the table at him. "Oh, and you know what else? Peggy lives on Beaver Street, and guess who lives a few doors down – Elvis' grandfather, Jesse Presley! She said he's lived there for years and he's good friends with her grandpa. Well, Peggy called me a while ago and said Elvis himself came this morning and gave his grandfather a brand new '57 blue and white Ford Fairlane– along with a *color TV*. He had that stashed in the trunk. She said Elvis also handed his grandmother a hundred dollar bill. Ain't that something? Peggy said he stayed a few hours with them, and then the next time she looked out the window, Elvis was leaving in the back of a pink Cadillac with pillows all around him and two husky bodyguards in the front seat!"

"So *that's* who it was," Vic mumbled, pointing at his son with his fork as he recalled a conversation. "A pal of mine stopped by the station today and was telling me about being down at Riggs

Motors on Broadway when a man pulled in – big fella, wearin' a white cowboy hat, white jacket and black string tie, smokin' a big ol' cigar, and drivin' a pink Cadillac. He got out and went inside and precedes to hand Mr. Riggs a check for a brand new '57 Ford. Said he didn't even dicker about the price. My friend said after the man left, Toby Riggs kept crowin' it was the easiest sale he'd ever made."

"That wasn't Elvis, that was his manager, I bet!" Tommy exclaimed. "What's his name? Colonel something…Parker? Yeah! Colonel Tom Parker."

"Yeah, that's it."

"You know, that Elvis…" Tommy mused thoughtfully, "Not only can he *sing*, but he's a darn good actor, too. When I took Peggy to see his movie, *Love Me Tender*, a couple of weeks ago, I was expecting it to be corny or something, but it wasn't. He did a real good job in it. The character he played even *died* in it, and he really did that scene well. The thing is…he's only twenty-one, and he's already made it in show business. It just…" he paused, glancing around at his family, who were all listening and looking at him. He cleared his throat and a small shrug lifted his shoulders. "It just kinda makes me wonder if…maybe I could try to…I don't know…be a singer or something." He looked around again and snickered self-consciously. "Anyway…"

"I don't see why not – we know you can sing, and you're handsome and talented," his proud mother declared.

"Wow, that would be swell, Tommy!" "Yeah!" Buddy and Jimmy exclaimed simultaneously, with true big brother hero-worship.

The family talked about the idea of Tommy trying to break into show business until the conversation tapped out and they lapsed into silence and went back to eating their dinner.

A few minutes later, a memory surfaced and Vic tipped his head back, motioning toward Louise with his chin. "By the way, I meant to tell ya, Al called and said that he and Goldie want to come spend Thanksgiving in Louisville."

"Uncle Al? That's great," Tommy responded as he spooned another helping of mashed potatoes onto his plate. "We haven't seen them in, what...years," he shrugged, unable to pinpoint the last time.

"No, we haven't," Louise nodded as she took a bite of her meatloaf. "We went to Evansville a couple of times and stayed with them for holidays, when you were little. But since Buddy and Jimmy came along, we quit doing that." That fact saddened her, as Vic's brother Al and his wife Goldie were the nicer of Vic's family members, but she was glad that they could at least talk on the phone every few months.

"They're gonna stay at Jack and Liz's house," Vic commented off-handedly as he forked a big bite of meatloaf. He shoveled it in his mouth and proceeded to chew as Louise turned surprised eyes on him. He chuckled softly, knowing what she was thinking. Swallowing and reaching for his glass of iced tea, he went on, "Since Tim and Shirley are both married and gone, Jack and Liz have a three-bedroom house all to themselves." He paused for a moment, thinking about his niece and nephew; twenty-eight year old Tim, married with two children, and twenty-six year old Shirley, who had married at eighteen and moved to Florida with her ex-soldier husband. They now had three children, and spent most holidays at home.

Louise perked up, her eyes zeroing in on Vic. In rapid fire, she gushed, "Let's have them here for Thanksgiving! They haven't seen our house, or the station...do you think Jack and Liz would come, too? Or are they going to spend it with Tim and his family..." she paused as Vic held up a hand.

"I called Jack. He and Liz are drivin' to Florida, and he said Tim's wife always insists they go to *her* people."

Hesitating for only a moment, Louise continued, "Oh, well...still, Al and Goldie can come... Jack and Liz's house isn't too far from here, so that will work out. Mama and I can cook everything…" she paused and turned her head to meet her mother's eyes. Lilly nodded in answer.

Vic smiled and when his wife turned back to him, he sent her a loving wink and nod. "I think they'd like that just fine."

₭ℓℂℜ

OVER THE NEXT several days, Louise and Lilly worked on the house to get it ship shape for the coming event. Doing what amounted to a Spring Cleaning on the rooms, they rearranged the furniture, scrubbed the floors, dusted every square inch, cleaned and put away anything and everything, and even washed the windows. No amount of fussing from Vic, who was worried about his very pregnant wife over-exerting herself, accomplished the least bit of good. As the holiday neared, both women wore themselves to a frazzle.

The closer the day came, the more fretting Louise did. The family tried their best to remember that part of her crankiness came from being so far into her pregnancy, but it was difficult for little boys to play and exist in a house without creating a mess. Louise wanted everything to be perfect for the holiday, and was on pins and needles trying to ensure that nothing went wrong.

On Monday before the big day, however, details unfortunately started to unravel.

Little boys will be little boys, and that morning as Buddy and Jimmy were getting ready for school, a tussle started in the bathroom. Hearing the bickering from the kitchen, Louise and Lilly's eyes met as if to say, "Are *you* going, or should I?"

Since it was more difficult for Louise to disengage herself from the chair she was sitting in, Lilly opted to go. "Hey, gimme that!" she heard Jimmy squawk, followed seconds later by the distinct sound of the toilet flushing just as she made it to the door of the bathroom.

"What'd you shove me for? Now look at what you've done!"

Buddy hollered as Lilly stepped into the room just in time to see something indefinable disappear down into the porcelain never-never land.

"James Alan, Victor Herbert, what are you two doing in here?" Lilly demanded as two guilty faces stood staring down into the empty receptacle.

Immediately, they began talking over one another. "*He* started it!" "He swiped my…" "He kept on…" "I did *not*, you made me laugh!" "I didn't make you do nothin'…"

Lilly put up a hand to stop the tirades. "Enough." She reached down and flushed the commode again, checking to make sure the water would go down fine. "What was it?"

Both boys' eyes opened largely and they exchanged glances, simultaneously sputtering, "N…nothing…"

"Nothing?" Lilly asked suspiciously, folding her arms across her chest and giving them *The Eye.*

"It's time for the bus!" Louise called from the other room.

Before Lilly could break into a fuss, Buddy injected, "We gotta go or we'll miss our bus."

"But my…*umph,*" Jimmy began, stopping short as he was elbowed by his brother.

Lilly stepped between them and ushered them on out into the hall. "Whatever it was, we'll worry about it later. Go on, now."

Once the boys were out the door, Lilly returned to the kitchen to find her daughter standing near the sink, leaning forward and resting her back.

One hand on her belly and one on her lower back, she asked, "What was all that about?" as Lilly went to the table, shaking her head and gathering the last few dishes.

"Those boys, they got to squabbling and something of Jimmy's ended up going down the commode before I could get in there."

Louise's eyes widened. "Oh no…I hope it doesn't cause a back up…maybe we should call Vic…"

Lilly shook her head again as she brought the dishes over to the sink. "It seemed to be clear. I'm sure it will be fine."

But, that set the dominoes in motion...

⁝⁞

"HERE YOU GO, Mom," Tommy greeted his mother as he put down the last of the bags of groceries he had purchased at the store on Tuesday evening.

"Did you get everything on the list?" Louise asked as she moved to the kitchen table and began going through the sacks.

"Yep. Well, mostly."

"Mostly?" she turned to him, brows raised.

He began removing his jacket, shrugging his shoulders at her question as if it were no big deal. "They didn't have any cranberry sauce left, or cans of pumpkin, or oregano, but I got everything else."

"*What?* Oh no!" she cried, urgently searching through the bags as if she could make his off-handed declaration false. "It's not Thanksgiving without cranberry sauce! And the pumpkin pies! How can I make pumpkin pies without pumpkin!" She grabbed another bag and began frantically taking out every item.

Tommy watched her for a moment, thinking he should have figured she would blow a gasket at the news since she had been getting her dander up at the slightest thing lately. "I guess I can try another store...but I heard some other customers saying they were having trouble finding those items, too..."

This was just what Louise didn't need. "And the orega-no...I've *got* to have fresh oregano...ours is old and the dressing will taste like soap if I use it. Oh, *why* did they have to be out? I should have bought it last week..." she grumbled with her head in the last sack.

Lilly turned from checking that night's dinner at the stove and watched her daughter for a moment. "Louise, it's just one dinner.

Everything will be all right. Don't let yourself get upset…"

Just then, Vic walked in the door and placed his lunch box on the counter. "Get upset about what?" he asked the group, noticing his wife seemed frantic. He was immediately concerned.

Louise glanced at him, her eyes snapping with frustration. "It looks like we won't have cranberry sauce, pumpkin pie, OR dressing with the turkey on Thanksgiving – and both the toilet and the kitchen sink are stopped up, to name a few things," she added sarcastically.

He walked over and stopped her actions, turning her into his embrace. He held her for a moment, gently rocking back and forth as he met Tommy and Lilly's eyes. "Try to calm down, Babe. Al and Goldie won't care if there's no cranberry sauce or pum'kin pie…"

"But *I'll care*," Louise whined against the front of his jacket as she relented a bit and allowed her arms to encircle his waist. "I wanted everything to be perfect…"

He reached up and touched her chin with a gentle finger, tipping her head back so he could look into her eyes. "The most important thing is for you not to overdo…"

"Hah," Lilly mumbled as she began putting the groceries away. "I've told her and told her that. Maybe she'll listen to *you*."

Vic gave Louise one of his heart-melting smiles and leaned down to brush her lips with a sweet kiss. "We'll figure something out. Okay Babe?" He waited until she nodded in acquiescence, and then gave her a gentle squeeze and stepped back. "Now, what's this about something stopped up?"

Having forgotten the bathroom incident with the boys, Lilly began explaining how the toilet and the sink had begun to work sluggishly, growing progressively worse as the day wore on.

"I'll try to plunge it," Vic murmured as he shucked out of his jacket and hung it on the coat tree by the door before heading down the hall, hoping he could fix it so they wouldn't have to call a plumber.

The next morning, the phone rang as Vic was working, for the fourth time, on the kitchen sink. Nothing he tried seemed to do any good, and he was beginning to think the obstruction was further down the pipe, maybe even in the ground. However, he dreaded trying to get a plumber out to the house on Thanksgiving Eve, as he knew they would charge an arm and a leg.

"You've just *got* to get this fixed," Louise fussed as she moved aside dirty dishes to try and get some breakfast on the table. "Oh, that phone!" she griped as she wiped her hands and crossed to the incessantly ringing object on the wall. "Hello!" she answered, with more force than she intended.

"L...Louise?" Goldie's voice stammered on the other end of the line.

Louise took a deep breath and raised the palm of one hand to her forehead as she tried to calm herself. "Oh, yes, hello, Goldie. So you made it," she managed, meeting Vic's glance over his shoulder.

"Yes, we had a good trip. Got in last night and had a good sleep. How are things going? I bet you're just about ready to have that baby by now, aren't you?"

"Um, yes...about two weeks. My due date is December 11."

Goldie hesitated, and then asked, "Is everything all right? Did I call at a bad time?"

"Oh no," Louise quickly assured her. "Just trying to get everything ready for tomorrow and I guess I'm a little out of breath," she hedged, turning her head from Vic's incredulous look.

"Well, all right, then..." Goldie returned, obviously feeling that there was something going on that Louise wasn't telling her. "What can we bring tomorrow, and what time should we come?"

The two talked for a couple of minutes about specifics, and then Goldie rang off with a cheerful, "See you tomorrow, and tell that handsome brother-in-law of mine that I can't wait for my hug."

Louise smiled at that and returned the sentiment as the two

hung up.

Just then, Vic stood up straight and reached for a rag to wipe his hands. Turning to face her, he leaned back against the edge of the cabinet. "I can't get the dang thing unstopped; the clog's too far in. I think it's time to call the plumber."

ℰℭℛℬ

VIC WAS RIGHT, the plumber did charge time and a half because it was coming up on a holiday and he was backed up on calls. When the boys got home from school and found out a plumber had been called; the guilty looks on their faces couldn't be mistaken.

"Boys...?" Vic inquired of his two rambunctious sons as he stood towering over them, hands on his hips.

"Yeah, Daddy?" Jimmy offered, raising contrite eyes to his father's face, only to quickly avert his gaze back down to the floor.

"What went down the drain when you two were roughhousing Monday morning?" Vic asked pointedly.

Buddy bit his lip, and then huffed out a sigh, knowing the jig was up. "Jimmy's toothbrush," he mumbled.

"What? B...but... How in the world?" Vic sputtered as the plumber threw him an amused look while he readied his industrial plumber's snake to go into the pipe he had taken apart in the kitchen. Vic figured the man had seen much worse over his years on the job, but still...

"It wasn't my fault!" Buddy protested.

"It was, too!" Jimmy reacted. "You took it away from me..."

"You were spitting toothpaste at me!"

"Only cause you made me laugh," Jimmy countered.

"All right, all right. What's done is done," Vic interrupted. "From now on, when you guys are in the bathroom at the same time – shut the lid on the commode. Got it?"

"Yes, Daddy," they both answered sheepishly.

"I know it was an accident, so I'm not gonna punish you. Just don't do it again, okay?"

"No, Daddy," they echoed.

Gazing down at them, Vic fought hard not to laugh at the whole situation. Controlling his levity, however, he ordered, "Go on to your rooms and wait for supper – and stay outta trouble."

They made tracks down the hall without a backward glance.

Vic shook his head, wondering what else could go wrong for one little holiday.

He didn't have long to wonder, as just then, he heard a woman's voice holler out in pain. *What now?*

He hurried through the kitchen and out onto the porch, only to look through the screen and see Lilly lying on the ground beside the door.

"Lilly!" he called as he rushed to her aid.

"What happened?" Louise hollered, her emotions immediately escalating.

"What happened Grandma?" Buddy and Jimmy echoed as they came skidding to a halt on the porch.

"I…I don't know…I was coming back from using the restroom over at Fleet's…I tripped on something…" she paused, wincing as Vic tried to gently take her arm and help her up. "I think my arm is broken."

"What in the Sam Hill is gonna happen next?" Louise shrieked, causing everyone to cringe.

"What's going on?" Tommy's voice asked as he came through the back door, having just arrived home from school.

"Come help me get your grandma up. She thinks she's broke her right arm," Vic called to him. Tommy rushed as he was bid, both of them carefully helping the older woman to her feet as she clamped her teeth and tried not to cry out.

"I'll call Dr. Denton's office and see if they're open," Louise offered as she quickly made her way back inside, mumbling about what else could go wrong.

The four males of the house helped Lilly onto the back porch and eased her down into a chair.

Buddy and Jimmy both knelt at her feet. "How'd you do that, Grandma?" "Does it hurt much, Grandma?"

"My lands, yes," Lilly whispered. She pressed her lips together tightly and glanced at Vic, striving to control the sharp discomfort. It was the first time she'd ever broken a bone and she was surprised at the amount of pain it was causing. Vic hunkered down next to her and tried to comfort her the best he could. "Back up a little, boys...don't crowd," he murmured, more than a little concerned about his mother-in-law, as he knew first hand just how much broken bones hurt.

In just a few minutes, Louise stuck her head out the door to tell them the doctor could see Lilly if they brought her right over. Vic nodded, already rising to his feet.

"Tommy, you go with us. We'll take her over to the doc's office in the car," Vic decided as he helped a stoic Lilly to her feet again. He reached into his pocket and retrieved the keys, tossing them to the teen. "Go start the car, let it be warming up."

Looking over at his wife, who stood in the doorway with her arms folded across her belly, he sent her a reassuring smile. "Don't worry, Babe. Everything'll be all right. We'll be back in a little while." Then directing his gaze at his two youngest, he admonished, "Help your mother with whatever she needs." With that, he began to carefully assist his wife's mother out to the car.

Louise sighed and shut the door, turning to meet the plumber's amused gaze.

"When it rains, it pours, huh?"

Louise wondered if she would someday find it all the least bit funny.

₧₧

"COME IN, COME in," Vic encouraged as he stepped back from

opening the front door at the sound of his brother's knock the next day. "Welcome to our home," he added as he closed the door behind his sister-in-law and held still for her hug.

"Nice, little brother," Al complimented as he looked around, in the act of taking his coat off. The weather had taken a chilly turn.

"Oh, I love this room," Goldie complimented as Vic stepped near to take her coat while she transferred a covered dish from one hand to the other.

"Thanks," Vic replied, smiling proudly. He took a good look at his brother and his wife, whom he hadn't seen in several years. They hadn't aged too much, in his opinion. Al had gone nearly bald, and what little hair he had around the back of his head was sprinkled with gray now, but he still resembled Vic quite a bit. Goldie was still a pretty woman, her blonde hair fixed in a neat hairstyle. She was wearing a nice pants suit in the latest style. He noticed they were both wearing glasses now, and wondered when that change had taken place.

Everyone else came into the living room, then, including Lilly, who was sporting a large cast on her right arm to stabilize the two fractures caused by her fall – one in her forearm and one above her elbow. As a result, she hadn't been able to help Louise with the meal at all, much to her chagrin.

"Uncle Al, Aunt Goldie," Tommy greeted, hugging his aunt and shaking hands with his uncle. Buddy and Jimmy followed suit.

"Where's Louise?" Goldie asked, looking toward the kitchen doorway as the lady of the house stuck her head around.

"I'm in here, finishing up. Come on in, Goldie."

She met Louise at the doorway and uncovered the object in her hand – a homemade pecan pie. "I made this at home and brought it…I hope that's okay."

Louise smiled in relief and gave the woman a hug. "That's perfect, since we won't be having pumpkin pie and all we were able to make for dessert was banana pudding."

After greetings and a little bit of catching up, Goldie insisted she help Louise get the meal on the table as Vic and the others visited in the living room.

Goldie paused next to Louise, reaching out a hand and feeling of her tight-as-a-basketball baby belly. "Goodness, that's rock hard. Gonna be a big baby boy, I bet. I'm so jealous," she added, meaning it, but not in a malicious way. Louise knew that the couple had never been able to have children, and it had been a source of sadness for them both, especially Goldie – although she had made peace with it long ago. She'd had two devastating miscarriages, and then never got pregnant again. Still, every now and then, a bit of wondering what it would have been like would hit her – like when faced with a pregnant woman.

"Yes, it's a big baby, I think…baby *girl.*"

Goldie grinned at her, knowing that Vic had told his brother that he figured it was a boy.

"Oh I know, I know. Vic thinks it's another boy – but he's wrong. I just know it." Then, with a hand on her overly tight belly, she whispered, "It just has to be my girl…"

"Well woman – now tell me you haven't cooked this whole meal by yourself, in your condition," Goldie fussed, thinking if she had, she would give Vic a piece of her mind.

"No, Vic and the boys helped all they could…" Louise admitted, and then leaned toward the other woman and joked, "So don't blame me for any booboos. I had wanted everything to be perfect for your visit – but it seemed like everything that *could* go wrong *did!* I couldn't get some of the things I wanted to serve, the sink *and* the toilet stopped up, and then Mama broke her arm!" she added, shaking her head.

"Goodness! Talk about *best laid plans going awry,*" Goldie laughed. "What can I do to help?"

Louise looked around and offered, "Make drinks, I guess. Go in and ask everybody what they want?"

"Your wish is my command," Goldie quipped as she turned

on her heel and went into the other room.

Just then, the timer buzzed and Louise opened the oven door. Realizing the turkey needed to come out of the oven, she grabbed two oven mitts without giving it a second thought and bent over grasping hold of the edges of the large pan. With a tug, she pulled it forward and was just picking it up when Vic stepped through the kitchen doorway.

"Babe!" he hollered, hurrying to her side. "What are you *doin*? Why didn't you call for me?" he scolded as he grabbed two towels and quickly relieved his straining wife of her burden. Her face plainly showed discomfort as he set the heavy roaster on top of the stove before dropping the towels and turning to take her by the arms.

"You okay? You hurt yourself, didn't ya," he stated accusingly.

She had, indeed, felt a sharp twinge, but as she stood still massaging the area, the pain slowly dissipated. "Yes, but...I...I think I'm okay..."

Taking charge, Vic steered her over to the table refusing to take *no* for an answer. "You sit here and rest. We'll get everything on," he ordered as Goldie entered the kitchen again.

"Louise! What happened?"

"She took the turkey out of the oven," Vic informed her, in truth, a bit in anger, and a lot in worry. "She said she felt a twinge."

"Oh *Louise*..."

"I'm all right. Don't fuss," Louise griped in embarrassed frustration, shooing them away and toward the stove. "Everything's going to get cold and be no good..."

"Okay, okay. Relax Mary Lou," Vic teased as his tension began to subside seeing that the danger seemed to have passed. Louise managed to smile up at him.

Then, the others came into the kitchen and everyone, except Lilly, helped to get the meal on the table and brought extra chairs in for their guests. Vic made short work of carving the juicy turkey.

Ten minutes later, the family was seated comfortably; inhaling the delicious scent from steaming bowls of food on the table as they all joined hands. Vic bowed his head and the others followed suit as he mumbled a short blessing over the meal.

When he finished and everyone echoed *Amen*, they began dishing food onto their plates and passing the bowls. In spite of all of the setbacks – the Thanksgiving meal was delicious, so everyone agreed as they started to dig in.

"Want me to help you, Grandma?" Jimmy asked sweetly, poised with the bowl of mashed potatoes in his hand.

Lilly smiled fondly at him, quipping, "I think you'd better, honey. I don't think I'll be able to manage a boarding house reach right now."

"Huh? What's that?" he asked, scrunching up his nose as he plopped a good amount of the thick, fluffy potatoes on her plate.

Glancing at him with twinkling eyes, she mused, "Oh, that's what you do when you live in a boarding house with lots of other people and only so much food. Nobody waits to be served. When the landlord sits down and says, "Let's eat," you reach out and snatch whatever you can get or go hungry."

Tommy grinned across the table at her. "Sing us the boarding house song, Grandma."

She met his gaze with a sparkle in her eyes. "You mean…*Bread and Gravy?*"

The teen nodded as he passed the bowl of stuffing, remembering the many nights when he was a child and she had sung the song to him while rocking him to sleep.

Lilly looked around the table and noting the confused expressions on Al and Goldie's faces, explained that the ditty was about a landlord with an attitude during the Great Depression, and that those who lived through the hard times, scarcities, and lack could laugh about it now.

Clearing her throat, she began to sing the chorus, *"On Monday we had bread and gravy. On Tuesday twas gravy and bread. On Wednesday and Thursday, twas gravy on toast – but that's only gravy on bread. By Friday, we said to the landlord, 'Can't we have something else instead?' So on Saturday morn, as if nothing was said – we had gravy…without any bread!"*

Everyone laughed at the silly song and Lilly's sing/song delivery. "Sing it again, Grandma!" Jimmy hollered above the din.

As Vic laughed along with the rest, he glanced at his wife sitting at his left. He was so relieved to see that she seemed to be all right after the fright he had experienced seeing her with the huge turkey roaster in her hands.

"I remember days as a child when it was about that bad," she chuckled as she reached for his hand.

"Me, too," Vic murmured.

"I remember me and Billy stayed with Daddy for a couple of weeks one winter in Bowling Green," Louise recalled, meeting Lilly's eyes. "The boarding house we stayed at was a little better than that, but not much. The only heat in our room was a pot-bellied stove that burned coal, and I remember me and Billy walking along the railroad tracks and finding pieces of coal to bring back and heat the room. Even with the stove going, it was still so cold in there you could see your breath," she added, the memory causing a shiver. "I was so glad when we came back to Louisville…even though all of us had to live in one room together – at least it was warm." She shook her head in amazement and looked around at her surroundings. "Compared to that, we live like kings, now."

She met Vic's gaze and they shared a loving smile.

Al noticed and he put down his fork and reached for his glass of iced tea, raising it above the table.

"A toast – to my brother and his wife and family on this fine holiday, for their comfortable home, and for a delicious meal with all the fixin's – and more than just gravy and bread!"

The others all grasped their glasses and agreed with a chorus of, "Amen."

Suddenly, Louise squealed, "Oh!" and bent over, spilling her glass of tea on the table.

"Oh Vic!" she gasped, both hands going to her belly to try and relieve the sharp pains zipping across.

"Louise! Is it time?" he asked worriedly, bending toward her trying to see her face.

"I…I think…" she gasped again, unable to form words as she tried to weather the contraction. Seconds later, a loud moan escaped and she raised her eyes to her husband's.

Everyone reacted at once, and to anyone looking in the window, they would have somewhat resembled the Keystone Cops as they all jumped up from the table and ran into one another in their quest to help.

Vic reached for his wife, shouting orders for his oldest to go start the car – Tommy took off like a shot. He told Buddy to run for Louise's coat and the boy obeyed instantly. The kitchen turned into chaos as everyone began to shout ideas for what they should do, while Lilly kept hollering that it was too soon, and Louise still had two weeks left to go.

Somehow, Vic got his cringing, moaning wife into her coat and out to the car for the trip down to the hospital. She kept repeating that she hadn't taken the time to pack a bag yet.

It had been an eventful Thanksgiving, indeed.

೩०ಛ

CHAPTER 18

The Crash

"A T LEAST YOUR babies don't come while you're in the shower," Fleet deadpanned as she and Louise sat in the kitchen a week later.

Louise nodded in response, knowing that not one, but both of Fleet's babies had come so fast, that she had been in the shower the first time and the bathroom the second. Flashing a grin over at her friend, she quipped, "Vic would trade me in."

"Nah, that man loves him some Mary Lou," Fleet shook her head. "He ain't gonna toss you out – even if you ate crackers in bed," she added with a snort. Louise chuckled and reached over to give her friend a swat on her arm.

"I'm just glad it was a false alarm," Louise replied as she relaxed at the kitchen table.

"Yeah, but you've dropped, I can tell. It won't be long," Fleet declared as she stood up to take her coffee cup to the sink. "Want me to wash these for you?" she asked, indicating the lunch dishes on the counter.

"Oh, that'd be wonderful, Fleet, thanks," Louise replied with a smile. "Bending over really hurts my back right now, and with Mama out of commission..." she paused for a moment. "Thanks for coming over today... with Mama gone to Aunt Sis's house to spend the day, well..."

"Say no more," the tall honey-haired woman replied, turning

on the water and letting it fill the plastic tub nestled in one side of the large sink. "Hey, how come they always call your Mom's sister, *Sis*? I never heard her name, but that is some story about her and your uncle getting back together. Did you say they found a house to rent?"

"Her name's Leona, but the whole family always called her 'Sis'. They rented a little house across the street from Churchill Downs," Louise answered, adding with a wry grin, "I hope Uncle Frank stays put this time, the rascal." She shook her head, pausing for a moment as she thought about her aunt and uncle having been fully divorced and her Uncle Frank had even remarried, but when his second wife died, he and Leona had rekindled their relationship.

"Yeah, if Alec ever did something like that to me – divorce me, marry somebody else, then come back and ask me back – I don't know if I'd take him back…much as I love that clown."

Louise laughed and took a sip of her hot tea. "Oh sure you would, Fleet. You know you couldn't live without him, clown or no."

Fleet laughed and nodded in agreement. "Just don't tell *him* that."

After a few minutes, Fleet glanced over her shoulder at her friend. "Al and Goldie are really nice, aren't they," she stated, having talked with the couple several times over the course of their visit. Although Vic's brother and sister-in-law had slept at their oldest sibling's house fifteen minutes away, they had come back every day and spent time with the family. It had been the most pleasant visits Vic had experienced with either of his brothers since he had lived in Evansville all those years ago.

"Yes, they are. I'm going to miss them," Louise sighed, thinking of the tearful goodbyes they had shared the evening before when they had left. The plan was that they were going to stop by the station and Vic would give their car a going-over before they got on the road to go back to Evansville. "I wish they could have stayed until the baby comes, but…" she sighed, reaching for the box of baby gifts Goldie had given to her the day they arrived. Pulling out a cute pair of pale yellow and white booties, which Goldie had told her she had knitted herself, she caressed the soft items.

"Those are cute. Same colors as the blanket I gave you at your shower," Fleet called over.

"Yes…I just wish I would have gotten some items in pink…" Louise murmured, a smile coming to her face as she thought about the baby shower Fleet and Ruth had arranged in September. It was actually the first baby shower anyone had given her, because no one thought of it when she was carrying Tommy, and they meant to when she'd had Buddy, but somehow had never gotten around to it. Then when she'd had Jimmy, she used mainly hand-me-down things from Buddy.

This time around, everything was different, and only added to her steadfast belief that she was, this time, going to have her coveted girl.

Fleet laughed and shook her head, leaning to wipe her forehead with her shoulder. "You and that girl fetish of yours. I hope you're wrong just so I can say 'I told you so'," she chuckled.

Reminiscent of their girlhood days, Louise teasingly stuck her tongue out at her friend, mumbling, "You'll see – I'll show you all."

Fleet snorted another laugh.

"Nobody seems to understand how important this is to me…" Louise tried to explain. A look of determination crossed her face as she looked over at her friend. "You've got your girl, easy as pie. You just said, 'I'd like to have a girl,' and wham! You got her." Placing both hands on her belly and giving it a fond caress, she went on, almost dreamily, "Everybody does. Ruth and Earl have two girls…almost everybody on this street has girls…Edna has two girls and two boys…Sonny and Sarah have two girls…Mama had three girls and three boys…heck, even

Gerald and his wife have three! But I've got all boys!"

Fleet turned around again, pinning Louise with a look. "Well, I'll say one thing – if it can be accomplished by sheer grit and orneriness, it's in the bag."

The two women shared a good laugh for a moment, and then Fleet grinned at her friend. "You've had a hectic couple 'a days, girl, and that doctor at the hospital told you to stay off your feet as much as possible. How 'bout you guys come over tonight for dinner. I'll make my special lasagna that Vic likes so much."

"Fleet, that sounds great," Louise agreed with a tired smile. "Dial the station and bring me the phone, will you? I'll tell Vic."

Fleet dried her hands and walked the few steps to pick up the receiver off the bright yellow wall phone and dialed the number, then hurried over and handed it to Louise. After just a few rings, the line connected and Vic's familiar voice answered, "Hello WAKY, Matthew's Service Station."

Louise laughed, remembering that her husband had mentioned he was determined to win the cash prize offered by the newest radio station in town – 790 AM, which boasted the call letters WAKY (pronounced Wacky). Since its first day on the air, when the DJ's had played, "Flying Purple People Eater," *on repeat all day long* – the station had lived up to its silly call sign. It had quickly become the city's favorite radio station, playing all of the newest "rock and roll" hits. The contest daring listeners to actually answer their telephones in honor of the station had created much wanted publicity all over town. Vic's friend, Charlie Borders, the manager of the Frisch's Big Boy Restaurant next door to the station, had won a small prize of $7.90 just the week before and the two men now had a friendly competition going that Vic could win as well. Even the grand prize, which was a whopping $79.00! All you had to do was answer your telephone with "Hello WAKY," the hope being that it was a DJ at the station calling you, and you'd win. It made it doubly hard when it was a business phone, but her intrepid husband was determined.

"Hey, handsome, it's me," Louise answered in a low, sultry voice, feeling better and happier than she had in quite a while.

On the other end, she heard the voice of her wonderful husband chuckling at her flirtatious greeting. "Hey Babe. How you feelin'? Any pains today? Well," he paused and laughed, "since lunch?"

Louise laughed, also, knowing he meant since he had come home and ate lunch with her. "No, I feel fine. Wonderful, in fact," she added, smiling up at her friend. "It's always a good day when somebody does the dishes for me." She winked in response to Fleet's chuckle.

"I hear ya," he answered and she could hear the squeak as he sat back and made himself comfortable in his office chair.

"I'm calling to see if you want to have supper at Fleet and Alec's tonight. She's making her famous *lasagna*," she added teasingly, casting a grin over at her friend who had returned to the sink to finish up the dishes. Fleet grinned back with a wink.

"Sounds like a winner. I'll try and take off early. Don't have much scheduled today."

Louise related the message to Fleet and then turned her attention back to her husband, asking, "So…did Al and Goldie call or anything?"

"No…I thought they were just going to head on over here when they got up this morning, but I ain't seem 'em yet…" he paused. "Oh, wait…here they are now."

"Oh good, well, I'll let you go, then."

"Yeah, okay. You take it easy now, you hear?"

Louise laughed joyfully at her protective husband. "I will. Give them my love one more time."

All of a sudden, Louise heard her husband yell, "What the… No! Stop!" and then a tremendous crash with glass breaking and all kinds of noise came through the earpiece, in the midst of which, she heard Vic's voice yell, "Oh, SH—!" and then silence.

Louise gripped the phone with both hands and screamed,

"Vic! Vic! What's happened? Vic! Are you all right? VIC!!!!" But the call had disconnected.

Fleet ran over from the sink and grabbed Louise's arm. "What is it?"

Louise met her eyes, tears already welling up and starting down her face. "I don't know! He was talking, then he said Al and Goldie had arrived, and then I heard a loud noise, like a crash...and the phone went dead...oh Fleet! Something terrible has happened!"

Horrified, Fleet's mouth dropped open at such a revelation. "Okay, just hang on, let's try to call him back," she suggested, grabbing the receiver from a just about hysterical Louise and running to the phone on the wall. Her mind instantly blanked, however, and she turned to look over her shoulder at Louise. "Dag nabbit, I forgot the number! What is it?"

Panic nearly made Louise forget it too, but mercifully, it popped back into her head. "Um...Taylor 9-9320," using the full word for the local exchange.

"Right, right," Fleet responded, nodding vigorously and mumbling the numbers as she dialed the new style yellow rotary wall phone. Dialing the "0" took the longest for the plastic circle to come back around and she fussed at it to hurry up.

When the dial completed the final turn and she heard the dreaded "busy" signal, Fleet turned with the receiver in her hand and stared at her friend's face, wet with tears, across the room. "It's busy...I'll try again," and she redialed, only to get that aggravating pulsing noise. "I'll call the operator," Fleet mumbled, as Louise looked on in alarm.

Fleet dialed a zero and waited a few rings until a bored sounding, nasally voiced woman answered. "Number, please."

"Yes," Fleet responded, "We were just talking to Taylor 9-9320 and we were cut off, and now I'm just getting a busy signal..."

"One moment please," the voice intoned. Fleet met Louise's

eyes, clearly worried about her extremely pregnant friend, who was staring at her unblinking, both hands gripping her belly, with tears lining her cheeks. Her face was flushed and Fleet worried about her blood pressure.

The operator came back on the line. "That number seems to be out of service."

"But...my friend was just talking to her husband and she heard a lot of noise and..." she began, but the operator cut her off.

"I'm sorry, ma'am. We'll send a technician out to check it. Thank you."

Fleet couldn't believe how disinterested the woman sounded! She opened her mouth to try and get the operator to understand, but clamped it shut again when she realized the woman had already hung up! "Well, how do ya like that? The hussy hung up on me!" Fleet fumed, staring at the receiver in her hand as if she wanted to reach through it and yank a piece of hair from the offending woman's head.

Louise stood to her feet, heart pounding, and gulping in air as if she had run all the way down the street. Turning first one direction and then another, her panicked state was making it hard to make a decision as she fretted, "I've got to see if everything is alright. Oh...where's my car keys...where's my purse..." she put both hands up to her head, tears streaming.

Fleet hung up the phone and hurried over to Louise. "Now, now, calm down. Don't get yourself in a hissy. Maybe it's not as bad as you think..."

Louise immediately rounded on her friend. "You didn't hear it! The awful noise, the crash, Vic yelling!" Placing one hand on her belly, she delayed a moment as she felt a twinge, but within seconds it had subsided.

Fleet noticed. "Okay, okay," she tried to soothe, knowing she had to get her friend to calm down. "I'll drive you..." she began, but stopped when the telephone began to ring. With a wide grin, she said, "See? I bet that's him!" and raced to answer it.

"Hello? Vic?" she began, only to stop and listen. Nodding, she said, "Okay…but Vic's all right…yeah…you're kidding!"

Louise had shuffled over and gripped Fleet's arm, staring at her friend's face and repeating over and over, "What's he saying? Who is it?" all the while trying to read between the words of the one sided conversation.

"Oh my goodness…" Fleet continued, holding up one finger to stave off Louise's questions as she continued to listen to the animated caller. Up close, Louise could hear the *squawk squawk* of a voice coming from the earpiece of the handset pressed against Fleet's ear. She had no idea who it was – but she could tell it wasn't Vic.

"Yeah, okay…thanks, bye," Fleet finally ended the call and took her friend's hands in hers.

"Vic's all right. That was Duke. You're not gonna *believe* what happened!"

₧₨

VIC COULDN'T BELIEVE his eyes. The sight sent fear ripping through his soul.

"OH SH—!" He started to yell, but didn't bother to complete the curse word as he flung the handset and took a flying leap that would have impressed Bob Richards, the recent Olympic gold medalist pole-vaulter. He would never have expected, in a million years, to see the big front end of Al and Goldie's 1956 Oldsmobile 98 headed straight for the side windows, with Goldie behind the wheel, her mouth forming a perfect "O" and her eyes as round as soccer balls.

Miraculously, Vic wasn't injured. Banged up a bit, shook up, and scared witless, yes, but otherwise intact. However, his desk and the stacks of products lined up on the windowsill were shoved out of the way by the impact. The large plate-glass windows shattered as the front end of the Olds pushed its way into the side of the station. It seemed to take place in slow motion, but in reality, Vic realized it was over in a matter of seconds.

From where he landed on the concrete floor halfway across the room, he shook his head a few times to gather his wits about him and get his bearings, just as Floyd came flying in the door. He had been out at the street changing the sign and had made a mad dash when he heard the crash. How, his eyes rounded with astonishment as he surveyed the damage.

"Great God A'mighty! You okay, Chief?" he asked his friend, rushing forward to help Vic climb to his feet.

"Yeah…I think so…" Vic began as he raised one hand to drag it back through his hair. Then, the thought clicked in his head that his brother and sister-in-law were in the car. Immediately, he and Floyd moved toward the Olds, its front end perched hazardously inside the building, while its back end was still out on the sidewalk.

"Goldie? Goldie, you okay?" Vic called as he picked his way carefully over broken glass and bits of brick and concrete, of which tiny particles and small pieces were still slowly raining down. "Al?"

"I think they' all right," Floyd commented, as they both could see the occupants begin to move and there didn't appear to be any blood. Vic saw, however, that he wasn't going to get to them from inside the office, so they reversed directions and exited the door, hurrying to the car.

Amazingly, the Olds had stopped before the windshield could be impacted, leaving the inside of the vehicle unscathed. Matter of fact, the front end hadn't sustained much damage at all. *These Olds are built like tanks,* Vic mused as he carefully opened the driver's door to find his sister-in-law sitting with both hands tightly gripping the steering wheel.

"Goldie? What happened?" Vic prompted, looking past her to

his brother, who was shaking his head in amazement.

"I let this woman drive *one time* on this trip, and this is what happens."

Just then, Vic realized they were drawing quite a crowd around the spectacle of a late model luxury car sticking precariously out of the glass walls of the station's office. Floyd had circled around to Al's side of the car.

"Oh my my my my! Eva-body okay, Boss?" Duke asked at Vic's elbow. Vic glanced over to find the whites of his employee's eyes impossibly large around his dark irises as he surveyed the incredible scene. "I was in de men's room and heard de crash...what was dat woman tryin' to do?" he asked as he took off his U-Haul cap and scratched his head.

"That's a good question," Vic muttered as he extended a hand and helped a shaken Goldie out of the vehicle. Al exited the other side with Floyd's help and came around to his brother and wife as they surveyed the damage. Al stood there with one hand on his forehead, shaking his head in disbelief.

Goldie raised both hands to her face in absolute mortification, her eyes huge as she looked around at the broken glass, brick, and hanging wires. "I can't believe I did this..." She paused and met her husband's eyes. "We were talking...you were telling me where to park the car and you bent over...I turned my head to look at you...and thought I was stepping on the brake, but..."

"You stepped on the gas, instead," Vic finished. They all stood there, gazing in shock at the destruction that had taken place, almost in the blink of an eye. Finally, shaking his head, Vic started to chuckle.

"I...I guess I did," she agreed, casting a glance at her brother-in-law. His mirth began to affect her and she started to giggle. Al soon joined them, and pretty soon, all of the bystanders began to chortle and snicker, guffaw, and out right belly laugh, now that the fear of someone being injured in the mishap had passed.

"Man, I don't think I've ever been so scared in all my life,"

Vic chimed in. "I was just sittin' there minding my own business, talking to Louise..." His eyes popped wide open and he muttered a curse word. "She's gotta be scared out of her mind, right now – I bet she heard the crash!" He veered around several people and made his way back inside, stepping over the debris until he found his office telephone. Picking it up, he clicked the buttons on the cradle several times with no success, before grasping the wire and giving it a gentle tug. It came right to him, having been sheared off at the wall by the impact. "Great, and I thought puttin' it on the desk was better than on the wall in the bay," he mumbled.

Turning to find Duke at his side, he laid one hand on the man's shoulder as he searched his trouser pocket for several dimes. "Here," he urged, pressing the coins into the man's hand. "Go out to the pay phone on the corner and call my house. Tell my wife I'm all right and for her not to worry. Then, call the police. Tell 'em to call the fire department. We better get them out here, just in case."

"Sho' nuff, Boss. Right away," Duke replied, nodding vigorously as he took off for the pay phone at a trot. Vic could hear the old man mumbling as he went, "My my my my my..."

Vic turned back again to survey the damage to his home-away-from-home and he shook his head in amazement.

"My my my is right. Man, what a mess."

ॐ

"CALM DOWN, LOUISE. I told you, Old Duke said Vic's not hurt, and neither is Al or Goldie," Fleet tried again to get her friend to relax.

"But I just don't understand how something like that could *happen*," Louise fussed, pressing one hand to the small of her back as she waddled over to the stove and fumbled around to put the kettle on for tea, completely forgetting that she had a still warm cup on the table. "And what if Vic's hurt, but Duke just didn't want to upset me?" she turned worried eyes toward her friend. She felt another slight twinge and gripped the handle to the oven to steady herself for a few seconds.

Fleet let out an exasperated snort. "You believe he called just to *lie?* I don't think so." Recalling the short conversation, the veracity in Duke's voice, and the plethora of *my my my's*, she went on, "He said even though the phone line was cut and things are broke up in the office, nobody got hurt. He said the car didn't get all the way in, and didn't even look all that banged up. Those big Oldsmobiles must be built like tanks." She watched her friend for a moment and reached out to pat her arm consolingly. "Come on," she ordered gently, "Quit borrowing trouble."

Louise stopped and hung her head, finally conceding to her friend's urging. She turned and met Fleet's eyes with a small smile. "You're right," she began, allowing the other woman to lead her back toward her chair.

They only got half way there, however, when Louise suddenly doubled over with a loud squeal, both hands immediately grasping her belly.

"Louise! Oh no, maybe you'd better sit down…or lay down…" Fleet gasped, wrapping an arm around Louise's shoulders and trying to coax her toward the hall. But Louise shook her head, her gaze on the floor, watching as a puddle began to form. Her water had broken.

Looking up and meeting the other woman's eyes, she mumbled, "I think it's too late for that."

❧ ❧

CHAPTER 19

The Rodeo Ride & The Baby

FLEET HELPED LOUISE into a kitchen chair and then hurried to the linen closet to bring back a towel to help her anxious friend dry off. Just as she reached her, Louise bent over with another contraction.

"Oh Fleet, this baby's coming quickly!" Louise panted through gritted teeth. Fleet could only watch her helplessly as a moan escaped her lips, while she attempted to weather the pain.

When it finally began to subside, Louise looked up at her friend, thankful that she wasn't in the house alone. However, the hormones hit with a vengeance and she was inundated with a fierce longing for her husband.

"Vic!" she gasped out. "Call Vic and tell him…" she stopped short. "Ooooh, doggone it, the telephone!"

"Do you know the number of that payphone out at the street?" Fleet countered.

"N…no, but…get the operator to connect."

Fleet hurried over to the telephone, quickly dialing zero and hoping she wouldn't get the same disinterested sounding operator she had the last time.

After just one ring, a friendly sounding voice asked, "Operator, how may I direct your call?"

"Yeah, can you connect me to the payphone in front of Matthew's Service Station at 4848 Shelbyville Road? It's right next to the Frisch's…"

"One moment, please," the voice responded and within seconds, Fleet could hear the ringing in the earpiece.

"It's ringing," she informed Louise, who was across the room, leaning forward in the chair with both hands on her belly. The phone on the other end of the line rang…and rang…and rang.

"They're not picking up…they probably can't hear it," Fleet groaned, replacing the receiver and biting her lip trying to decide what to do next. "Maybe I can call the Frisch's next door…" she mumbled, quickly dialing zero again instead of wasting time looking the number up in the book. Another operator connected her to the restaurant, but this time, the phone was busy. Fleet hung up and called Ruth and Earl's home, but once again, their telephone merely rang with no one picking up.

"Ahh!" Louise gasped as the contraction took its toll. "Ooo ooo ewww, ahhhhh!" she growled as she ground her teeth together and tried to hold on through the sharp pains. "Oh Fleet!" she gasped again, "*Do* something!"

"I'll call a taxi," Fleet quickly offered, but Louise shook her head miserably.

"I don't think there's time. It feels like it's coming!"

Alarmed, Fleet hurried to kneel in front of her panicked pal. "No! Now, you hold on, girl – you can't have this baby here!"

"I don't…think…I have a choice!" Louise cried, tears pooling in her eyes. "Can you…take me to the hospital?"

"Of course," Fleet agreed, climbing to her feet once more. "Where's your keys? I'll go warm up your car…"

The contraction abating, Louise sat back a bit, breathing hard. "Um…in my purse…in the bedroom." Fleet didn't hesitate as she ran down the hall, quickly retracing her steps and pulling on her coat. Opening the front door, she called over her shoulder, "I'll be right back…" but nearly skipped to a stop as she looked outside. "Where the heck is your *car?*"

Louise's head dropped back as a memory surfaced. "Oh *no*, I forgot – Vic took it to the station to check the brakes when he went back after lunch. He left the pickup, right?" meaning Vic's '48 Chevrolet. She watched her Fleet slightly bob her head up and down. "We'll have to go in yours, then," Louise groaned, pressing on the table next to her as she tried to rise to her feet.

Fleet turned around, shaking her head in the negative. "It hasn't been running good…Alec took it to Vic at the station yesterday…"

Up on her feet, Louise tried not to let Fleet's obvious dismay make her feel even more flustered. "We'll go in the pickup, then." She waddled over to a hook on the wall and grabbed the extra set of keys.

"All right," Fleet agreed, although there was a bad feeling weighing in the pit of her stomach. She hurried over to Louise and helped her into her coat. "You pack a case yet?"

Louise sucked in a breath, pressing a hand to her lower belly, and inclined her head toward the bedroom. "On the floor by the closet."

Fleet hurried down the hall once more and came running back with the item.

"Leave a note," Louise requested.

Fleet rushed on as she was bid and quickly scribbled something on a scrap of paper on the table, leaving it propped against the sugar bowl. "Okay, let's get you out there. Hang on to me," she murmured as the two shuffled slowly out the door, only pausing long enough for Fleet to lock it behind them, before continuing on.

Somehow, between Louise pulling and Fleet pushing, they managed to get her up in the cab of the old Chevy. However, if anyone had been watching, their efforts would have looked downright comical. Fleet made sure Louise was settled, firmly shut the door, and then ran around to the driver's side. Climbing up into the cab, she reached to put the key in the ignition and froze when she saw what looked like a long gearshift lever rising up out of the floor.

"Wait – is this a *manual?*"

Louise felt the beginnings of another contraction and started to moan. "Yeah, why?"

"I CAN'T DRIVE A STICK!"

Louise groaned, trying to focus on Fleet's perturbed face. "You'll have to!" she gasped out, adding, "C'mon Fleet, you can do it."

"I'll…I'll take you to Vic…" Fleet offered, but Louise, tears once more in her eyes, shook her head. "It's twenty minutes to the station – in the opposite direction from the hospital. I don't think I'll last that long before this baby pops out!"

"Oooohh," Fleet groused, muttering a few salty words. "Okay, but if I tear the transmission out of this rust bucket, don't blame me."

Trying not to scream out in pain, Louise burst out instead, "I don't care about this blasted truck. Just hurry!"

Shaking her head and wondering how she always seemed to get herself into such situations, Fleet mumbled, "Hang on," and started up the motor. "Here we go." Biting down on her lip, she pushed in the clutch, and put her hand on the knob at the end of the pole sticking out of the floorboard. Wobbling the loose fitting mechanism around and around, resembling someone stirring their coffee, she searched for reverse, cringing at the awful grinding noise coming from under their feet until she found the right slot. Glancing over at the grimacing face next to her, she focused again on the task at hand and tried to let out the clutch and give it gas to back up.

It promptly died.

"*Dang* it!" Fleet yelled. "This is why I made Alec get an automatic when I started driving!"

Nodding miserably, Louise gasped, "I know…me too…just…just try again."

Fleet pressed her lips together and repeated the process,

resulting in the motor dying three more times before she managed to back it out of the driveway. As she put it in first, she stole a look at Louise and quipped, "In between pains, you might want to be praying we get there in one piece!"

Louise tried to laugh, but it came out sounding more like a whimper.

Miraculously, Fleet got the truck moving forward, but quickly found out that the steering seemed extremely loose, necessitating the driver to aggressively twist and turn on the oversized wheel just to keep it on the road. The truck's tires ran up over the curb and back down with a hard jolt, eliciting a high-pitched squeal from the passenger side.

"Sorry!" Fleet yelled as she fought the large steering wheel.

Managing to slowly follow the road through the neighborhood, only slowing to look both ways at two stops, Fleet halted the beat up vehicle at the stop sign on Breckinridge Lane and waited for traffic to allow her to move out onto the main thoroughfare. Struggling with the steering and the shimmying, she managed to get it out just enough into the flow of traffic when she killed the motor again. A horn blared behind them.

"All right, all right! Hold your horses!" she growled over her shoulder, scrambling to restart the engine. More grinding of gears and the truck began inching forward again, but it took all of Fleet's strength to turn the wheel enough to make the corner. The back tire again ran up over the curb and dropped off, resulting in both women bouncing willy-nilly on the coil-spring bench seat.

That seemed to trigger another contraction, and Louise let out a screech. "Ahhhh, Fleet, hurry! Hurry!"

"I'm tryin', I'm tryin'" Fleet flung back, swallowing down her fear of driving fast in a vehicle she was afraid of, before she added, "For once, I'm glad Alec's mom and sister insisted on taking Alexa for the day."

Louise didn't answer as she was concentrating on getting through the pain.

Fleet checked the traffic in the rearview mirror as the truck moved along at a good clip. Everything finally seemed to be going well. She looked over at Louise again, and grinning proudly, she opened her mouth to say she thought she'd gotten the hang of it when she looked forward again and saw the brake lights on the car ahead. She let out a screech as she fought to steer around it, nearly side-swiping the other car in the process.

Fighting to get the ridiculous old bucket of bolts headed straight once more, Fleet quickly prayed that they could just sail through each traffic light so that she wouldn't have to deal with the clutch again. Glancing at Louise to gauge her condition, she mumbled, "Eight more miles...you gonna make it?"

After a few moments, Louise turned her head and tried to grin as she joked, "I hope so...unless we can find a cop or a taxi driver with nothing better to do."

Fleet laughed and then mumbled a swear word when the next traffic light turned yellow. She carefully pressed the brake and the clutch as she maneuvered the truck into neutral at the light. When the signal turned green, she moved the gearshift, pressed the gas, and promptly killed the motor again.

"Ohhhh, this stupid thing!" she yelled, slamming her palms on the steering wheel in frustration before frantically trying to start the ignition again. Horns blared and a driver roared around them, rudely gesturing out his window, and yelling something about "stupid women drivers" as he went by them. Fleet rolled down her window and bellowed after him, "Blow it out your ear, you jerk!"

"Fleet!" Louise squealed, gripping the dashboard and trying not to screech as the truck lurched, bucked, and shimmied like a bull in a rodeo. *Now I know what bull riders and broncobusters go through.* The thought crossed her mind that if the situation weren't so serious, it would be hilariously funny. "If you don't quit that, I'm gonna have this baby right here!" she yelled after a particularly hard lurch.

"I can't help it!" she bellowed in return. "You made me drive this no good piece of junk!" Then glancing over at Louise again, she added, "Sorry honey...just hold on...and try not to *push*," she added with a cheeky grin.

Louise flashed her a pout. "Easy for *you* to say."

A minute later, clamping her lips tightly as the most recent contraction began to abate, Louise fought irrational giggles at the absurdity of it all. "And you thought *I* was wild that time you taught me how to drive. This is just the kind of shenanigans Lucy and Ethel would experience on *I Love Lucy*." She paused a moment, shaking her head. "All we need now is to be pulled over by the cops."

Ten seconds later, they heard the unmistakable tinny wail of a siren, and Fleet met Louise's shocked expression, before looking up into the small, tarnished rearview mirror to see that they were being hailed by a motorcycle cop. Judging from the expression on his face, he was definitely not amused.

"What *else* is gonna happen?"

❧❦

"MAN, YOU PICKED the right day to come back home," Vic laughed across at his oldest brother, Jack.

"Yeah, fancy meeting you two here, huh?" Jack responded. The three brothers chuckled as they sat together in the waiting room of the old City Hospital.

"Don't it beat all – both of us being in crashes today, and both of us here with our wives hurt," Al added, shaking his head at the coincidence. Jack took a swig of a bottle from a brown paper sack, wiped off the top, and handed it to Al. He took a drink and passed it to Vic.

Thinking it was sure a funny place for a family reunion, Vic asked Jack, "So, what happened, again?" He took a deep swallow from the covered bottle and coughed at the strong taste. Jack reached over and snatched the item from his hands, then proceeded for the second time to tell the story of how a dump truck veered in front of their car, causing him to steer off the road and hit a guardrail as they were exiting the Second Street Bridge. "I figure the wife's just got a touch of whiplash, but I thought we'd better have it checked out."

"Yeah, same here," Al agreed. "Goldie seemed all right at first, but by the time the police got there, she said her neck was hurting." Then, glancing at his brothers, he quipped, "Man, I'm glad I bought that tank. My old Rambler would've folded right up like an accordion." The others nodded in agreement. "But Jack – you should have seen twinkle toes here," he added with a grin, aiming a thumb at Vic. "I bet he never moved so fast in his life – he made a flying leap like he thought he was Superman or something."

Vic laughed along with his brothers. "That's cause I'm still a young buck, not old and broke down like you two."

He dodged as his brothers took playful swipes at him, acting a bit like they did when they were young. They came back with good-natured jokes as they all chuckled and he confessed there were some days he didn't feel like such a young buck anymore. "Kiddin' aside, though, I thought my number was up for sure."

"I wish I'd been there to see it," Jack commented, shaking his head at the mental image of Al's big fancy Oldsmobile perched half in and half out of the building. "What happened after the fire department got there?"

"Not much. We hooked the wrecker up to the back of the car and dragged it out, they checked everything to make sure there wasn't any danger of a spark from loose wires or leaking fuel in the car, and we answered questions for the reports," Vic explained. "The cop had a sense of humor. He asked me if I wanted to press charges for *breaking and entering*. I thought about it, but I said, 'Nah'," he teased with a chuckle.

"I don't see how it could be breaking and entering, since you were *open*," Al shot back with a wink.

Jack's head wagged side to side in amazement. "And that you were on the telephone talking to your wife when it happened, that just beats all."

With that, Vic's eyes widened. "Speakin' of Louise, I should call her. She's probably worried sick."

Al's mouth dropped open. "I can't believe you haven't called her yet!" Then, as Vic got up to move over to the payphone on the wall, Al called, "If she's anything like my wife, she'll have your hide."

Vic winked in agreement as he dropped coins into the slot and dialed his number. After a few rings, Lilly answered the phone, sounding a bit out of breath.

"Lilly? It's Vic."

Without acknowledging his greeting, Lilly started right in on him. "I've been gone to Sis and Frank's and when I got home a few minutes ago, I found a note on the table. All it says is, *Louise worried about Vic, went into labor. Taking her to hospital. Fleet.* I've been calling and calling, but the phone at the station is busy!" she blustered. "What happened? Why was Louise worried?"

Vic quickly informed his mother-in-law of the particulars and then asked, "How'd they get to the hospital? They call a cab?"

"I thought they took the car, it's not in the drive."

Vic's eyes widened. "Is the pickup?"

"No – don't you have the truck with you?"

"No, I took the car to the station after lunch and left the truck at home!" Vic exclaimed.

"Then, that's how they went," Lilly deduced.

"But the pickup's standard transmission – I thought Alec said Fleet can't drive a stick."

"Well, apparently she did – unless someone has come along and stolen the old thing. I can't imagine who'd want it, though," she added with slight sarcasm.

Feeling like a heel for not having contacted his wife sooner,

Vic ended the call and hung up the phone. *I can't believe I was on the telephone with her, knew she heard the crash, and forgot to call her back! The worry probably caused her to go into early labor.*

Berating himself, he hurried back to his brothers.

"Louise is havin' the baby – Lilly says she here at the hospital!" he added before taking off at a dead run for the maternity ward. Having been through two pregnancies with her before, he knew exactly which floor it was on.

Open-mouthed, his surprised brothers watched him go.

ℰℐℂℛ

THE FIRST THING Louise recognized when consciousness returned was her husband's voice speaking softly somewhere nearby. She opened one eye, and then the other, peering through her lashes, trying to make sense of her surroundings. Familiar images registered, such as the ceiling of the maternity ward at City Hospital. Her head was turned slightly and she saw that she was in the last bed in the row, next to the window. The darkness outside told her it was evening.

Then, slowly, the events began to come back to her…

The motorcycle cop had, indeed, pulled them over, which was a feat in itself, complete with the passenger-side tires bumping haphazardly up onto the sidewalk. He parked his motorcycle in front of the Chevy, dismounted, yanked his jacket down over his hips, adjusted his cap, and stomped to the driver's window, obviously prepared to give the woman behind the wheel a dressing down. However, he took one look into the passenger side as Fleet exclaimed, "My friend's about to have her baby!" and immediately sprang into action.

Louise couldn't have dreamed when she had awakened that morning that she would be receiving a police escort to the hospital, and if she hadn't been doubled over in excruciating pain for most of the trip, she might have found it exhilarating. *And yet...*

Fleet had followed the policeman the rest of the way, mumbling that she was grateful that he kept the other drivers out of the way so that she wouldn't have to do more than slow down at intersections, and not have to come to a complete stop and kill the motor. He had arrived at the hospital first, parked, and ran inside as Fleet lurched Vic's old service station truck to a stop at the emergency room doors. Out of one eye, she watched Fleet shove the rickety gearshift into first, and mash down on the emergency brake. Then, the longest twenty seconds of Louise's life passed as they waited in the cab of the truck for the cop, a nurse, and an orderly with a gurney to hurry out to assist.

They had made short work of wrangling her out of the cab and onto the stretcher. Just before the swinging doors had shut between them and she was rolled away, she had heard the nurse at the admitting desk asking Fleet and the uniformed policeman questions. Then, it was a harrowing ride down endless halls, most of it completed with her eyes shut tight, listening to the nurse's attempt at humor while trying her best not to yell as she withstood yet another contraction.

The welcoming party took her straight to the delivery room, and after a quick check and an even quicker preparation, a staff doctor had begun talking her through the delivery. A call was put in to Dr. Denton, but she was told they couldn't wait for his arrival. The doctor on duty gave her a shot for pain, but there wasn't enough time for them to administer a saddle block, the painkiller she had received with her previous three deliveries.

After some fierce pains and heroic pushing, the baby had been born. Louise had fought off the encroaching sleepiness brought on by another shot while she repeatedly asked the nurses and the doctor to tell her if she'd delivered a boy or a girl. Her last conscious memory had been the nurse's answer...

Now, she focused on her husband in the soft light of the bedside lamp as he carefully held a small bundle in his arms, wrapped in a hospital baby blanket. He was cooing and speaking sweet baby talk to the infant as others looked on fondly. Louise's awareness cleared just enough to realize who the people were, and she smiled that her in-laws were there to share the momentous event.

At that moment, Vic glanced up at her, his face transforming into his most fetching dimpled grin, his teeth shining white against his tanned face in the lamplight as he whispered, "Hey babe. How d'you feel?"

Goldie, Liz, and Vic's brothers immediately shifted their attention to Louise as she aimed a sleepy smile of welcome their way.

Then, her gaze once again met her husband's and she smiled lovingly at the picture of the two of them – he and their new baby. It was an image she knew she would never forget. Her eyes twinkling impishly, as she murmured with a dry mouth, "See? I told you I was having a girl."

He closed his mouth, but his lips still formed the grin as he inclined his head in acknowledgment of her statement. "Yep. You sure did."

"Congratulations, Louise!" chorused the others gathered near the bed.

Louise smiled happily as she met each one's gaze. Once again, her eyes finding her husband's, she wanted so much to ask to hold the baby, but extreme lethargy swiftly overtook all else.

Her eyes drifted shut as she silently celebrated. *At last I have my Anita Louise!*

₭ℓCR

JACK LOOKED AROUND to see if any hospital personnel were near before removing the brown bag-covered item from his inside coat pocket. Unscrewing the cap, he took a deep swig, wiped the top, and surreptitiously offered it to his brothers. "In lieu of smoking a cigar in celebration, since that crotchety nurse put up such a fuss," he kept his voice low as he leaned near. To this, he added a few derogatory names for the nurse in charge of the maternity ward, who had given the order to extinguish earlier when Al had produced several of the foul smelling items and passed them around. All three brothers had quickly lit up.

Al chuckled, reached for the bottle, and snuck a swig as their wives glanced at one another and rolled their eyes. Vic passed the baby to Goldie, accepted the disguised bottle and joined his brothers in the covert action, glancing around and feeling much like a schoolboy doing something naughty. He took a large mouthful of the strong brew and gasped a quick breath as his eyes watered.

"Man, what *is* this stuff?" he mumbled as he pulled the bottle up enough to see the bright red, broken seal at the top, and read the label. "Five Brothers Kentucky Straight Bourbon Whiskey. Five Brothers?" he asked, wondering where he'd heard of that brand before then. He took another big gulp, feeling the effects burning all the way down his throat to his belly.

"Yeah," Jack responded, reaching for the packaged item, capping it, and slipping it back in his inside pocket. His words were just a bit slurred. "It's bottled in a li'l brewery in Ow'nsboro. The old man used to drink it. Always said he had friends that worked there."

The brothers nodded in unison, remembering back through the years when their father had indulged in an occasional night of over-imbibing. It seemed to happen after a mysterious package would arrive in the post – usually a box stuffed with straw, the bottle hidden deep within.

Vic wondered for a moment if the old man had been drinking, or was even *drunk*, the night he had gambled away everything they owned. The thought turned his stomach and he wiped the back of his hand over his mouth. His head began to feel a bit fuzzy and he belatedly wondered if he should have taken that last big swig. Sure, he indulged occasionally, on holidays like the Fourth of July and New Year's Eve, but normally it was something tamer, like beer. There were a few times when he'd had whiskey, but this stuff would, as they say, "Put hair on your chest."

He glanced over at Louise, asleep in her hospital bed and smiled, thinking she'd be fussing up a storm if she were awake. *She sure don't like for me to drink...always says I get silly and act a fool.*

"So, what are you all going to name this newest Matthews?" Goldie asked, she and Liz awww-ing and cooing as the baby in Goldie's arms stretched and yawned adorably.

"I think...I think Louise has a name picked out...*Annie? Annette?*" Vic murmured, reaching up to scratch his head and snicker. "Danged if I didn't forget. Guess I didn't pay much attention, 'cause I figured it'd be another boy," he added sheepishly. "I'm jus' glad to have you guys here to cel'brate with me this time," he announced, flashing a silly grin at his companions.

Just then, noises at the other side of the ward alerted the family that visiting time was about to come to an end. Orderlies were bringing in the little rolling bassinets to begin the transferring of the newborns to the hospital nursery for the night. Moans, babies' cries, and soft complaints were heard all over the large room.

Once the floor nurse got to them, Liz, who had taken the baby for a few minutes of holding, carefully placed her in the woman's arms. The nurse laid the infant in the conveyance and the family watched as an orderly wheeled her away with the others. Then, the woman turned back and produced a piece of paper, handing it to Vic.

"Mr. Matthews, if you don't mind, would you go ahead and fill out the birth certificate?" she asked. "I'll come back and collect it in a few minutes" she added without giving him a chance to answer before moving over to the other side of the room.

Vic stared at the form, especially the line for him to fill out the name of his new daughter.

"Whatd'ya going to name the lit'le darlin'?" Jack slurred, leaning forward to try and get a view of the paper. Vic's heart rate sped up as he realized he didn't know, and time now seemed to be of the essence. He raised his gaze to his wife's peacefully sleeping face.

"I think we should try and wake Louise," Goldie warned, trying desperately to remember the name Louise had told her just the week before that she intended to name her little girl. She rose and went to the side of the bed, laying a hand on Louise's shoulder and giving her a gentle shake. "Louise?" she spoke gently. Louise moaned softly and moved her head, as if to say *leave me alone*. She mumbled something unintelligible. "Louise? Wake up, honey…Vic needs to fill out the birth certificate and…" she waited as Louise again mumbled something, trying to open her eyes, only to allow them to drift shut again, obviously unable to stay awake.

Goldie turned toward Vic. "Looks like it's up to you, Vic."

Vic wished he hadn't taken that last big swig of old Five Brothers. *Five Brothers? But there's only three of us…'less you count the three that died…but that would make six…* he shook his head at his ramblings and made himself focus on the task at hand.

Slowly he realized his now bumbling two brothers were trying to be of help. "How 'bout Elizabeth? I like that name," Jack recommended. "Well, how 'bout Goldie, then," Al contributed.

Jack mentioned another name, followed by Al with something else. Liz and Goldie shared their opinions and suggestions. The bombardment of names were beginning to swim around in Vic's head and he wished fervently that Fleet hadn't already gone home; he was sure she'd know what Louise wanted. Turning to the women, he asked, "Could one of you find a payphone and…call the house? Ask Lilly?"

"I'll do it," Goldie volunteered and rose from her seat, exiting the ward on her errand. While she was gone, the others continued to volley names at Vic, each combination sounding less appealing than the last. Even people from the next bed got in on the act. Through it all, Louise slept like the dead.

After a few minutes, Goldie returned. "I called your house, but the phone just rang and rang. Don't know where everyone is at."

"I gotta come up with something!" Vic grumbled, exasperation building by the second. It never occurred to him to tell the nurse they would give her the paper the next day.

Jack looked over toward the door to the ward and tried to suppress a hiccup. "Uh oh, that nurse's coming back. She's headin' this way…"

"I think you should pick a name that means something…a family name…" Liz cautioned.

Al snapped his fingers. "I got it! How about…remember Jack, the old man used to tell us that our mother always wanted a girl, after having six boys…and she would have named her Linda something – after her two grandmothers?"

Jack scratched his head, searching his memory. "Yeah…Linda…Linda…Elaine? Linda…Helen?"

"Linda Ellen!" Al shouted, immediately clamping a hand over his mouth when he realized how loud it had come out. The people visiting with the new mothers in the beds across the aisle looked over at him.

"Yeah, that's it. Linda Ellen," Jack agreed, swaying a bit on his chair. Looking over at Vic, who was staring at the piece of paper, he leaned over and tapped him on the arm. "What'dya say to that, Chief?"

Vic looked up, clearly uncertain, his eyes a bit blurry. "I don't know…what if Louise doesn't like it…"

"I think it's kind of pretty," Liz offered. "It's different. Lindas are usually named Linda Sue or Linda Jane."

The nurse arrived at their sides. "You have the form filled

out? I don't mean to rush you, but…" she offered, but her expression said she wondered why the family hadn't already picked a name before the birth.

Vic looked around at his family members. "You think Louise'll like Linda Ellen?"

The others nodded encouragement.

Vic glanced once more at Louise's sleeping face, took a deep breath, and nodded once in agreement. "Okay." He bent over the paper, filling in the name and murmuring as he wrote the letters, "Linda…Ellen…Matthews." He signed his name and handed it over to the nurse. She took it, uttered a quick thanks, and turned to exit.

Vic grinned at his co-conspirators. "Well, looks like we've got ourselves a little Linda. Never thought it would happen…but we've got our girl."

As the others fondly agreed, Vic turned his head back to gaze lovingly at his deeply sleeping wife. To him, she had hardly aged since he had first fallen in love with her all those years ago. In his mind's eye, he could still see that big wooden door swing open and there she stood, a vision of loveliness in champagne lace. A hazel-eyed beauty, with a smile that set his heart on fire. And now, she was his very own.

She's got her girl, now. Maybe everything'll get back to normal…

ജ○ര

CHAPTER 20

The Admission

LOUISE HAD DRIFTED in and out of a medicine-induced sleep. Having very few memories of the hours after delivery, she could only recall vague words and voices.

The next evening, after her husband had spent the day overseeing the repairs to the station, she looked over to see him walking through the ward in her direction. Smiling, she noticed with appreciation that he had made it a point to go home, shower, and change out of his perpetually stained uniform before coming to see her. Their eyes met for just a moment before the baby in Louise's arms made a soft sound and immediately yanked her attention away from her husband.

She refocused on the tiny face scrunched up in a grimace and gently ran a finger over the wispy strands of dark hair on her little girl's head. Readjusting the baby's position in her arms she hummed to her softly. As Vic reached the bed, Louise looked up and smiled a silent greeting, accepting his kiss as he leaned down.

"Hiya," he mumbled a second before his lips touched hers.

"Hi yourself," she whispered back.

He sat carefully on the bed, reaching to caress the baby's delicate skin with the back of one finger, before bringing around his other arm and producing a small bouquet in a glass vase. He flashed his dimpled grin, crooning in answer to Louise's smile, "For my two beautiful girls."

"Thank you, honey," Louise responded, leaning forward to touch his lips with hers again. Tilting her head toward the bedside table, she added, "Put them over there for me?"

"All right," he whispered, leaning up to do as she asked. He resettled once more, watching her actions with the baby with gentle amusement. Finally after a minute, he asked, "How you feel?"

Without looking at him, Louise answered, "Sore. Tired. Aggravated at the nurses. But...happier than I've ever been in my life," she added as she drew the baby closer and pressed tiny kisses to the tiny cheek. Angling the baby a little toward him, she sighed adoringly, "Isn't she beautiful?" Then, she seemed to remember the events that led up to her delivering the baby a week early and she looked up at him, scanning his features to reassure herself that he truly wasn't hurt. "So...tell me...why in the world did Goldie drive their car into the side of the station?"

Vic chuckled quietly and shook his head. "That was the da...darndest thing I've ever seen. There I was, mindin' my own business, talking to you on the phone, when I look up and WHAM, I think my number's up and I'm scramblin' to get outta the way of the front end of an Olds." Then, his words halted as their eyes met again. "By the way...I'm sorry that all the drama caused you to go into labor early. You, uh...she's really okay, right?"

At that, Louise smiled broadly and nodded, looking back down at the sleeping infant in her arms. "Oh yes. She's perfect. Just like I knew she'd be. And really, she was only a week early, so that's not too much."

Vic changed his position a bit in order to get more comfortable. "That's good. I'm glad the office is the only casualty. Things woulda been a lot worse if Al and Goldie weren't drivin' the civilian version of a tank," he snickered. "An expensive, luxury tank. Only scratched the paint and broke the headlights, but other than that, nothin'."

"That's good," she said, a bit distracted as she concentrated on the baby. Vic shook his head, idly wondering if Louise would be concerned if he'd actually been hurt in the crash. Then, ashamed of that thought, he chastised himself. *Aw, cut her some slack, she's got other things on her mind right now.*

They spent the next half hour alternately between talk about the craziness of the day before, making over the baby, and chatting with people visiting new mothers in the nearby beds. Louise was just telling Vic about her lunchtime visit from her brother and sister-in-law, Sonny and Sarah, when suddenly, a loud voice declared from the direction of the main aisle, "Where's that newest Matthews I've heard so much about?"

Vic looked up and sent his best friend a grin as Alec and Fleet sailed down the room, with Earl and Ruth following in their wake and making a beeline for Louise's bed.

"Hey girl! You don't look too worse for wear," Fleet greeted as she dragged a chair up next to the bed. The men shook Vic's hand as Ruth circled to the other side and leaned down to give Louise a hug.

Reaching for the baby in Louise's arms, Fleet murmured, "Come here Anita Louise."

Vic visibly blanched. *Oh no...THAT's what she wanted to name her...oh man...how'm I going to tell Louise...I hope she won't be too upset...*

Ruth settled herself at the foot of the bed as Fleet sat back in the chair, comfortably cradling the quietly fussing baby. "So *you're* the one that was causing all that commotion yesterday," she accused in a singsong voice, chuckling a little when the baby yawned and blinked up at her.

"I'm so glad Anita is all right. I was a little worried at first because she's a week early, but she's fine," Louise enthused. "Perfect. Look at that little face. Did you ever see a prettier baby?" she added as she reached to touch the edge of the baby blanket.

"She's a darling, all right," Ruth agreed.

"Oh, I don't know – our Alexa is pretty darn cute," Alec interjected as he leaned over his wife's shoulder to view the baby. "But yeah, this one's pretty nifty. Especially considering the amusement park ride my *wife* took you on to get here – or so I understand," he teased, laughing when Fleet smacked his leg and peered up at him, the tip of her tongue darting out.

"So I can't drive a stick shift like A.J. Foyt! Big-time race driver! Sue me. That baby was comin' and Louise refused to wait for an ambulance. At least I got her here in one piece."

"*That* you did, my darlin'. *That* you did," he agreed, leaning down to give his wife a quick nuzzle.

"Was the truck all right, Vic?" Louise asked. She shot him a look, wondering why he suddenly seemed distracted. "Vic?"

"Hmm?" he startled, meeting five sets of eyes that were curiously trained on him.

"Was the pickup all right after Fleet's attempts at stripping the gears?"

"Hey!" Fleet countered amidst the others' laughter. Feigning insult, she continued, "See if I drive you to the hospital the next time you have a kid."

Louise grinned playfully at her friends, enjoying the camaraderie that had always existed between them. It took her mind off just how uncomfortable she was at the moment.

"Oh, this will be my last baby, believe me. What a day! First, on the telephone with Vic I get scared out of my wits, and then it took forever to find out he wasn't hurt. That was bad enough – but that *ride*...it was like a never-ending roller coaster – I'll never forget that as long as I live," she laughed and shook her head in amazement, her eyes meeting her best friend's. "I was sure you'd be beeping the horn for that motorcycle cop to pull over and bring Anita into the world by himself..."

"Babe..." Vic interrupted. "There's something I need to tell you..."

"What, honey?" Louise turned her head to look at him again and raised her eyebrows, completely unsuspecting. Wondering what he was about to tell her, she tried to decipher the confounded look on his face, but she hadn't a clue.

"I...that is...me and Al and Jack...that is..." he paused, running a hand back through his hair in frustration. Opening his mouth, he looked as if he were going to blurt something out, but he clamped his lips shut when Earl interrupted, "Hey, look who's here."

The assembled friends turned as one to see Vic's brothers and their wives walking past the last few beds to get to Louise's own. It crossed Louise's mind she now had so many visitors, some of them might be asked to leave.

"Oh good, you're awake," Goldie's dulcet voice crooned as she glided around the bed to Louise's left and leaned in to give her a hug. She returned the embrace, giving her sweet sister-in-law a kiss on the cheek.

"I'm so glad you were here to welcome Anita," Louise greeted, "and I'm glad no one got hurt yesterday. Thank you for coming." Turning her eyes to the other three standing at the end of the bed with eyes like saucers, she added sincerely, "All of you."

Oblivious to the suddenly strained atmosphere, Ruth immediately reached for the wrapped bundle in Fleet's arms. "You've had your turn, now it's my turn to hold her."

Fleet obligingly and carefully passed the baby to Ruth. Vic looked on with a tight smile, although he exchanged a silent communication with his brothers and their wives.

Ruth gazed into the baby girl's face as she raised her up to brush a feather-light kiss on her forehead. "Oh, she's precious. Just precious," she whispered fondly.

Louise, by this time, was getting a bit fatigued. Yet, she was, at the same time, pleased that so many of their friends and family cared enough to come for a visit. She shifted a bit on the bed and smiled at her in-laws. "It was a bumpy ride getting her here, but I'm relieved to say everything is fine now," she commented as she watched her long-time friend fuss over the baby.

Vic cleared his throat and lowered his eyes. "I still feel bad that I was talking to you on the telephone and got you upset."

Earl gave Vic a playful push. "Yeah, Chief, now what is this about a car crashing through your service station?"

"Oh please, let me just hide my face if you're going to tell it again," Goldie moaned, and everyone laughed.

VIC SHOOK HIS head thinking *here we go again,* and launched into another retelling of the story. He stole nervous glances several times over at Louise, half afraid that she would be upset by the details, but she didn't seem to be paying attention. Just as it had been earlier when they had talked, his words about being the most frightened he'd ever been in his life while being run over by the car seemed to skim right over her head. Rather, all of her attention seemed to be centered on their baby girl lying asleep in Ruth's arms.

Once he was finished, Fleet – not to be outdone – took up the tale of the impending birth from her perspective. People around them had been sending looks of aggravation at the small crowd that had congregated around the last bed in the row. Now they stopped their conversations and listened to the auburn-haired woman's descriptive reenactment of her and Louise's wild ride from Buechel all the way downtown, complete with sound effects of their motorcycle police escort. Louise corroborated details of the story several times, adding her own feelings and impressions of Fleet's comedic attempt at driving Vic's old pickup. Each time the story was told, it seemed to get funnier and funnier.

However, the whole time Fleet was telling the story, Vic sat in a chair and stewed, deep in thought about how to break the news to his wife that he had filled out the birth certificate for their little girl with the wrong name. Every time he heard the baby referred to as *Anita Louise*, he cringed. Should he wait until they were alone? But…their friends were already becoming used to the wrong name. His siblings and their wives kept giving him the eye, with subtle body language, wondering why he hadn't told her yet. He knew he would have to take the bull by the horns and just do it.

He moistened lips that had gone dry from nerves. Fleet seemed to be finished with her story, and while Louise was reaching for the baby, right before another conversation could start, he took a deep breath and blurted, "Her name isn't Anita Louise. It's Linda. Linda Ellen."

Silence met his statement. He swallowed and took a chance to meet his wife's stunned expression. Frozen in mid-reach, she said nothing, just looked at him, her mouth open a bit as if she'd almost turned to stone.

After a few moments, Fleet cleared her throat. "Oh, um…okay. I thought…" Then she stopped, bouncing her stare from Louise's shocked expression to Vic's clearly shamed one.

The others exchanged uncomfortable looks, but they could see storms brewing.

Before another comment could be made or questions asked, a voice came over the intercom and announced, "Attention visitors. Visiting hours will be over in ten minutes. Thank you." Orderlies with rolling bassinets immediately began their nightly vigil of taking the babies back to the hospital's nursery.

As one, the Matthews' visitors realized that the couple had some important talking to do and they each rose from their chairs or perches on the end of the bed before making their farewells. In thirty seconds, they were walking out the door together.

Glad they were at the end of the row, which gave him a few more moments, Vic approached the bed. She had taken the news even worse than he'd initially dreaded and he briefly wondered if she was about to have a conniption. He opened his mouth to start, but she cut him off. "What did you say?"

"I didn't name her Anita Louise. I'm sorry, babe," he added with a self-conscious shrug.

"But...but *why*? You knew..." she sputtered, trying to form her thoughts into words.

"See...Jack had this bottle of bourbon and I took a couple of swigs," he paused, grimacing as he realized how that sounded. But it was the truth, as stupid as it was. "The nurse came around and handed me the birth certificate and told me to fill it out...I couldn't remember the name you'd picked out...we tried to call home, but couldn't get Lilly, or Fleet..." again he paused his quickly delivered monologue. "So...Al and Jack suggested the name Linda Ellen – it was..." he faltered, trying to gauge how mad his wife was, or *hurt*... "They remembered that our mother had always wanted a girl, kind of like you did, and she was gonna name her after her own grandmothers...my *great* grandmothers...so I thought that might be good..."

Tears came to Louise's eyes. His heart sank. "I'm sorry, babe. When I woke up this morning, I coulda kicked myself for not just tellin' the nurse we'd do it today..."

"You were *drinking* and named our baby a name we hadn't discussed?" she finally asked, her voice rising with each word.

"I'm sorry sir, but visiting hours are over. I'm going to have to ask you to leave," the nurse's voice interrupted. From the look on her stern face, which seemed as starched and stiff as her crisp white uniform and cap, it was obvious that she knew she was disrupting something important. "Rules are rules, and they must be followed – to the letter." She took the baby from Louise's arms and placed her in the bassinet. Seeing that the couple was just staring at one another, she touched Vic's sleeve and repeated, "You need to leave, sir. You can come back first thing in the morning," she added helpfully.

With a huge sigh, Vic mumbled, "All right, I'm goin'," and stepped closer, bending down to try and give his wife a kiss goodnight – but she turned her face away.

"Goodnight Vic. I'll talk to you tomorrow."

He hated leaving with her acting so aghast and hurt, but there wasn't anything else he could do. Feeling defeated, he turned toward the door and slowly walked out.

℘◯℃

HER NAME ISN'T Anita Louise. It's Linda Ellen. Linda Ellen. Linda Ellen.

Louise fussed with the covers, unable to sleep.

Why did Vic do that? It had taken her so by surprise she hadn't had time to process what he'd said. They hadn't even discussed naming the baby that, should it be a girl. She'd told him several times the name she'd picked out – Anita Louise. The name she had always wanted to name a little girl of her own should she ever have one. She'd told him her reasons why she wanted that name. And he forgot? And now, it was too late. Louise had asked the nurse about it after Vic walked out the door, but the woman had indicated that once the paperwork had been sent to Frankfort, which it had, and the name was published in the newspaper, which it had been, it was too late. *Too late...*

Turning her head to look out the tall windows at the end of the ward, near her bed, her eyes slowly filled with tears. Postpartum blues had hit with a vengeance once Vic and the others had gone. Louise didn't know if her tears were because of that, the mix-up about her daughter's name, or a combination of both, but whatever the reason, tears turned to sobs as she gave up trying to get her feelings under control.

Why did everything in her life seem to be hopeless and working against her?

It was one of the longest nights of her life.

༄ ༅

CHAPTER 21

The Attack

"JIMMY, BUDDY, STOP running in the house. Go on outside and play," Louise scolded as she fastened a pair of tiny white patent leather shoes on the baby. Bouncing up and down, five-month-old Linda squirmed, attracted by her brothers' shenanigans and wishing to join in the fun. She couldn't, of course; she was much too young.

It was the first week of May, almost Easter, and Louise had gotten the most darling Easter outfit for her little girl, as well as new outfits for the boys, new slacks for Tommy and Vic, and even new dresses for Lilly and herself. She had suffered a small twinge of guilt about spending so much, but she'd pushed it aside, maintaining that she worked hard and had waited years to enjoy life, and now she deserved it. After all, she reasoned, you only live once. There was a beer commercial that played during one of her favorite television shows whose slogan repeated in her mind and now floated through again, "Live life, every golden minute of it…enjoy Budweiser, every golden drop of it!" Of course, she didn't drink beer, but the snappy slogan really resonated within her heart.

"There now, pussycat. How do you like your new Easter outfit?" she asked the baby in a singsong voice as she scooped her up and settled her in her arms.

Linda, Louise mused. "When your daddy first named you

Linda, I didn't like it. I wanted to name you *Anita Louise*, but he beat me to the punch...him and those brothers of his," she told the baby as she bounced her on her hip, both of them looking into the dresser mirror. The baby reached out one tiny hand toward their reflections, emitting a cute giggle. "But now...I think they were right to do it. It suits you," she murmured, pressing a kiss to her baby girl's soft cheek.

Thinking back to the early days after her little girl's birth, Louise shook her head when she remembered how she had cried and fussed over her name. She'd let herself get downright depressed over it, as if it were the end of the world. The next morning after a fitful night with practically no sleep, she had grabbed the nurse's arm as soon as she was near and asked if she would check again about the possibility of them filling out another birth certificate. The nurse, however – a large, buxom woman with a no-nonsense personality – had given her an emphatic NO, without even checking. She had insisted that all birth certificates were filed the following morning after receipt in the office, and nothing short of going to court to change the name would alter it.

Louise had pouted, sulked, and treated Vic with quite the cold shoulder, until the day before she was to be released from the hospital. She had been standing at the large windows looking into the nursery, gazing with pride and pleasure at her longed-for little girl, when an elderly woman standing next to her struck up a conversation. The woman asked which was her baby, and then had pointed out her own grandchild, a robust, dark-haired boy she called, "Little Pete." After a few minutes, Louise had commented about the name she had chosen for her little girl and the circumstances as to why that wasn't her name.

The old woman had pondered this for a moment, admiring Louise's baby sleeping peacefully in the hospital bassinet.

"Linda...that means *beautiful* in Spanish, you know. And in Old England, Ellen meant *bright, shining light*. So I'd say he picked a wonderful name for your baby girl. It fits her, from what I can see." She paused for a minute, both of the women standing together companionably as Louise thought about what the woman had just told her.

The elderly matron cast a sidelong glance at Louise, nodded with sage wisdom, and continued with a glimmer in her eye. "I wouldn't make him stay in the doghouse over it."

Louise had thanked her and then had slowly made her way back up to the ward, the old woman's words reverberating in her mind. *Linda Ellen...it does have a nice ring to it,* she finally admitted privately. When Vic had come for his visit that evening, he found a much more agreeable Louise returning his kiss of greeting.

Now, she turned back to her bed. Sitting the baby down, she began to remove her Easter outfit so it wouldn't become ruined before Sunday. Taking a quick look over at the crib pushed up into the corner of the crowded bedroom, she hummed, "Oh, I'll be so happy when we get a bigger house and you can have your own room. Would you like that, sweetie?"

The baby just gurgled and responded with a few unintelligible sounds as her mother worked at changing her clothing.

Louise had been badgering Vic, claiming that they needed a bigger house. For the past month, she had been scouring the newspaper for homes for sale and even taking the kids along with her and Lilly to tour new home subdivisions, imagining them acquiring her dream home. *Four bedrooms, full basement, garage, two bathrooms... When we get that, then everything will be perfect. I'll have no more worries or concerns. We can live in comfort, and not be cramped together in a small house. Surely then, everyone will be happy and content.* She refused to acknowledge, however, that none of the other family members seemed to mention being uncomfortable in the house on Granvil Drive.

Although they had not been in the Buechel house for very long, in just these few short years, Louise had become more and more dissatisfied with it. She constantly complained to Lilly and to Vic that there was no storage space, since it had no basement, and the bedrooms were too small for the now six people to live comfortably. When everyone was around the kitchen table, there was hardly any room to maneuver, she would remind him. And the one lane driveway – they always seemed to be playing musical vehicles now that Tommy had his own car. If friends came to visit, they were forced to park out on the street! "It's not the thirties anymore. The Depression is over. It's nearly the 1960's! We shouldn't have to live like sardines anymore," she would tell her silent, moody husband. He would just listen and nod, never sharing his thoughts.

Finished with the baby's change of clothes, Louise picked her up and made her way into the kitchen, going over her list of plans on everything that needed to be done for Easter Sunday. *We have to dye the Easter eggs, make the baskets, buy the chicken and everything for Sunday dinner...oh and I need to buy film and batteries for the camera...and maybe more flash bulbs in case we get stuck inside, since the darn forecast is for rain...*

The boys came back inside just then, but Louise immediately shooed them back out the door. They whined and complained that they had nothing to do and so she relented a bit, giving both a cookie as she told them to take a ride around the block on their bicycles. The two just looked at one another, lifted shoulders with identical sighs of boredom, took the cookies from their mother, and went back outside.

"Come on, Jimmy, let's find something to do," she heard Buddy say as the back door slammed shut behind them.

ᔕᗢᘓ

VIC UNCONSCIOUSLY RUBBED his chest against an unfamiliar feeling and drew in a deep shuddering breath as he poured the last of the coffee from the station's stained pot into a grease-smudged porcelain coffee cup with the Frisch's logo on the side. Always taking his coffee black, he lifted it to his lips and took a sip. He grimaced at the strong brew, but took a large gulp anyway, thinking it might boost his energy. His nerves, however, felt frazzled and he seemed more tired than usual.

Once spring had arrived, customers seemed to be coming out of the woodwork – or their winter dens, as Floyd liked to say. Vic figured there were many reasons for that. One explanation – he'd had lots of weekend fuel customers with people taking Saturday or Sunday drives out to take a look at the new building going up right next-door to the station. From the looks of it, it was going to be huge. Vic had never seen anything like it before and it seemed that everyone wanted to take a gander at its construction.

A large sign at the edge of the property indicated it was to be called simply, "The Mall", and the Courier had said it would be the first enclosed suburban shopping mall in the state of Kentucky. The sign said it would house an A&P grocery, Kaufman-Straus, Rose's Department Store, and many other smaller stores. The newspaper had also said it would have a children's play area, including some painted concrete turtle characters to climb on, and an oversize chess set. When he had first heard the news, Vic wondered if it would take business away from the downtown department stores, but he'd quickly dismissed that notion. *Who'd want to wander through a warehouse when you could drive right up to the store you want downtown, get what you need, and get out?*

Often, Vic made it a point to try and stand out in the back of the station and watch the progress when he had a few minutes, knowing he was viewing a piece of history in the making. However, those minutes had been few and far between, lately.

"You need to slow down, son," his friend and mentor, Doc Latham, had told him just the week before when he had stopped in from seeing a friend in the "East End" and filled his car up with gas.

"I know, I know, but I got too much to do to stop. I'll take a break later," Vic had waved off Doc's concern. Now, his words came back to niggle at Vic's consideration. *Maybe I should slow down...but how?*

"Have you prayed about it?" Doc had asked, and Vic's conscience pricked once again. No, he had not.

Putting down his coffee cup, he reached into his pocket to retrieve a cigarette, and found the package empty. Taking it out, he frowned down at it and crushed the paper in his fist, before sending it across the office and toward the trashcan in the corner. He missed. With a scowl, he noticed he had done the same thing on about four other occasions, and they were lying all around the base of the can. With another tired sigh, he trudged the few steps over and bent down to pick them up. When he straightened, he felt light-headed for a moment. *Mmm, too much caffeine, maybe...or maybe not enough,* he mused as he headed over to the cigarette machine, unlocked the front, swung it open, and took out a pack of Lucky Strikes, telling himself he would put the money in for it at the end of the day.

Ripping off the top of the wrapper, he took out a smoke, slipped his hand in his trouser pocket for his lighter, and lit the end of the cigarette. Walking a few steps to the front windows as he stashed the new pack in his shirt pocket, he stood for a few moments with his feet spread, taking in deep drags of the flavored smoke and blowing it up over his head in circles. Silently surveying his domain, he watched the cars come and go as Floyd and Duke worked quickly to see to their needs.

A new model Olds 98 was just rolling away from the pumps and that immediately put him to remembering another Olds – one heading his way and giving him barely a moment to jump out of the line of trajectory. Remembering that sight made a shiver run through his body. Never had he been so frightened.

Vic turned his head and looked over at the sidewall of windows, his new desk, new telephone, and repaired concrete blocks. The Phillips team had done a good job of putting things to rights after the accident. Now, you couldn't tell it had even happened.

But that sent Louise into early labor...and then me, Al, and Jack named the baby wrong...oh man. What a day that was. At least Louise finally warmed up to our little girl's name...thank goodness.

With another drag on his cigarette, he gazed to the right a bit, his eyes lighting onto one of the U-Haul trailers that had been returned in a pretty sad condition earlier in the week. The renter had not made sure of the connection onto the hitch of his car, and the trailer had broken loose in heavy traffic, spinning and smashing into a guardrail. Luckily no one had been injured – but that was another expense Matthews Service Station had to eat, because the trailers were his responsibility. Insurance was offered at the time of rental, but not everyone took it. That guy hadn't. He claimed it was Floyd's mistake that had caused the accident. Vic knew better, but there was no way to prove it. *Just another thing added to my plate. Like I need something else. Now, I gotta get that trailer fixed before it can be rented out again.*

Just then his eye caught movement and he shifted his gaze to the left. Charlie Borders was coming over from the Frisch's next door, carrying a covered dish. Vic smiled at his friend's thoughtfulness. *He musta looked over here and saw I didn't leave for lunch, so he's bringin' me something.* He nodded at Charlie as the man stepped up on the sidewalk in front of the office and walked to the open door.

"Hey there, Matthews," Borders greeted, handing him the bowl. "Thought I'd take a break, stretch my legs, and see how the repairs are coming along on my Ford. Had a little of your usual left over from the lunch rush. On the house," he added with a friendly wink.

Vic peeked under the napkin and noted the hot, greasy chili, crackers already crumbled onto it just the way he liked. He had smelled it before Charlie even reached the door. Nothing smelled like Frisch's hot and spicy chili. His nostrils celebrated and his mouth watered at the aroma.

"Thanks, pal," he uttered as he accepted the gift, turning to sit at his desk and scarf down the offering. He chased the first mouthful with a swig of his coffee. "I ran into a snag on your Ford," he mumbled between bites. "One of the plugs in the back broke off when I put the muscle to it. Gonna take longer to fix."

Vic didn't add that he had yelled a few choice words in frustration and threw the wrench clear out the bay door. His son, Buddy, had been at the station when it had happened, and he had run to pick up the tool for his father. The picture of his son witnessing him allowing his temper get the best of him flashed across Vic's conscience and he scowled at the memory. The guilt pinched at him with the knowledge that his son had heard him cuss.

"Well, that's okay," Charlie replied. "I'll get the wife to pick me up again. Hey," he added with a teasing grin. "You get that all-important call yet?"

Vic knew he meant a call from the WAKY radio station and he glowered at his friend playfully as he took a big mouthful of the deliciously thick concoction, relishing the spicy burn as it flowed down into his gut. He'd deal with the heartburn later. "Not yet, but I *will*," he answered, adding a few salty names for his friend that would rival the heat of the chili. Both men chuckled at their jovial competition.

"Sorry to hear about your man breaking his foot the other day," Charlie offered as he perched on the edge of the desk. Having noticed business had picked up lately; he guessed that Vic would feel the absence of his extra employee. "That's a tough break. You gonna hire somebody temporary to replace him?"

Vic thought about the freak accident. A one-dollar gas customer had recklessly pulled away too quickly, rolling over the foot of his part-time man and crushing several bones. He would be out at least a month, the doctor had said.

"I don't know. It's such a doggone pain to find good help, especially if they know it's only for a short time. But business has picked up, so I'll probably have to…" he paused as he heard the driveway bells ding and his name being called.

Floyd, outside at the pumps, yelled, "Hey boss, we're covered up out here! Can you give us a hand for a few?"

Vic looked past Charlie and saw cars waiting at both pump islands, and he let out a tired breath. Taking another big bite of his food, he muttered, "Better go. Thanks for lunch." He swallowed quickly and added, "I'll get you done as soon as I can."

"No hurry," Mr. Borders replied, giving a wave as he headed back across the little bridge to his restaurant.

Vic jogged out to the car waiting at the first island and helped out, checking oil and fluid levels, washing the windows, and counting out the S&H Green Stamps for the customers. Not only did he pride himself on his station giving the customer their money's worth, he knew that any new customer could be an undercover quality supervisor for Phillips. You never wanted to take the chance on disappointing one of those guys – or gals, as he'd heard through the grapevine that they even had a few women on the job. Good marks could mean promotion, advertisement, and awards… Bad marks could mean sanctions or even fines, and would surely kill his chances for Manager of the Year. It added to his stress level, but that's just the way things were.

Functioning together, the men caught up and before long the three of them were finally able to walk together into the office to put the cash and checks into the register.

Good, this is shapin' up to be a good day. We should close out the day in the black. I need to replace the money in the bank account that Louise spent last week on all those Easter clothes and do-dads. Thinking of Louise brought to mind something their son Tommy had mentioned in passing the night before – something about earning his letter in football, "But, a lot Mom would care. All she thinks about and talks about and cares about is the baby." It had hurt to hear Tommy say that, but shaking his head, Vic had to wonder if he was right in his assessment. It did seem that all Louise cared about was the baby…and getting a bigger house.

Thinking of that made him grit his teeth. *We're makin' it right now, keeping the bills paid, food on the table, and buyin' all kinds of extras – and now she wants a bigger house. We just paid off the second mortgage on the one we got! And I screened the back porch in like she wanted. I'd like to start puttin' some money away for a rainy day… I sure didn't think she'd do this when she told me she wanted another baby. Not that I'd trade in our little girl…she's precious…but man, things have just got to loosen up…*

Just then, the office phone started ringing, and the drive bell on the lot dinged – two sets of doubles. Two more cars. Vic's chest hammered and the headache he had been ignoring all morning took a turn for the worse. Duke jogged out to tend to the customers as Floyd answered the phone.

Vic sent his right-hand man a wave with a half grin as he heard him say, "Hello WAKY, Matthew's Service Station, can I hep' ya?" before he turned and headed back into the bay to work on Charlie's car, his half-eaten lunch forgotten. He gritted his teeth against the vibration he felt in his body – he knew he was tense. Too tense. But he couldn't do a thing about it. People just kept piling more and more on his plate and there was no end in sight. He hadn't slept well in months and he didn't eat right. He seemed to get less and less rest as the days and months went on and now he was up to three packs of cigarettes a day; although he had switched to filtered, telling himself that it would make a big difference.

Nearing the rack where Charlie's Ford was perched, his ears suddenly began to buzz, his heart sped up, and black spots swam before his eyes. He shook his head to try and clear his vision as he felt a spasm of pain radiate across his chest. It was so intense it took his breath away and he reached up with one hand, pressing on his breastbone to try and relieve the constriction. *Oh man…what's happening…* he thought as he felt himself begin to blackout. The spots blocking his vision prevented him from seeing the air hose on the floor and he tripped. *Louise*...he whispered, his beautiful wife's smiling face was his last thought before he lost consciousness.

He didn't know his head was about to strike the edge of the lift. He didn't hear his friend just emerging from the office yell a warning to watch out. As he fell forward, his forehead ricocheted off the hard, unmovable metal and he hit the concrete floor with a sickening thud. The cigarette pack somehow flew out of his pocket, bounced off the wall of the grease pit, and landed at the bottom.

෫ଓଡ଼

BACK AT HOME, Louise was just getting ready to go out and run some errands when the telephone rang. Her brow furrowed and her heart sped up for a moment as she went to answer it. *Who could this be?*

It was Floyd on the other end.

"Miz Matthews," he started respectfully. "Dis here's Floyd. I'm sorry to have ta tell you, ma'am, but...they just took Vic to the hospital in an am'blance."

Louise's mouth dropped open in shock. "Wh...what?" The hairbrush in her hand clattered to the floor at her feet, unnoticed.

"We not sho'w what happened, but he musta tripped or something' and he fell and hit his head on the rack. Knocked hisself clean out. He was still out when the am'blance pulled away," he added softly, a hitch in his voice on the last word.

Her world seemed to drop out from under her feet.

CHAPTER 22

Desperate Prayers

I T HAD BEEN hours. Louise had lost all sense of time.

Vic lay unconscious within the white sheets of a hospital bed. One strong, calloused hand lay across his chest; his tanned skin had been scrubbed clean. His face was pale – what she could see of it beneath the large bandage on his forehead. Louise sat in a chair at his side holding his other hand, her eyes never straying from watching the long black lashes now motionless against his cheek.

She gazed lovingly at his face. *He looks peaceful. He looks almost de... NO!* She jerked her mind away from the word. *He's alive.* Unconscious yes, but *alive.* She laid a hand on his chest again, as she had done countless times since her vigil had begun, needing to feel the movement of his breaths to gain reassurance of that fact. *Vic...do you know I'm here? Do you know how much I love you? Do you know how much I long for you to open those beautiful brown eyes and smile at me? How I long to hear your voice?*

The doctor and several nurses had arrived and departed, words were spoken, predictions given, and encouragement offered... thus far there had been no change. The doctor had said the next twenty-four hours would be critical to Vic's survival. She wasn't sure how many of those had already passed, but she resisted glancing at the clock on the wall to track time. Somehow, she felt that if she weren't watching it, it would move slower and work to their advantage. She knew she was being silly, grasping at straws, but she couldn't help it.

I should pray for him…but I haven't really prayed in a while… She felt numb. Thoughts wove their way in and out and Louise admitted to herself that she felt almost rusty at talking to God. Would He even listen? She wondered if perhaps this had happened as some form of punishment for not going to church regularly, not praying, not giving…for letting other things become more important. *I don't know…I just don't know…* Her heart squeezed as though it was constricted and tied up in a tight knot; so tight she felt smothered.

Vaguely hearing the soft squeak of the door to the room open, she couldn't bring herself to turn to see who had entered. She figured it was another nurse coming to check Vic's vitals.

"Louise?" a man's voice softly prompted.

Louise slowly turned her head and recognized two dear people, Doc Latham and Irene Waller, standing just inside the doorway. Louise tried to smile in welcome, but her face felt frozen – she didn't even realize tears were still wet on her cheeks.

Irene moved forward at once, coming to stand beside Louise's chair. Doc automatically walked around to the other side of Vic's bed.

"We came as soon as we heard," Doc explained, his eyes trained on the man in the bed, a fond expression on his face. Louise could see the love he had for Vic, and she knew that the preacher had, from the day he and Vic met during the '37 Flood, considered the younger man as a son. Watching him now, that was abundantly clear. "How is he?"

Louise looked back at her husband's face. "No change. He's unconscious. They're not sure if it's just because of hitting his forehead, or something else, too."

"I spoke to the doctor, he gave a cautious prognosis," Doc agreed, laying his large, gentle hand on Vic's shoulder.

"Louise, are you all right?" Irene asked softly as her arms

gently came around Louise's shoulders. The older lady pressed her smooth, powdered cheek against Louise's. Raising one hand, the distraught wife covered one of Irene's with a warm response. At the concern evident on the faces of these two precious friends, Louise felt her heart speed up and pound even harder, dread and fear surging to the surface.

She nodded in answer to the question. "Mama's watching the kids…I'm just…waiting for him to wake up…but so far…he hasn't." Tears began again to silently slip down Louise's cheeks.

Without further ado, Doc reached down and took Vic's hand in his left, reaching his right across the bed to Louise as he murmured, "Let's pray right now."

Louise took hold of Doc's offered hand, her other grasping Irene's as if it were a lifeline and she was worn out from treading water in the ocean. For some reason, it made her tired brain recall the time when she had ventured out too far from the beach in Miami. Unable to get back past the high waves and strong current, she had been forced to wait until her hero, her Vic, had swum out to get her. Just one of the many times he had come to her rescue. Now, if she could only come to his!

She closed her eyes as Doc's resounding voice began to plead words she herself had been unable to articulate.

"Father in Heaven," Doc began, his deep strong voice seeming as if it were commanding the attention of Heaven. He prayed for Vic and for Louise, stating that he knew the Lord saw and understood the situation. With great passion and feeling, the earnest preacher asked the God of the universe to heal the dear man lying on the bed, and to allow him to wake up and be fine again, with no permanent damage.

Irene squeezed Louise's hand as she tenderly added, "And Father, we lift up our sister to you. She's a good wife to Vic and a wonderful mother to the children. Please give her strength and faith to believe. In Your Holy Name…"

"Amen," all three softly intoned. Louise felt a tiny shiver

course through her body.

"Thank you," she whispered as she released their hands and reached for a tissue from the box on the bedside table, wiping her eyes and blowing her nose as the visitors stood quietly.

The three made small talk for a while as they waited for some form of change from the man on the bed, but he remained unmoving.

Finally, during a lull in their conversation, Louise glanced self-consciously toward them and before she could clam up, she asked, "Do you...do you think God punishes people for not doing what they should do, even when they know they should?"

Doc and Irene both smiled understandingly at their friend. For a moment, Louise wondered if either of them had ever experienced such doubts. Doc seemed to carefully consider his words before he answered, "I wouldn't say that it is God *punishing* us, as much as it is that He perhaps pulls back His Hand of protection, at times, and allows the devil to...spank us...so to speak. But – it is *always* for the sake of bringing us back into the fold, never out of some sort of pleasure in our pain, and normally after a long period of waiting for us to do right on our own."

Louise looked away from his penetrating eyes and cast her gaze back down at her hand still joined with her husband's. Doc went on, "One thing I do know is that God's Word is true – and in there He tells us that if we feel guilty for something, all we have to do is ask His forgiveness and He forgives. He doesn't play cruel mind games with us. The devil does that, and then blames it on God, and we fall for it. In Psalms 103:12, He even says that He removes our sins as far from us as the east is from the west. Thus is the way of our good God," he smiled gently. "However, the key is that we must *ask*."

Louise nodded, pondering all they had said and prayed.

A few minutes later, the kind preacher and the dear lady said their goodbyes, promising to visit again soon. They left with parting words of encouragement for Louise to hold on to God's

Word and not lose faith.

Alone once more with her silent, motionless husband, Louise closed her eyes and began to talk to God, asking Him to forgive her for everything that came to mind. As far back as she could remember, all the way to when, as a child, she had walked over to another little girl on the playground at school and slapped her – merely because her sister Edna had told her to do so. Louise had known it was wrong, but she had done it anyway. Now, after all these years, she asked God to forgive her. Moving on in her memories, anything that she had done or said that was or could have been wrong, she asked God's forgiveness.

When she was finally finished, she felt a bit better, but worry still maintained its grip upon her heart as she gazed at her beloved Vic's handsome features. Now, she noted for the first time that his face was starting to show his age. From the years gone by, yes; but mostly from the mountain of stress and responsibility that he carried day after day. His hair was beginning to show a few strands of silver, and the crow's feet next to his eyes belied hours of squinting in the sun and frowning in concentration. She realized that she hadn't really looked closely at him in quite some time, and for that, she felt truly ashamed. He was her Vic! He was her true love, her knight on a white horse.

"Oh Vic," she whispered as tears began to pool again. "Please don't leave me." Her heart squeezed even tighter as one tear spilled over and tracked slowly down her face. "I'm so sorry that I haven't been the wife to you that I used to be… I love you so much…You'll always be my only true love…my first love…"

In her mind's eye, she pictured that first moment when she had opened the door of her family's two-room apartment and saw him standing there. The cap in his hands had been damp from the rain, and his chocolate brown eyes had stared into hers as he asked, with a note of hopefulness, if she was Edna. Oh, how her heart had immediately flown from her chest, straight into his hands.

She saw images of their magical days of courting...eating hamburgers and drinking chocolate malts, laughing together over the silliest things, sitting on his lap in their friend Earl's father's old black hearse, enjoying rides at Fontaine Ferry, dancing on the Idlewild, kissing in front of her parents' apartment. She remembered how proud he'd been when she had won that singing contest at the Knights of Columbus, his eyes twinkling, and his smile a mile wide. But then, she remembered his anger and shock when he'd found out about her lies and half-truths. She felt again the agony of their terrible misunderstanding, finding his letter a mere day too late, and the awful years when they were apart. During those long, lonely, miserable years, she had missed him dreadfully. She'd dreamed of him and longed for him until she thought she would lose her mind, believing that she was destined to live a wretched, unhappy life. Her only saving grace had been her sweet son, Tommy.

Shaking those thoughts away, she pictured how Vic had looked the first time she saw him after four years of being away from one another...how handsome he was, and so strong and mature. From then on, he was her best friend, sweetheart, and protector as they waited for her divorce to be finalized so that they could be married. She thought about how sweet Vic was when her daddy died and how he had taken care of all the details and been her rock to lean on. And then, their wedding, such a lovely day...and their wedding night, so wonderfully magical.

Images of those early years of their marriage swam through her mind; they were so much in love. A memory surfaced of him driving his taxi, following her down the street to whistle at her and make her laugh. She saw him out in front of the jail the morning after she and Alec had bailed him out – he had looked so sheepish and ashamed. She pictured him working hard at so many different jobs, waiting for his big break, all while being such a wonderful husband to her and a loving father to Tommy. She remembered their first Christmas together, and every holiday thereafter. The days, weeks, months, and years had moved on as they had experienced life together.

Life. That thought made her think about the reality of their home life. Through all the years of living with his mother-in-law in the house, Vic had always made it a point to be patient and get along, even when Lilly was at her most obstinate.

The years had just seemed to flow swiftly by, like a fast-moving stream headed toward the Ohio. She wondered where so many years had gone – sixteen years of marriage, raising Tommy, working hard, navigating the ups and downs of life together, starting their own business, having sons of their own – and finally a little girl.

With that thought, her conscience pinched again and excruciatingly, she saw her own actions as if she were standing on the outside looking in. Lilly had told her more than once that she would be sorry for emotionally neglecting her boys and even Vic by concentrating her energies and attention on the baby. She had ignored her mother, stubbornly refusing to admit that she was, in fact, doing that very thing. Oh, why had she allowed herself to become so obsessed? Why did she allow the devil to make her unhappy and feel so unfulfilled? Comparing now to all those years ago when all she had wanted was to be reunited with her one true love, she didn't even feel like the same person.

Vic had never given Louise cause to be jealous or think that he was unhappy, but always let her know how much he adored her and the kids. Did she show him how much she cherished him in return? Had she told him often enough? Did he know that she wouldn't be able to go on if something happened to him? Had she taken him, and his love and fidelity, for granted? *Oh Lord, he's such a good man...*

Her heart compressed so tightly, her chest hurt with the effort to breathe as the tears continued to flow. She held Vic's hand firmly, their fingers entwined, with her tears dropping onto his skin. "Oh Lord...forgive me for times when I've hurt the boys...or Vic...I didn't realize...I didn't mean to..." she whispered, eyes squeezed shut. "Please forgive me...please don't take my Vic away from me...I couldn't bear it..."

She gave in to the tears and let them fall. Minutes passed as she quietly sobbed.

And then...

"Hey babe," came a voice, soft, weak, and achingly familiar.

Her eyes flew open and when they met the beloved warm brown gaze of her husband, looking at her with such love, she felt the constricting band that had been around her heart begin to loosen its grip. He was awake!

"Hey, yourself," was all she could manage past the lump of emotion in her throat.

ℰℭ EPILOGUE

"WHAT HAPPENED THEN, Grandma?" asked David, Linda's youngest son.

Ninety-year-old Louise reached for a tissue, raising a shaky hand to wipe away tears as she looked around her back porch at her family. They had gathered to celebrate the Fourth of July, grilling hamburgers, and enjoying one another's company. It hadn't taken long for someone to request Louise finish the story she had paused during their last family get together.

"Oh honey, I thanked the good Lord for giving your grandfather back to me," she answered as her daughter leaned in to give her a hug. "Vic asked how long he'd been out, and told me what he remembered of the moments before it happened."

"So he was okay?"

"Oh, he had a ways to go, but he made it. His skull had been fractured, but besides that, the doctors gave him a thorough examination and said that he'd suffered a heart attack. He had passed out from that and fell, hitting his head on the steel rack. Too much stress, work, cigarettes, and greasy food," she added with a chuckle. "After that, I made sure he took healthy things for lunch...he hired extra help, worked less hours, and quit smoking – oh, but he was a bear during those early days."

Everyone laughed.

"We all started going back to church again, and things were much better. He truly gave his heart to the Lord, and to my knowledge, he never uttered another word of profanity – at least

243

not around *me*," she added with a twinkle, making everyone laugh again.

"What about the station?" asked her grandson, Will, Linda's oldest.

"Oh, we were very fortunate there. Vic, of course, had his trusty men, Floyd and Duke. But since it was during one of the busy seasons, his friend Hap sent one of his mechanics over to the station to help out with the repairs until Vic got back on his feet. Matter of fact," Louise paused, lifting one finger into the air and furrowing her brow at the recollection, "it was Gary Hilliard, the man who had robbed him and Vic had dropped the charges." The family uttered awed gasps at that.

Louise looked around at them, nodding as she shared their amazement. "Hilliard worked tirelessly, above and beyond the call of duty. His gratitude for what Vic had done for him had never waned. I saw him again many years later, his daughter grown and married by then, and he still mentioned his thankfulness toward Vic."

A soft smile adorned her countenance as she thought of how proud she was of her husband for what he had done for that out-of-luck family. She knew most businessmen wouldn't have. *No, they would have taken their "pound of flesh" and been proud of themselves for it.* With a shrug, she continued. "Anyway…once Vic was back at work, he hired another mechanic to share the load and Gary went back to Hap's…probably because Hap could pay him more. Then once The Mall was finished, business was booming!"

A small smile adorned her face as she remembered how, during his recovery, her Vic had hated feeling "weak as a kitten" and had fussed and worried about particulars at the station until Hap had stopped by the house and gave him his word that he was making sure those details were covered.

"For the rest of his life, though, that old head injury would give him headaches," she recalled. Then with a snicker, she added, "I thought of it as his barometer, letting him know when he'd done too much, because when he would get too stressed or tired is when his head would hurt. I'd have to remind him that he had others looking out for things, it wasn't all on his shoulders alone anymore."

Jim spoke up as he lounged in a chair on the porch. "We all helped out during the summers, and every time school was out. I loved working at the station," he added quietly, an expression of fond nostalgia on his face.

"Yeah, didn't Mom remake one of Dad's old uniforms to fit you?" Buddy asked with a laugh. All of Louise's grown sons, Tom, Buddy, and Jim, remembered when Jim – Little Jimmy – was a boy of nine, hustling around the station in his miniature uniform, with a grease rag hanging from his back pocket just like his Daddy, his U-Haul cap so big it slipped down over his eyes. But, he had always been a good helper.

"And what about Mom?" Will asked with a mischievous grin, reaching over to teasingly poke his mother.

"I'm afraid I was too young – and your Grandma wouldn't let me get dirty," Linda added with a laugh. "I did get to go to Daddy's big mail box out at the street – on busy Shelbyville Road no less, and get the mail for him sometimes. Man, the station got a lot of mail!"

"So, you wanted to name Linda, Anita Louise?" Tom asked Louise. "I didn't remember hearing that before. I bet you *did* give him what for when he went against your wishes."

Louise nodded, turning her head to look at her daughter with a loving smile. "Yes, I was mad at him for a while, but I got over it. I followed the advice of a very wise woman, who told me not to keep him in the doghouse too long. And she was right, the name Linda did fit my little girl, probably better than the name I'd picked out. So in a way, I should have probably thanked Jack for passing around that bottle of Five Brothers."

Everyone erupted into laughter and shook their heads, delighted at the fact that Louise, their dear mom and grandmother, had never lost her spunk.

"I used to not like my name," Linda admitted with a shrug when things quieted down again. "But once I found out the story – that it was our great grandmothers' names, and knowing that Daddy named me…it meant more to me."

"Well, I love it," Steve, Linda's husband chimed in as he leaned over to steal a kiss.

"So, what happened to the station after that?" Georgie, one of the grandkids asked as he grabbed a handful of potato chips. "It's not still there, right?"

"No, it isn't," Louise answered with a soft sigh. "My Vic passed away too soon, for all of us, and eventually the station was torn down and replaced with a Moby Dick Restaurant."

"Well, that's lousy!" Georgie snorted in disgust.

"Yes it was. But, Phillips pulled out of Kentucky in later years when there became more and more competition for the gasoline business. Ah, well. They were good years while they lasted." She lapsed into silence then, remembering more good and bad events during the years Vic operated his Phillips 66 service station.

"Vic used to say that he'd always wanted his own business, and when he finally got it – it turned out to be *almost as much* as he hoped it would be."

"What did he mean, Mom?" Tom asked.

"Oh, you know…almost as much money as he dreamed he'd make. Almost as much success as he hoped he'd achieve. Nothing is perfect; life brings aggravations and trouble as well as good times and prosperity."

The others concurred as Louise reached out to lovingly grasp the hands of those on either side of her, namely Buddy and Jim.

"His *bold venture* wasn't everything he hoped it would be…but it was *almost,* and I'd say that's pretty darn good."

Amen.

THE END

The real Vic and Louise – and her beautiful smile!

Want to see more pics of the real people, like Uncle Billy? Visit the author's Pinterest page for this story –

pinterest.com/linda4him59/almost-as-much

Previous books in this series:

Book 1 – Once in a While

www.amazon.com/gp/product/B00P39GYIK

Book 2 – The Bold Venture

www.amazon.com/gp/product/B01340HSGQ

Dear Reader,

Thank you for finishing my trilogy! I hope you enjoyed reading about my family and Louisville in the 30's, 40's, and 50's. If so — would you please consider leaving a review on Amazon and let others know that you enjoyed it and that maybe they will, too? It would also be greatly appreciated if you would share these stories with your family and friends who you think might enjoy them as well. Thanks!

Writing these stories was a truly gratifying and sometimes cathartic experience. I've loved sharing the funny, sad, scary, and heart-warming stories that I've heard from my mom my whole life, plus adding some of my own concoctions to spice up times when, like Mom said, "They were just living, nothing exciting happened." I've also grown closer with my mom, the real Louise, as we worked on details for the stories together. At 92, she's still sharp and has such a great sense of humor; I wish you all could meet her. Perhaps you did, just a bit, through reading her story. And although my father, the real Vic, died when I was quite young, writing these stories made me feel like he was alive again, at least for a little while, and I was able to enjoy being with him.

DEDICATIONS

I have so many people to thank for helping to make this work of fiction happen. First of all, Jesus my Savior, who gave me the courage to attempt such a project, and who always answers a heartfelt prayer of, "Help me please, I'm stuck!" Next would be my husband and best friend, Steve, who is my biggest fan and is always full of encouragement and wonderful help. Countless times, I have gone to him feeling as if the story was stuck in quicksand, but with his wisdom and common sense – as well as his interest and knowledge in the story itself – he always helped me find the right path again. My beta and friend on this book, Judy Glenn, was a constant source of encouragement as I sent her chapters. Comments like, "You made me laugh," or "Just so you know, you made me cry, and I'm not usually a crier," gave me the boost to keep going. Thanks also go to the many friendly and helpful members of the Facebook group *Clean Indie Reads*, for their encouragement, knowledge, and helpfulness. I've learned so much since joining the group. My friends at the office, Mary June, Verna, Wanda, Kathryn, Sherry, and Terry, who were more inspiration than they know, always interested and asking how much more on the story I had written over the weekends. Their genuine interest means the world to me. I thank God for you guys! Thanks to my fans of the first two stories who begged me for a final installment – I was so honored that they wanted more! Thanks goes to my wonderful editor, Venessa Vargas, for fitting me into her busy schedule to polish, tone, and cull out my many repeats and stumbles; and Kathryn Lockwood for her final combing of the manuscript. Thanks to my brother, Buddy, for the funny anecdotes and memories that I'd never heard and was too young to remember at the time, like Hello WAKY and Five Brothers! And last, but certainly not least – to Mom, the real Louise – without you, there would be no story. Love you!

ABOUT THE AUTHOR

Linda Ellen lives in Louisville, Kentucky with her husband of thirty-five years. A lifelong avid reader, and after encouragement from her family and friends, she tried her hand at writing in 2009 and never looked back. Prior to the release of her debut novel *Once in a While* (fashioned from the real-life story of her parents' romance), she has written 30 well-received Fan Fiction works, including short stories, missing scenes, novellas, and four full length novels, based on the TV show *Dr. Quinn Medicine Woman*. Linda keeps very busy with her work in her church's prison ministry and writing every spare moment she gets. Many more plans are under way for books and series, both historical and modern day. To keep up with the latest news on her books, including trailers, cover reveals, release dates, and book signings, visit and "like" her Facebook page, *Linda Ellen – Author*. Also, if you "Follow" her on her Amazon Author Page, you will be notified when she publishes her next book.

For a special treat, go to her Pinterest page to see many pictures related to all of her stories:
pinterest.com/linda4him59

Linda loves to hear from readers. You can contact her in any of these ways:

Email:

Linda4him@gmail.com

Twitter:

@LindaEllen54

Facebook:

facebook.com/LindaEllen.Author

Follow her on her Amazon Author Page:

http://goo.gl/rFj5Ci